Wilder: The Guardian Series

G.K. De Rosa

~2015~
#1

Cover Designer: Masa Licinia

Published in 2015 by G.K. DeRosa LLC
Palm Beach, Florida
www.wilderbook.com
ISBN: 978-0692443408

To my husband, who encouraged me to follow my dreams and my mother who taught me to always be young at heart.

G.K. De Rosa

Table of Contents

Prologue

A violent clap of thunder burst through the night sky, and Celeste shot up in her bed and screamed. The shrill cry echoed through the quiet house. Her heart raced as she looked out the bay window as a brilliant flash of lightning lit up the black sky. Movement at the foot of her bed turned her attention away from the window, and she froze panicked. She heard a muffled whimper and a sniffling cold nose tickle her feet. She giggled. Relieved, she scooped up her new puppy and held him close to her thundering chest. Slowly, her breathing returned to a more normal rate.

Suddenly, Celeste's bedroom door swung open and her mother raced in, her long brunette curls a tangled mess.

"Celeste, sweetie, are you alright? I heard you scream and came as fast as I could." Her warm caramel colored eyes were fraught with concern for her young daughter.

Celeste nodded silently, not taking her eyes off the storm that surged outside of her window. And that's when the deafening sound of an approaching police siren pierced the rainy night.

There was a loud banging at the door and Celeste's eyes shot to her mother's nervous ones. "Stay here," she told her and sped down the stairs, grabbing her pink fleece bathrobe on the way down.

Celeste slipped out of bed and cradling her puppy tiptoed to the top of the staircase.

"Are you Olivia Wilder?" asked the police officer, his face grim and his tone professional.

"Yes I am," she answered, a slight tremble in her voice.

"I'm sorry to disturb you at this time of night Ma'am, but I'm afraid there's been an accident. It's your husband..."

Chapter 1

Celeste sighed. "Why aren't boys in real life like the ones in the movies, Rocky?" she asked her sleepy German Shepherd. In response, the dog cocked his head quizzically to the side before flopping down and letting out a prolonged sigh. All Celeste Wilder wanted was to find a guy who would sweep her off her feet like she had so often seen in the movies. Surely that would fill the empty void inside of her. She had just finished watching one of her all-time favorite movies, *Titanic*, for probably the millionth time and it left her completely wrapped up in the fantasy world of endless love, romance, and adventure – until, that is, she was snapped harshly back to reality by a squeal from her cell phone. She saw it was a text message from her best friend Brian.

On my way.

She glanced at her watch. She had completely forgotten that they had agreed to go to the library to study for their American history final. She grabbed her books and quickly stuffed them into her backpack.

As she headed down the hallway, Celeste paused outside the closed door of her mom's room, carefully turning the handle to peek inside. Her mom was still sleeping, her short brown hair swept across her face – no doubt recovering from another overnight shift. Celeste's mom, Olivia, was the head nurse at Oak Bluffs Hospital and often worked shifts that ran late into the night. She took her job very seriously, which meant lots of lonely evenings for Celeste.

Beep, beep!

Celeste ran back to her room and peered out the window at the black, sporty Mustang sitting in the driveway. "Ugh. Back to reality, Rocky." Pulling her curly, golden-blonde hair into a hasty ponytail, she grabbed her bag and headed outside to meet Brian.

It was a beautiful day, one she would have preferred not to have to waste cooped up inside a library. At least with Brian there, it would be somewhat bearable.

Brian hopped out of his Mustang with a beaming smile, his sandy brown hair ruffled by the wind. Brian Kennedy embodied the typical boy next-door good looks. Proudly sporting his letterman jacket with the St. Alice Crusaders' emblem in royal blue and gold, he looked like he could have just stepped out of a J. Crew magazine.

"Ready for a mind-numbing day of studying American history, Cel?"

The Oak Bluffs Library was built at the turn of the century, and stood as a historic landmark building. They walked through the atrium and Celeste couldn't help but stare at the imposing columns and vaulted ceilings lined in mahogany. As beautiful as it was, to Celeste it had always seemed a bit creepy. The never-ending rows of massive book shelves and dark recesses seemed like the perfect setting for a horror movie.

She and Brian found a quiet corner and settled in. "So what do you think living in New York City will be like, Cel?" Brian whispered.

Celeste grinned.

"I have no idea, but I know it'll be amazing! I got my NYU welcome package in the mail last week, and everything seems so unreal. I can't believe my dream of moving to New York City is actually happening. I got into the dorms on campus, and I'm going to be in a double with a random roommate. I'm kind of freaking out about that part though. What if she's weird or doesn't like me?"

Brian chuckled.

"Calm down, I'm sure she'll be totally cool and everything will be great. I mean, she won't be as cool as me, but then again not many people are."

Celeste giggled, but then her expression grew serious.

"I really don't know what I'm going to do without you, Brian. I've had you right next door for fifteen years. You've been there for me through it all. How am I going to get through college without you?"

"Don't worry. You won't be that far away. I'll come visit on weekends. It's not like there's going to be much going on here in Oak Bluffs once you leave. I'm sure I'll be bored out of my mind."

Celeste threw him a grateful look.

"I think the more important question is, what am I going to do without you, Cel? School has never been my thing. Whose homework am I going to copy when I'm at community college?"

"Maybe it's about time you start doing your own homework, Brian. You need to figure out what you want to do with your life."

Brian grunted. "You're starting to sound like my dad."

Her eyes dropped to the book in his hands and she made a face.

"Well, I guess we'd better actually start studying, because if we don't pass Mr. Wilson's final, neither of us is going anywhere."

They spent the rest of the afternoon delving into American history, quizzing each other until they couldn't memorize another date if their lives depended on it.

Brian got to his feet and stretched.

"We should get going," he reminded her, with a look at the clock behind the main desk. Celeste's mom was scheduled to work another night shift, so Brian had invited her over for dinner.

As they drove home, the soft rumble of the engine lulled Celeste into a semi-conscious state. Her mind began to drift and vivid memories came flooding in.

"Olivia, Celeste, I'm home!"

"Daddy!" said Celeste as she came bounding down the stairs in her pajamas.

"It's so late Kristof, I was getting worried," said her mom rushing out of the kitchen.

"Just some issues at work, nothing to be concerned about. I've got some unruly clients in town that's all."

"Daddy, when I grow up I want to be a private investigator just like you."

Out of the corner of her eye she saw her mother cast a nervous glance at her father. He laughed and threw her over his shoulder. "It's way past your bedtime young lady."

Celeste giggled as she hung upside down and her dad carried her up the stairs back to bed.

"Hey Celeste, are you going to get out of the car?" asked Brian, impatiently holding the door open.

"Oh sorry, I didn't realize we were here already."

"Yeah, I got that. What were you thinking about?"

Celeste paused just outside the Kennedy's front steps.

"Nothing really," she said, avoiding his scrutinizing eyes.

As Brian turned to walk inside, she interjected, "Hey, thanks for always including me in your family dinners by the way. Sometimes I feel like I spend more time with your family than I do with my own mom."

"Yeah, of course, that's what best friends are for right?" he said. "And you should give your mom a break. It's not her fault she has to work all those long night shifts."

"I know. I just wish we had spent more time together over the past few years, you know, like we used to. In a couple of months, I'll be gone."

"I thought I heard you two out here," said Mrs. Kennedy opening the door.

Celeste put on a bright smile as she walked in and gave her a hug. Mrs. Kennedy was an elementary school teacher,

13

and the perfect mom in Celeste's eyes. She was always home when Brian and his sister came home from school and dinner was always on the table promptly at 6:30pm. Little Maxi came running up, her unruly black curls tumbling in abandon as she jumped into Celeste's arms. Maxi—Maxine—was Brian's seven-year-old sister. She positively worshipped her older brother and, by extension, Celeste as well.

"I'm sooo glad you're here, Celeste! You have to sit by me!" Maxi chimed in her singsong voice, grabbing her hand and leading her to the table.

"Celeste, I'm glad you're joining us for dinner," said Mrs. Kennedy, giving her an affectionate smile. "You haven't been here in weeks."

Celeste grinned. "Yeah, it's been crazy, what with school almost over and finals and everything. Mom's been complaining she hardly sees me either, what with her schedule and mine. And in a couple of months I'll be off to New York."

"Aren't you nervous to move to such a big city after living in little old Oak Bluffs?" she asked.

"Kind of, but I'm definitely ready to graduate from little St. Alice Catholic High School. I feel like we grew up in a protective bubble, and I can't wait to see the real world out there."

"Well we're certainly going to miss you," finished Mrs. Kennedy.

"I suppose we'll see even less of you while you're in college, as I'm sure you'll be studying hard," Mr. Kennedy said. "But I hope you'll stop in to see us whenever you're home. Brian could use some more encouragement in figuring out what it is he wants to do with his future. There's more to life than sports, you know," he added, looking pointedly at Brian.

"It's not like I'm going to spend the rest of my life at a community college, Dad. I'll figure it out. I just don't know what I want do yet. Celeste's just lucky," Brian said, grinning at her. "Tell them about the campus tour," he said, hoping to change the conversation before his dad, a lawyer, grilled him any further.

As she said goodnight, Celeste thought about how much she was going to miss these family dinners with the Kennedys. Brian walked her home even though it was just next-door – he always did, and as they stepped up on the porch, he pulled a crumpled brown bag from his jacket pocket.

"I was going through some of my old stuff last night," he explained, "and I found these stashed away between my collection of Legos and Mighty Morphin Power Rangers. Remember our walkie-talkies?"

Celeste opened the brown bag and her eyes lit up.

"Oh my gosh, yes! We had so much fun with these." She giggled. "Remember how we used to drive our parents crazy talking to each other all night?"

"Over and out." Brian quipped.

"That's an affirmative."

"Listen, I know we're going to be too far to use these things soon, but I just wanted you to know that I'll always be here for you, no matter what, okay?"

Celeste swallowed hard and felt a lump in her throat.

"And in the meantime," Brian said, "we can play with these all summer." And he pulled her into a bear hug.

Celeste squeezed him tightly and wiped her eyes when the tears threatened to spill over.

That night, Celeste couldn't sleep. Alone in the house, it was just too quiet. She sat up and looked across the room to where she'd left her walkie-talkie. She was tempted to turn it on and see whether Brian was still up. She peeked out through the curtain of the big bay window facing his house but saw only darkness. She opened the window hoping that the cool night air would help her sleep.

She scolded herself, whispering, "Celeste, you are fine! You're practically eighteen and you'll be living on your own in New York City in a few months. Grow up and stop being so childish!"

She slipped back down under the covers and felt Rocky's cold, wet nose nudge her cheek. She closed her eyes determined to sleep but heard a rustling outside her window. Rocky whined. She sat up and swept the curtain aside. Outside, perched in the oak tree just a couple feet from her window, she could just make out the outline of a large black bird.

It reminded her of pictures her grandfather had shown her after they'd watched the old Humphrey Bogart film *The Maltese Falcon.* She'd been curious as to what a falcon was and he had found pictures of the predatory creature and shown them to her. The peregrine falcon, he told her, was the fastest-moving creature on Earth. She stared at the bird in fascination.

Could it be a falcon?

She was about to lean further out the window to get a closer look when Rocky, catching sight of the strange visitor, let out a menacing bark. The bird immediately took flight and disappeared into the night.

"Well that was weird, huh?"

She crawled back into bed and closed her eyes, willing herself not to think about the curious creature.

Celeste drifted off to sleep and into a dark dream. She found herself surrounded by birds. They filled the air, thousands of them, not unlike the old Hitchcock horror movie *The Birds*. They filled the towering oak tree outside her window, chattering and squawking with urgency, as if they were trying to tell her something. Frightened, she tried to shoo them away, but they wouldn't budge. The largest stared at her intently, as if looking into her mind, its eyes a vivid, hypnotic blue. She felt strangely exposed as she stared back into its oddly human eyes. She awoke, startled, her breath coming rapidly. She tried to shake off the memory of the dream, but she found herself thinking of the strange bird's stare all night long.

Chapter 2

"Good morning sweetie."

"Mom, what are you doing up at this hour?" said Celeste as she stumbled drowsily down the stairs, her curly hair wild like a lion's mane.

"I got home a little earlier than usual and four hours of sleep is plenty of time if that means that I get to spend some quality time with my daughter."

Mrs. Wilder got to work in the kitchen to prepare a special Sunday breakfast. As Celeste watched her mom hustling around the kitchen, she thought about what Sundays used to be like. If she closed her eyes a bit, she could almost see her dad's warm smiling face and just about hear him saying, "Celeste, you can go to Brian's later. Sunday is family day, and we need to help Mom make breakfast. Go get the eggs from the fridge, and I'll let you stir the batter for the waffles."

"Okay Daddy. Can I use the electric one?"

"I don't think that's such a good idea, sweetie," interjected Mom. "We don't want you to lose any of those precious little fingers!"

She handed her the whisk and Celeste giggled as her father made *whirring* noises as she stirred.

Celeste snapped out of her daydreaming as the delicious smell of batter and syrup began to fill the kitchen.

"Yum waffles my favorite!" she said.

"That's why I'm making them," Mom answered with a smile.

"I'm glad we're doing this Mom. I wish we did it more often."

"I know. I really wish we did too. I'm sorry I've been so busy at the hospital lately."

It made Celeste wonder if it was easier for her mother to delve into her work at the hospital instead of dealing with the reality of losing her husband. Since she hadn't been able to save him, helping strangers had become her life.

"Sweetie, I was thinking we should probably go through all of your things before your big move. I've seen clothes in your closet from when you were in grade school! You know you're not going to be able to bring everything up to your tiny dorm at NYU," she said.

"Yeah, I know, I just don't know if I'm ready yet. As much as I want to move to New York City, it's all kind of scary," said Celeste.

"I know, baby girl. I wish your father were here with us now. He would be so proud of you. You have become such an amazing young woman, and you are going to love NYU just like he did. I know it!"

That afternoon, when Mrs. Wilder headed back to the hospital, Celeste decided to stop at the library. A book she had been dying to read had just arrived. It was another beautiful day, perfect for sitting outside in her sunny backyard and

19

working on her tan while escaping into a good book. As she searched through the stacks of the Best Sellers section, she couldn't help but feel like she was being watched. She glanced around furtively, but saw no one nearby. In fact, the library was practically deserted.

Of course, it's a beautiful Sunday afternoon, who else would be cooped up in a dark library?

She found the romance novel she wanted, the newest one from the series she had been obsessing over, and made her way to the checkout desk. She turned the corner and abruptly collided with someone. She dropped the book, which slapped against the marble floor with a disconcertingly loud thud, echoing through the cavernous room.

"Oh, I'm so sorry!" she blurted, without looking up as she bent down to pick up her book. As she stood back up, her heart skipped a beat. Before her stood a towering, well-built young man with wavy, raven hair, chiseled jaw, and eyes as blue as the summer sky. Celeste felt her cheeks grow hot. Embarrassed, she flushed even redder.

"No problem. Sorry, I should have been watching where you were going, I guess," he said, eyes twinkling.

Looking into those deep blue eyes, Celeste was completely at a loss for words. She watched helplessly as he walked away, disappearing further into the library.

Way to go, Celeste.

She stumbled to the checkout counter trying to gather her wits. The librarian behind the counter cleared her throat. Celeste looked up, confused, as if she'd forgotten why she was there. The librarian held out her hand and Celeste handed her the book and then fumbled for her library card. She looked around, but the mysterious stranger had disappeared. Oak Bluffs was a small town and she pretty much knew everyone that lived there. There was no way a guy like that would go unnoticed, not in this town. Who could he be?

Celeste didn't know what it was about him, but for some reason she just had to find out. And she knew exactly who to ask.

The next day at school, during her fifth-period art class, Celeste approached Natalie Meadows. Natalie was one of the most popular girls in school, beautiful and confident, and involved in every after-school activity that mattered. Celeste had always thought of her as a brunette Barbie, with her shiny, perfectly styled hair, flawless skin, and with long model-like legs. Not to mention Natalie always had the perfect Ken doll on her arm. Although they didn't travel in the same circles now, Natalie and Celeste had been good friends in grade school. They had been best friends actually, but that was before her father died and everything had changed.

"Hey, Natalie, got a sec?"

"Hey, Celeste," she replied, glancing at her watch. "Yeah, I guess. What's up?" Celeste hesitated and then plunged right in.

"If anyone would know, you would," she said, and was rewarded by one of Natalie's warm smiles. "I saw this really hot guy at the library over the weekend, and, well..." She hesitated. "It's just that he took me by surprise. He looks older than us, probably in his twenties, but I've never seen him around before. Tall, black hair, gorgeous blue eyes—any idea who he might be?"

Natalie's eyes sparkled in recognition and studied Celeste, who was doing her best to act nonchalant. Natalie hadn't seen her friend this animated about anything in years, and it made her long for the free-spirited, fun companion she once had.

"Well, my friend, this just happens to be your lucky day. If it's who I think it is, Becky said that Jessica's sister, Dani Lynn, met this really cute guy at the community college orientation." Natalie pretended to search her memory as Celeste brightened up. "Wow, what did she say his name was...? Oh, yes, Nico something. He's got a brother, too, Roman. They're foreign," she whispered, conspiratorially. "From somewhere in Europe. Imagine anyone from Europe moving here!"

Europe? She wouldn't stand a chance with him, Celeste thought, her spirits crashing. Natalie squeezed her arm.

"Listen, Dani Lynn's having a party at her off-campus apartment on Friday. She invited him and like half of the population of Oak Bluffs. I'm sure he'll be there. We should totally go."

"Go where?" Brian asked, coming up behind them. Natalie threw him a flirtatious look.

"It's a party on Friday. You should come, Brian. It's a bunch of college kids from Oak Bluffs. You might as well get to know some of the other incoming freshmen before the fall semester."

Brian looked at Celeste and shrugged. "Yeah, I'm definitely in," said Brian, "as long as Celeste comes."

Celeste looked oddly flustered.

"What do you say, Celeste? What's the big deal? Let's go!"

"Okay. I'm in."

The week flew by without too much excitement. Celeste had barely been aware of any of it, her thoughts almost exclusively on Dani Lynn's party. Would he be there? Could she talk to him without making a total idiot of herself? As she lay in bed wondering what tomorrow would have in store, she heard something outside. She got out of bed and walked over to her bay window, and as she opened it a small pebble whizzed by her head.

"Ouch!" squealed Celeste.

She leaned out the window and saw Brian doubled over in laughter.

"Sorry Cel! I didn't mean to hit you!" he said.

Celeste was not amused, and slamming the window shut she pulled the curtains closed. Outside she could hear Brian apologizing and begging her to come out for a second. She threw on a pair of shorts and with a quick glance at the mirror, headed downstairs to see what was going on.

"What are you doing throwing rocks at my window at this time of night? You scared me to death!"

"I'm sorry Cel, I was trying to call you on the walkie-talkie for the past half hour and you weren't responding."

"Have you ever heard of a cell phone?"

"It went to voicemail so I came over instead."

"Okay, what was so important?" she asked impatiently, but Brian's attention was focused elsewhere.

"Whoa, that is a huge bird up there," he said pointing.

Celeste followed his finger, squinting to make out the figure in the tree.

"Is that a falcon?" her stomach churned nervously at the thought.

"I don't know, maybe," he said. "Yeah, now that you mention it, it does kind of look like a hawk or a falcon or something."

"Let's try and get a closer look." Celeste approached the tree cautiously, but Brian stopped her.

"Wait, I can go grab binoculars from my room."

"You own binoculars?" she asked incredulously. Celeste looked up at the sight line from his room to hers and took a couple steps back. "Please tell me you do not look into my room with your binoculars!"

"Look, it's not like that Cel, I swear. I worry about you sometimes, that's all. I know you are home alone a lot so I wanted to keep an eye on you," he said while awkwardly looking down at his feet.

"Literally, I guess." She could see he was embarrassed. "Whatever Brian, I can't deal with this right now. It's late and I have to get some sleep. This scary bird thing has me on edge. I think I saw the same one the other night too, and I had a nightmare about it. Just promise me you'll stop being weird and watching me through binoculars!"

Celeste gave him a good-natured punch in the stomach and turned towards her front door.

"Hey Brian, wait, what did you want to talk to me about?"

Brian paused, already half way across the yard. "Oh nothing, don't worry about it. It's late like you said."

Celeste glanced up into the oak tree before hurrying back inside her house. As she settled back into bed, she couldn't help but think about the unusual bird and hoped she wouldn't have another nightmare.

"Look, I'm really sorry about last night," said Brian as he ran up to Celeste in the cafeteria the next day at school.

Celeste could barely hear him over the boisterous talking and clatter of lunch trays as their classmates enjoyed the thirty-minute respite from class.

"It's fine, I'm over it," said Celeste, "I know you thought you were being protective and what not, I get it."

Placing his warm hand on Celeste's, his face grew serious and he said, "You know I really care about you, right?" She looked down at his large hand covering hers protectively then quickly looked away, surprised by his admission.

"Am I interrupting something?" asked Natalie as she sat down next to Brian.

"Nope!" they said in unison. Celeste pulled her hand away awkwardly, hoping Natalie hadn't noticed.

"I gotta get to class," said Brian, "but I'll see you girls tonight." As he walked out, Celeste caught a lingering glance back at her.

"Is everything okay?" asked Natalie.

"Oh yeah, everything's fine. I can't wait for the party tonight actually. Thanks for the invite."

"No prob! I think it will be really good for you. And who knows, maybe you and this mysterious guy will hit it off – that is if Brian lets you out of his sight." Natalie gave her a mischievous grin.

"Huh? Oh... no it's not like that with Brian and me. We're just good friends."

"Oh yeah? Are you sure about that?"

"Yes totally! You know we've known each other since we were practically in diapers. He's like a brother to me. I could never think of him romantically, Nat."

"I don't know, I mean he's changed quite a bit since you two were in diapers. He's gotten totally hot—don't tell me you don't notice? He's definitely got a six-pack under that shirt from all the working out for basketball and wrestling. And the way he looks at you sometimes with those bright green eyes, it seems more than friendly to me."

Celeste briefly thought about the night before and the binocular fiasco, but she quickly pushed it out of her mind. "No way Nat, and sure I'm not blind. I can see that he's cute, but it's just not like that with us."

"Okay, well if you don't want him then he's mine!" laughed Natalie.

Later that night as Celeste rummaged through her closet for something to wear to the party, she couldn't help but think about what Natalie had said about Brian. She had to be wrong: Celeste never noticed Brian looking at her in any special way. They were just friends, best friends, and she couldn't imagine it any other way. She finished off her outfit with her favorite necklace – a simple gold chain with three intertwined gold hearts, a present from her dad on her tenth birthday. Her dad had said it symbolized their family, the three of them, together forever. She felt the familiar twinge of loss, but pushed it away. She gazed critically at her reflection in the mirror, she always felt her hazel eyes were drab and she wished her button nose would perk up a bit at the end. Sighing, she added a bit of chocolate mousse eyeliner and a dab of cotton candy lip-gloss and heard Brian's car horn outside. She grabbed her purse, patted Rocky affectionately on the head and rushed out.

There had to have been at least a hundred people at Dani Lynn's party. Some were crammed into her apartment while the majority spilled out into the courtyard of her apartment complex. As Celeste walked in, the loud, drunk bodies packed into every corner overwhelmed her. She felt an indescribable urge to run back to the car, but Natalie caught sight of her and Brian before she could make her escape.

"I'm so glad you guys made it!" said Natalie accompanied by two pretty girls. "You know Jessica, and this is her sister Dani Lynn."

Celeste nodded and Brian threw Dani a charming grin.

"Come on in guys, the keg's in the back. I have to go do some damage control downstairs," said Dani as she rushed by.

Celeste looked over at Brian who was staring in the direction Dani had run off to. She noticed how striking Dani had become since her high school days, and obviously Brian had too. She had always been pretty, but now she had a certain alluring quality she never had before.

"Okay so Dani pointed Nico Constantin out to me, Celeste. Let's go introduce ourselves," said Natalie, grabbing Celeste's arm excitedly.

"Who's Nico Constantin?" asked Brian returning his focus to the conversation.

"Oh you know, the mysterious stranger Celeste bumped into at the library over the weekend."

Celeste noticed Brian's face tense up, but he coolly shrugged it off. "Nope never heard of him." He looked at her disapprovingly.

"Oh yeah, I guess it must have slipped my mind."

"Well, I'm going to grab a beer. You girls want something?" asked Brian.

"Sure!" the girls said in unison.

As soon as Brian walked away, Natalie hurried Celeste over to the cramped kitchen. She pointed at the back corner of the apartment where a tall dark-haired boy was talking to a group of giggling girls.

"Look, is that your mystery man?"

"I'm not sure," answered Celeste trying to get a look over the crowd on her tiptoes. "He has his back to us so I can't see his face."

"Well get over there Celeste! It looks like you're going to have to get in line to talk to him. Look at all of those girls all over him!"

Celeste's heart was pounding as she stared at the dark-haired stranger from across the room. "I don't know about this Natalie. What am I supposed to say? 'Uh, hi, I'm the girl who bumped into you in the library, nice to meet you'?"

"Who cares? Just get over there! Come on, I'll go with you," Natalie said, pulling Celeste by the arm.

The girls made their way over to the other side of the apartment, weaving through the dense crowd of college kids and stopping just a few feet away from their target.

"I can't do this," said Celeste, stopping in her tracks.

"There's no backing out now," said Natalie as she squirmed through the crowd with Celeste in tow and tapped Nico on the shoulder. He turned around with a stunning smile and Celeste found herself face to face with him.

"Well hello ladies, how can I help you?" he asked, warmth exuding from his voice.

Both girls were silent for a moment as they stared in appreciation of this gorgeous and impeccably dressed young man. His aqua button-down shirt was meticulously ironed, and his midnight blue designer jeans seemed custom made. He was tall, his black hair neatly gelled back, with matching dark eyes and a teasing grin that would melt any girl's heart.

"That's not him!" whispered Celeste under her breath.

"Oh hi," said Natalie, "we just wanted to introduce ourselves, my name is Natalie Meadows and this is Celeste Wilder."

Celeste nervously twirled a golden curl around her finger. Nico observed both girls, his interest clearly piqued.

"We are Dani Lynn's friends and she asked us to check up on you since you're new in town. She's been too busy running around trying to make sure she's the perfect hostess."

"Well that is very kind of you, ladies. I am Nico Constantin. It's a pleasure to meet you Natalie, and you Celeste," he said. He took Celeste's hand, and he could feel her pulse quicken as he bent his head to kiss it. He felt exhilarated.

Brian appeared out of nowhere as Natalie and Celeste sat mesmerized and too thunderstruck to say a word.

"Hi, Nico, right? I'm Brian," he interjected.

"Hello Brian, nice to meet you," he said, extending his hand.

"That's quite a grip you got there," commented Brian, grimacing slightly but not letting go.

"You do as well, my friend. Let me guess – you're a wrestler?" asked Nico.

"Yeah, actually I am. How'd you know?"

"I used to wrestle in high school myself. We should have a go one day."

Brian eyed him cautiously. "Yeah, sure."

"You know, I must say that everyone in Oak Bluffs is so friendly and welcoming. I think that I am really going to like it here."

Natalie finally found her tongue and asked, "So why are you here in Oak Bluffs?"

"My brother and I had been living in New York City for the past couple years, and he just graduated from college. We were looking for a change of pace after the hustle and bustle of the city. We had an uncle that lived here many years ago, and we visited him once when we were young. It seemed like a quaint and quiet town so we came on a whim. I'm not much for academics, but my brother insisted I get my degree, so I enrolled at the community college and here we are," explained Nico.

"Your brother?" asked Celeste trying to keep the excitement out of her voice. Natalie threw her a conspiratorial glance.

"Yes, my brother Roman. It's just the two of us here. We got an apartment on the other side of campus."

That must have been who I met! There was a definite resemblance between the two brothers now that she looked more closely at him. Nico was a bit shorter and leaner than the brother she met at the library. But they both had the jet-black hair, olive skin, and incredible looks.

"So where's your brother tonight, Nico?" asked Natalie.

"He's not one for these kinds of affairs. I'd have to drag him out of the house kicking and screaming."

"Oh, too bad," she said, with a devious glance at Celeste.

"So Celeste, you said your last name was Wilder? I've met a couple of Wilders in my day, mostly in Germany," said Nico.

"Yeah, that's actually where my family is from originally, but I don't know any of my relatives over there."

"Well, who knows, maybe I've met some of your distant relatives," Nico said with a half smile. He paused momentarily, reminiscing about a time long ago, but quickly recovered. "Germany really is a beautiful country. I'd love to show you pictures from my travels there someday."

"Oh sure, sounds fun," said Celeste, drawn to his warm smile.

Natalie grabbed Brian by the arm. "Let's go get refills on these drinks." She turned back and gave Celeste an encouraging look as she walked away.

"So, you said you've been to Germany?" Celeste asked, suddenly alone with the attractive stranger.

"Yes, I spent four years there at a boarding school in Berlin while my brother was in London attending university the first time around."

Celeste was soon captivated by all of Nico's stories of Oktoberfest in Munich, wild nights in Ibiza, strolling the Champs Elysees in Paris, gondola rides in Venice, and so much more. It appeared as though Nico had already lived an entire lifetime of adventures, a seemingly impossible feat for someone so young.

"I've always dreamed of traveling around the world. I wanted to backpack across Europe the summer of my senior year, which is in a couple of weeks now. I'm pretty sure that that won't be happening."

"Why not? You never know what may happen or how your life can change in the blink of an eye."

Celeste knew how true that was. Her life had completely changed when her father had died. Unexpectedly, Nico took her hand and led her out to the balcony. The party had started to die down now, and they were finally able to get a seat outside.

"It's such a beautiful night out, don't you think Celeste?" he asked.

She grinned. "Oh yes, it is. I love a full moon, there's something magical about it." Celeste found herself completely swept up in the conversation with Nico. It was odd how at ease she felt with him.

"So tell me a little about you. I've been going on and on about my life, and I haven't let you get a word in."

"Trust me, your life is way more exciting than mine is," she said.

"Maybe for now," he said with a knowing smile.

There was something about being around Nico that sparked feelings inside of her that were completely new and slightly startling. She couldn't figure out what it was, but there was something about this boy.

"I really missed seeing all of these stars when I was living in the city," he continued.

"I'm going to miss that about Oak Bluffs. I'm actually moving to New York City in the fall to go to NYU," explained Celeste.

"Well now that certainly sounds exciting. You must be a smart one then, aren't you?" teased Nico.

"I don't know about all that, but going to NYU is something that I've wanted to do for as long as I can remember."

"I don't know if I like this—I just moved here and now you're leaving?"

Celeste smiled shyly as Nico watched her intently – almost too intently. She was actually relieved when she saw Brian and Natalie approaching the balcony to join them.

"I think I'm ready to head home Cel, are you ready?" asked Brian.

"Oh yeah sure," she said, regretting having to leave so soon.

Nico took her hand and planted a sweet kiss on her cheek. "It was a pleasure to meet you, Celeste Wilder, and I hope to see you again very soon."

Chapter 3

When Celeste awoke the next morning, she had an overwhelming feeling of hopefulness, a sensation she hadn't felt in a long time. She glanced at her favorite family picture nearby on the nightstand; it was from her fifth birthday party, and everyone looked so blissfully happy, she thought. Celeste had on her favorite pink party dress, her dad was wiping icing off of her cheek, and her mom looked so young and beautiful.

"This is going to be a good day, Dad," she said out loud.

She got out of bed and was cheerfully humming as she made her way downstairs. Since her mom was still sleeping she decided to surprise her with breakfast in bed, and quickly got to work making some crispy bacon and eggs. As she hustled around the kitchen, she thought of the party (and Nico, of course) and a little smile crossed her face. She could totally do this—she could go out and have fun and meet interesting boys like a normal teenager. She resolved that this summer would be different: no more moping around the house and feeling sorry for herself. She was going to be graduating soon and everything was about to change. She snuck into her mom's room and left the tray with the delicious breakfast on her nightstand as well as a note saying she'd gone to meet Natalie.

As head of the prom committee, Natalie had been running around all morning searching for decorations to turn the school's stark gym into an authentic roaring twenties-themed casino. Celeste couldn't believe that prom was just a week away. She hadn't even planned on going really.

"Of course you're going!" exclaimed Natalie. "You have to, it's our senior prom!" Celeste had caught up with Natalie outside of The Party Store and now they were walking side-by-side basking in the pleasant morning sunshine.

After a few lame excuses, Celeste finally gave in to Natalie's theory that if Celeste didn't go to prom she would be missing out on one of the most important nights of her life.

"And you should totally take Nico," continued Natalie with a wink. "You two seemed pretty friendly last night."

Celeste laughed. "He is really friendly actually and seems super cool. He's been to all of these amazing places. And the way he talks, it reminds me of someone so much older. But I kind of like it, he's such a gentleman."

"Of course *you* would love that. He seems like he popped right out of one of your romance novels."

As Celeste was about to tell her that she doubted she would ever see him again, her phone started ringing. She didn't recognize the number, so she picked it up with a tentative, "Hello?"

"Why hello Celeste, it's Nico, the charming young man you had the pleasure of meeting last night. Please tell me you haven't forgotten about me already?"

Celeste responded with a nervous little chuckle and said, "Of course not. Hi - how are you?"

Nico explained that he had gotten her number from Dani Lynn (who had gotten it from Natalie – *so sneaky!*) and said, "I hope I'm not being too forward, but I would really enjoy seeing you again today."

"Oh..."

"I would really like to show you those pictures of Germany that we were talking about last night. Why don't you come by my apartment this afternoon?"

Celeste found herself searching for words, thinking, *Should I go to this total stranger's apartment after just meeting him? But he's not really a stranger, after all Dani Lynn knows him...*

She resolved her inner struggle with an impulsive, "Sure!"

When Celeste hung up the phone she was grinning from ear to ear. "I can't believe I just said yes."

"Me either! It's about time you start acting like a normal teenager, and on that note, you're coming to help me do some more shopping. This is going to be the best prom ever!" said Natalie as she dragged Celeste into another store.

***

Nico had texted Celeste his address and as she turned into his apartment complex, her heart was racing. What was she doing? This was so unlike her! She tried to steady her nerves as she examined herself in the mirror, applying a little cotton candy lip-gloss and tucking a loose strand of blonde hair behind her ear. She forced herself to get out of the car and then knocked hesitantly on the door. Within seconds, it swung open, and to her surprise the handsome stranger from the library stood in front of her. He was wearing a tight-fitting black t-shirt and a pair of dark blue jeans that hung flawlessly from his hips. His bright blue eyes twinkled as a shade of a smile crossed his perfectly sculpted jaw and the five o'clock shadow completed his roguish look. Celeste stared speechlessly until she finally gathered the nerve to murmur a hello.

"You must be Celeste, I'm Roman, Nico's brother. He told me he was expecting you, please come in." Roman inhaled deeply as she walked in, her scent intoxicating. He could hear her heart racing and the blood pumping through her veins.

As Celeste squeezed through the door that Roman was holding open, her arm brushed against his and it was like thousands of tiny electric shocks went through her. She tried to suppress a little "ooh" as she walked by him. The intense attraction that bubbled up inside her was even more powerful than what she had felt last night towards Nico. There was no doubt that Roman was incredibly gorgeous, but Celeste had met cute boys before and never felt anything like this.

Nico came barreling down the stairs and gave Celeste a quick kiss on both cheeks – very European, she thought. At that, Roman retreated to what must have been his bedroom. Celeste thought she caught a glimpse of disapproval as Roman stalked out of the room, but it must have been her imagination. The apartment was huge and immaculately decorated—not at all what Celeste had expected from two twenty-something year old guys. It was a mix of new world and old, classic with large stately pieces of furniture and yet still boasting a modern black and white vibe.

Nico led Celeste into the expansive living room, which had floor to ceiling glass windows overlooking a peaceful lake and lush green grass.

"Wow, what a beautiful view!" she said, walking toward the wall of windows.

"My brother and I enjoy the tranquility of calm scenery and quiet towns like Oak Bluffs. When you've traveled as much as we have, this is the perfect respite."

He stopped in front of the massive black leather couch where he politely offered her something to drink and pulled out his shiny silver laptop.

"I'm glad you came. I wasn't sure if you would," admitted Nico.

"To be honest, I wasn't sure I would either!" said Celeste nervously as she took a sip from her drink.

"Well, then I guess I lucked out. Where should we start? Berlin? Rome? London? We have the whole world in front of us, Celeste," he said his dark eyes alive with enthusiasm.

"I've always wanted to go to all of those cities. They seem so beautiful and mysterious."

"Well, maybe one day you will," he said.

She shot him an appreciative smile. "So when was this picture taken of you in London? Natalie was just there last summer." Celeste noticed that oddly none of the pictures had date or time stamps on them.

"Hmm, I think that was about two years ago – before we moved to New York," Nico confirmed.

"You look exactly the same!"

"Why mess with perfection?" Nico retorted with a witty grin, then quickly moved on to other pictures.

Celeste studied Nico furtively as he flipped through the photos on his laptop. She couldn't help but compare the two striking brothers. Nico had a kinder smile with a cute snub nose and softer features, while Roman's expression was a bit stern, with a straight-edged nose and his thick eyebrows furrowed more often than not. They looked through countless photos of historic sites and beautiful landscapes, intermingled with the occasional goofy selfie of Nico. Roman was in quite a few as well which prompted Celeste to ask a bit more about him.

"Roman and I are very close; we've spent a lot of time together. Our parents wanted us to explore the world so we did just that—a semester here, a summer there. We are a couple of world class travelers, my brother and I."

"That's so great. So are your parents still living abroad?" asked Celeste.

Nico paused, gazing out the window. "No, actually, our parents passed away awhile back. It's just Roman and me now."

"Oh, I'm sorry Nico." Celeste couldn't imagine what it must be like losing *both* parents. "My dad actually died when I was young too, so I know how hard it is. He was killed in a car accident when I was ten," she said, fighting back the tears. Celeste rarely spoke about her father to others; she was surprised as the words tumbled out of her mouth so easily.

Nico quickly pulled a handkerchief out of his pocket and gently wiped the single tear off Celeste's cheek.

"Enough of that," said Nico. "Come on, let's get out of here and grab some lunch. I've been home all morning, and I need to get out," he said, taking hold of her hand and giving it a comforting squeeze.

Before they left, Celeste made a quick stop at the bathroom to make sure her mascara hadn't smudged, and on her way out she bumped into Roman.

"We have to stop meeting this way," he teased, holding her arm to steady her after the near collision.

He *had* remembered her from the library, Celeste thought giddily. She had wondered if the intense connection had only been one sided. Encouraged by this new development she said, "Nico and I are going out to lunch. Why don't you come with us?"

"Oh I don't think Nico would forgive me if I intruded on his date with such a beautiful girl."

Celeste could feel her face flush and she glanced down momentarily but when she looked up again, Roman was gone.

"No, nothing happened Natalie, I swear we just had lunch. He's a really nice guy, fun and super sweet. I'm really glad I met him and his brother Roman!" squealed Celeste as she lay in her bed chatting on the phone.

After she recounted the entire series of events of the afternoon, she laid back in her bed, completely content and dozed off.

Nico returned from his lunch date to find Roman waiting sulkily on the couch with arms crossed.

"What do you think you are doing, little brother?" asked Roman with a slight edge to his tone.

"Relax, I'm just trying to get to know her, Roman," he countered defensively.

"Do you have any idea how dangerous that is? What if she finds out about us? You know what she is..." warned Roman, rising from the couch to follow Nico.

"She doesn't even know what she is!" said Nico. "And don't think that I haven't noticed that you've been sneaking off at night. I know exactly where you've been going."

"Well at least I have been discreet about it. And although we do *need* to keep an eye on her, we still have to keep our distance."

"Look Roman, you can do whatever you want to do, but I'm doing it my way."

Roman's eyes blazed angrily. Suddenly his incisors burst out, protruding from his upper lip. With fangs bared, Roman lunged across the room at Nico and growled menacingly, "You will do as I say little brother."

***

"Earth to Celeste, come in Celeste, come in Celeste."

Celeste was awoken by the fuzzy, static-filled sound of Brian's voice coming through her walkie-talkie. It was already dark outside and Celeste wondered drowsily how long she had been asleep. She reached over for the walkie-talkie on her bedside table and replied, "I hear you loud and clear Brian – go ahead..."

"I'm coming over, so let me in!"

41

Celeste got out of bed, splashed some water on her face and went downstairs to let Brian in, who she found waiting impatiently on the other side of the door.

"Thank God you're finally awake," said Brian as he walked right in and plopped down on the couch. "You've got to help me out, I don't know what to do."

"What's wrong?" asked Celeste.

"Natalie called me and asked me to be her date to senior prom," he answered, his copper flecked brows creased in concern.

Celeste took a breath to hold back the laughter that was bubbling up inside of her. "So what are you so worried about?" she asked, trying to keep her face serious.

"I don't know! I totally panicked and said that my mom was calling me, and I had to call her back, and I practically hung up on her. That was two hours ago, and now I don't know what to say."

"Well, Natalie is a lot of fun, she's beautiful, and I think you would have a great time going with her. Why wouldn't you say yes?" she asked.

"I don't know, honestly, I guess I had always figured we would go together," Brian answered sheepishly, looking up to catch Celeste's eye.

Celeste had to stop and think about that for a few seconds. It's true; she had always thought they would end up going to prom together too. For so many years there had never been any other boy in her life besides Brian. But she knew that Natalie really liked him, in a way that she didn't think she ever would, and Brian deserved that. She wanted Brian to be happy more than anything else. She wouldn't be selfish with him, not when she cared so much about his happiness. So with a slight twinge of wistfulness, she said, "Aw, come on Brian, we can still hang out together while we're there. I'll even save you a dance. I really think you should go with her."

Brian looked at her for a moment with serious eyes. "Yeah I guess you're right." He was quiet for a second, and then he added, "So who are you going to take then?"

Celeste shrugged off the question. "I wasn't planning on taking anyone."

Chapter 4

Roman stared at the computer as his mind wandered remembering the last time he was in Oak Bluffs. It had been so long ago, and yet sometimes it felt like it was just yesterday. His parents had been with him and his brother back then, when they first came to live in this small town, and perhaps that's what drew him here again. Well, that and finding out about Celeste Wilder, of course. At the thought of her, he felt a twinge of hunger; he walked over to the mini fridge hidden in his closet. Bottles of deep red liquid filled the refrigerator, and with a displeased look on his face, Roman gulped one down. After centuries of suppressing his nature, he still found it difficult, but he had promised his mother that he would not become the thing he hated—that he would not give in to the monster inside of him. His beautiful mother, who had always felt so guilty for what had befallen their family because of what she had done. She never gave up on them. She was the one that insisted they were better; they were not like the rest because they were the first of their kind.

Roman could remember everything so clearly, walking into their home, which was normally so neat, everything in its place and that time it looked like it had been ransacked by some supernatural force. The door had been taken off of its hinges; there was furniture upturned and broken shards of glass strewn across the floor. And the blood... There was so much blood everywhere. All of the myths about vampires being killed by a stake through the heart seemed so trite, and yet there laid his beloved parents with wooden stakes protruding from their chests. Roman had taken their bodies and buried them with the utmost care in the backyard, hoping to save Nico from the tragic scene he would have forever seared in his mind.

Nico barged into Roman's room and tore him away from his dark musings.

"I'm going out. Are you going to be okay here by yourself?" asked Nico sarcastically.

"Enjoy yourself Nico, and please try to keep out of trouble, okay?" Roman's older brother tone was back, and Nico knew the fight from earlier had been forgotten.

"Of course," said Nico as he sauntered happily out of the house.

Roman was feeling a bit on edge, and felt the need to get out of the house as well. He thought a long walk would help clear his mind, so he headed out with no particular destination in mind. As he walked, he thought about Celeste and the uncertain future before her. He resolved to call Stellan to discuss it further in the morning.

Celeste took a big bite of the cheesy pizza and looked over at Brian who was wiping his greasy chin with a napkin. He was totally engrossed by the movie. She had let him pick and of course he had chosen *Super Bad*, a movie she had no interest in.

"Come on, how can you not like this movie?"

"It's so stupid!"

"No it's not, it's hilarious! And there's even some of that romance stuff you like. Boop!" he said and poked her nose.

She giggled and swatted at his finger. "Brian, you know nothing about romance and obviously the writers of this movie don't have a clue either!" she retorted.

After he left, she had been clearing away the living room table and tidying up the kitchen when Rocky whined at her, looking up at her with big pleading eyes.

"Oh no! I forgot to take you out – poor guy!"

She hurriedly snapped on his leash and took him outside as his tail wagged furiously in excitement. The streets were so quiet she could hear the muffled sound of Rocky snuffling through the grass searching for just the right spot. As she passed by a tall oak tree, she heard a rustle and saw a bat hanging upside down from one of the lower branches!

First a falcon and now a bat? What's going on with all of these weird winged creatures all of a sudden?

Slightly spooked, Celeste made a quick 180-degree turn to head back towards her house and found herself suddenly face-to-face with Roman. Before she could speak, Rocky let out a startled bark. He sniffed the stranger suspiciously and growled, his hackles raised in alarm.

"Oh hi," said Celeste, unconsciously running her hand through her disheveled hair. "You surprised us, and nothing much gets by Rocky."

"In a former life I used to be a ninja," quipped Roman with a sly smile.

"What are you doing out here?" she asked.

"Well, I could ask you the same thing…"

"I live right there," Celeste said pointing at her house with the white picket fence and wrap-around porch, "and I'm just taking Rocky for a quick walk before bed. So what are you doing here, really?"

She eyed him questioningly with a hand on her hip.

"I'm not sure actually, I just started walking and somehow I found myself here," admitted Roman.

"You walked all the way from your place to here? That's more than a couple miles, isn't it?" Celeste asked.

"I've had some things on my mind, and I thought a good long hike would help. I went through town, kept walking, and found myself here admiring all of these beautiful turn-of-the century houses," he said.

They continued their casual conversation for a couple of minutes, and Celeste couldn't help but notice that he kept glancing over her head at the tree behind her. Finally she interrupted, "Did you see the bat up there?"

She turned around to point it out to him, but it was gone.

"No, I didn't see anything. Actually, I didn't think bats were native to Oak Bluffs."

Celeste thought she saw a flash of concern in his eyes, but it was gone as quickly as it had appeared. "They're not. I've grown up here my entire life, and I've never seen one until today."

"Well, I better walk you to your house just to be safe, we certainly don't want one following you home."

Roman accompanied Celeste to her front door and then he paused at the threshold.

"Thanks for protecting me from the scary bats," she said jokingly, anything to break the silence.

He took her hand in his and she felt the familiar sparks, like tiny little explosions all over her skin. For a moment he looked at her longingly as if there were something more he wanted to say, but then he dropped her hand and with a quick goodnight hurried off into the darkness.

"We have a problem," said Roman as he marched in the door and hurried up the stairs to Nico's room. He found him passed out in bed, and Roman could smell the faint scent of liquor in the air. He shook Nico roughly until he finally opened a drowsy eye.

"Wake up!" demanded Roman.

"Okay, okay, I'm up, what is wrong with you?" asked Nico as he tried to sit up and snap his mind awake.

"There's another one of us here in town."

"Another pair of devastatingly handsome brothers?" teased Nico.

"This is not a laughing matter, Nico. There's a vampire in Oak Bluffs. And I don't believe this one shares our predilection toward blood bags."

Roman went on to tell him about his midnight stroll, and how he had felt the vampire's presence through town and as he tracked it, it led right to Celeste's house. "It can't be a coincidence that it was in a tree not fifty feet away from her door."

"Okay, but what would he want with her?" asked Nico, "Unless he knows what she is..."

Roman had thought of that too, but there shouldn't have been any vampires who knew about the Wilders. Their family secret had been kept guarded by powerful magic for centuries in order to protect them. Suddenly, a terrible thought crossed Roman's mind – Fabian. He was certainly powerful enough to have found out, but would he dare interfere?

Nico interrupted Roman's thought with, "It could just all be a coincidence. Maybe the vampire saw her out somewhere and followed her home. She is a rather striking young woman, and you can't deny the appeal she seems to have with our kind. I know I feel incredibly drawn to her."

"I suppose it's possible. I have seen it before with others like her, but I've never experienced it myself," said Roman.

Nico looked over at him skeptically, saying "Oh no?"

"Regardless of what the reason is that this visitor has dropped into Oak Bluffs, I think it's time to consult with our dear friend Stellan, and the sooner, the better."

The following morning, Roman pulled out his shiny midnight black Porsche 911. He rolled the top down, and revving the engine, readied himself for a road trip with his brother. They hadn't seen Stellan in over fifty years, not since after their parents had died and they had fled Oak Bluffs. Stellan, like Fabian, was a very powerful sorcerer; however, unlike Fabian he did not practice dark magic. He had been close to their mother before they were all turned, and although he generally did not associate with vampires or any of what he termed "evil creatures," he had always made an exception for them. Over the years, they had often sought his guidance, and he had proven to be a trustworthy and faithful friend. In fact, it had been Stellan who had informed them of the Wilders' presence in Oak Bluffs.

***

Celeste tossed and turned in her bed as nightmares filled her subconscious. She was walking home from school when an enormous bat swooped down from the darkening sky and attacked her. She screamed as it tore at her face and hands with its claws and tried to bite her with its sharp fangs. Just as she thought she was dead for sure, a burly gray wolf with three-inch incisors bared had pounced on top of them, and she was able to roll away from the snarling fury. As she turned to run away, she glanced up in the sky and caught a glimpse of a colony of enraged bats descending upon the wolf.

At a distance, she heard an ominous grumbling and the asphalt began to crack and crumble. From the opening the most frightening creatures began to emerge – slithering, snake-like animals, six-legged demon hell dogs, horribly disfigured ghosts, and other demons of all hideous shapes and sizes. Celeste shut her eyes in terror. It seemed like the gates of hell had opened up and spit into her backyard all the vilest creatures of the underworld. In a panic, Celeste, previously frozen and unable to move, found her legs under her and took off running. As she turned to look back, she saw that the demons (the only word she seemed to have to describe them) were chasing her. To her surprise, she found that the more she ran, the faster she got and the less fatigue she felt. After what seemed like she had been running forever, she turned around to find that nothing was chasing her anymore. She was alone in the middle of an unfamiliar town where she collapsed on the spot.

Celeste awoke with a start, her heart pounding and drenched in sweat. She went to her bathroom to splash cold water on her face. As she stood looking in the mirror at her tear-stained reflection, she felt so weak in the knees she thought she might pass out. "It was only a dream," she said to herself out loud, hoping that the sound of her own voice would steady her. She pulled herself together and shuffled down the stairs looking for her mother.

Although Celeste was practically eighteen, she felt she needed some soothing words from her mother to forget all about her terrible nightmare. She found her mom in her hospital scrubs bent down in front of the refrigerator pulling out a variety of leafy green veggies and piling them on the counter.

After taking one look at Celeste's pale drawn face, she dropped everything and rushed over to her. "What's wrong sweetie? Are you okay?"

"Yeah, I'm okay, I just had the most horrifying nightmare," she explained as she nestled into her mom's warm embrace.

"What did you dream? Maybe you'll feel better if you talk about it. That always seemed to help when you were younger." Mrs. Wilder sat her daughter down at the kitchen table and began preparing her a cup of soothing chamomile tea.

Celeste had completely forgotten about that, it had been so long ago. When her father had first passed away, she had been plagued with horrific dreams for weeks. She was so young, only ten years old back then, and she must have buried those memories along with everything else around that traumatic time. She explained the dream to her mother, and found that she was shaking. She felt like she was reliving the whole thing again.

"This wasn't the first weird dream I've had about birds and bats. It seems to be a new trend. And I even saw a bat outside the other night, *and* there's a falcon nesting in the oak tree outside my window. It's all so strange."

At the mention of the bat, her mom looked slightly disconcerted. "Everything is going to be okay, sweetie," she said, hiding the preoccupied look in her eye.

***

Stellan's house looked exactly as Nico and Roman remembered it. It was immense, sprawling over five acres of land in a remote wooded area and seemingly untouched by modern civilization. It was rustic, completely built of the wood from the towering oaks native to the surrounding forest and exuded a cozy feeling of home.

As the brothers got out of the car, Stellan appeared, greeting them wearing his signature tattered blue robe. Sorcerers, unlike vampires, did age, although at a much slower rate than humans, and if they were great ones they could spell themselves against aging all together. Stellan chose the former and though he was several hundreds of years old, he looked to be only in his late sixties with graying hair past his shoulders and a lengthy beard. His kind gray eyes brightened at the sight of the boys.

Roman looked at him fondly, and asked, "How are you doing old man?"

"Now Roman Constantin, I know you have better manners than that. Your parents taught you to respect your elders," he scolded. Smiling, he said, "It has been far too long, my boy," and he yanked Roman into an awkward embrace. Nico, just steps behind, happily joined in on the long overdue reunion.

"It's been much too long since I last laid eyes on the two of you. I'd like to start with some pleasantries, but from your tone when we spoke last night I imagine this is a rather urgent matter we need to discuss," said Stellan, ushering the brothers into the expansive great room. The fire crackled and hissed as Stellan threw another log in the fireplace. Though it was late spring, it was much cooler in the countryside and the fire was a necessity to keep the dampness from creeping into the stately home.

Stellan situated his horn-rimmed glasses on his long aquiline nose, settled down in his brown leather club chair and looked at Roman expectantly. Roman, pacing in front of the fireplace, began by recounting the story of the new vampire in town and his concerns for Celeste's safety.

"What if this has something to do with Fabian?" asked Roman nervously. "Do you think it's possible that he has found out about her?"

"There's always a possibility, but the question is why would he even want to interfere with guardian affairs? Those are matters beyond his concern, unless of course, he stumbled upon her while tracking the two of you. But you two haven't been associating with her, have you?"

Stellan looked questioningly at Roman then Nico. "Humph." He didn't need a response; it was obvious by the looks on their faces. "What did I warn you two about before you came back to Oak Bluffs?" said Stellan, his voice rising as he moved to the edge of his seat. "You must not get involved with her; it is too dangerous for all of you. The only reason I told you about her was to protect you both, and now it seems I've done quite the opposite. Not to mention that I have put her at risk as well."

All three men sat in silence contemplating their next move. It was of the utmost importance for them to protect the secret of the Guardian. For centuries there has been a balance between good and evil—without guardians the world would plummet into chaos with all the creatures of the underworld running rampant. There have always been certain family lineages around the world which are burdened with the task of keeping the world safe for humans. These families have been protected over the ages by supernatural forces, and the knowledge of their existence has been limited to a select few who made up part of the Council. It just so happened that Stellan was one of the select few, and with that knowledge came the responsibility to protect the guardians and their secret. Roman and Nico's mother, Lilliana, having come from a line of great witches had also been tasked with the same obligation, that is, before Fabian intervened in their lives.

"Is it true about us being somehow drawn to her?" interjected Nico.

"Yes and no. I have heard of some cases where supernatural creatures are irresistibly drawn to guardians, but I've only ever seen it happen with a few vampires and werewolves. Since those two species are the closest to their former human selves, I imagine that is why the attraction is the greatest. As you know, there must always be a balance between good and bad, light and dark, and it seems that their light attracts your darkness and unfortunately the opposite is true as well," Stellan explained.

"Well, I definitely feel something," said Nico.

"And you Roman?" asked Stellan.

"Perhaps..." he answered with a guarded expression.

"She must be a very strong candidate if you are both feeling something so soon."

"She's also not bad to look at," added Nico.

Roman shot him a murderous glance.

"So what are we going to do?" asked Nico.

"We are going to protect her," answered Roman with a menacing sparkle in his eye.

Celeste found herself not wanting to spend the day alone after her mom left for work, so she decided to give Natalie a call. She paused to think about how quickly she and

55

Natalie had become so close again. It was like they were back in grade school and no time had passed at all. Spending the day with cheerful, bubbly Natalie would surely get her mind off of her disturbing dream.

"Yeah, come on over, I was actually just planning on heading to the mall to get black gloves and a matching clutch for my prom dress. We can go together!" said Natalie over the phone.

Celeste loved people watching, and the crowded mall on a weekend was a perfect place for it. She casually observed the happy couple walking in front of her hand in hand, whispering and giggling, oblivious to anyone else around them. She longed for that intimate connection with someone someday. She turned back to Natalie who was gushing over the fact that Brian was taking her to prom. Celeste listened happily as she recounted all the details of their phone conversation. When the topic changed to her dress, Natalie suddenly looked at Celeste in dismay.

"You don't have a dress yet?"

The rest of the afternoon focused on finding Celeste the perfect dress. "You want something that's not too 'costumey' but still clearly 1920's style," opined Natalie.

After what seemed to Celeste like hours, she found a sophisticated black flapper dress, knee-length with a matching bejeweled headpiece complete with a fancy white feather. She made a mental note to ask her mother to let her borrow her long pearl necklace, which would perfectly complete the ensemble.

"Okay, so you have the picture-perfect outfit, now you just need the perfect date to go along with it," said Natalie with a smile. "Decisions, decisions, oh which of the Constantin brothers will you take?" she teased.

"Ha-ha, Nat, and I was planning on going solo actually."

"No! We are ladies and should always be escorted by a handsome gentleman – especially for a Roaring 20's Casino," Natalie said affecting her most sophisticated accent. "Just leave everything up to me. I'll make sure you have the appropriate arm candy to immortalize the momentous occasion of our senior prom picture."

"That's what worries me," said Celeste.

***

After a lengthy discussion, Stellan, Roman and Nico had decided that the best course of action would be to determine if this new vampire was indeed a threat.

"We have to find out what brought this guy to Oak Bluffs and what he knows," said Roman.

Stellan agreed, "Yes, I believe an interrogation is needed."

"Don't worry, we'll find him," Nico finished.

Roman seriously hoped that this had all been a terrible coincidence, and that they could convince this intruder to leave Oak Bluffs without further complications. As they drove back into town, the sun was setting over the hills in the distance, making it perfect timing for vampire tracking. The two brothers split up to cover more ground, hoping to find the vampire before he caused any trouble.

After all the shopping, Celeste and Natalie were starving and headed to the center of town for a bite. Oak Bluffs had a town square reminiscent of old Western movies. There was a lush green park in the center surrounding the Town Hall and a brick paved sidewalk encircling it. The girls were greeted by the familiar neon red sign of Ralph's Diner and the jingling bell as the door swung open. Ralph's was a 50's themed late night hot spot with the high school and college crowds alike, but even on a quiet Sunday evening the place was packed. The girls ordered a couple things to snack on from the waitress in the poodle skirt and sat back to watch all the action around them. They were sitting in a booth next to the pinball machine, and the tall red-headed boy playing the vintage *Star Wars* game seemed completely enthralled by it, so much so that every so often he'd back right into the booth and cause the whole table to shake.

Natalie looked at Celeste, utter annoyance written on her face. "Excuse me, you're spilling my soda all over the place. Can you try to calm down over there?"

At that the boy stopped playing abruptly, and turned around with a conciliatory smile. "Sorry girls, I guess I just don't know my own strength. Let me make it up to you by buying you drinks." He flashed his gleaming white teeth and revealed a charming dimple on his left cheek.

"Well, it is the least you could do especially since you spilled all of ours," retorted Natalie, but her teasing tone was back.

Still smiling, he put his tan leather jacket down in the booth next to Natalie.

As he walked away, Natalie said to Celeste, "What is up with all of these new boys in town? Has Oak Bluffs CC suddenly moved up in the college rankings? This is so great!"

Celeste just rolled her eyes and laughed. A few minutes later, the cute boy was back with three frosty beers in his hands.

"Can we please start over?" he asked. "I'm Patrick." He had a cocky swagger about him – this was exactly the kind of guy that Celeste hated. But she put a smile on her face for Natalie's sake as she could tell her friend was intrigued.

Natalie smiled and gestured to Celeste, "This is my friend Celeste, and I'm Natalie. How come I've never seen you before?"

Patrick sat down with the girls, and explained that he had just started at Oak Bluffs CC as Natalie had guessed. He had pale skin with a few freckles on his nose, coupled with the ginger hair and name; Celeste guessed he had to be of Irish descent. "I'm from Woodfield. It's even smaller than Oak Bluffs and this was my closest option for college," he finished.

As they sat talking, out of the corner of her eye, Celeste saw Roman stalk into the restaurant. Without looking around, as if he had sensed that she was there, his eyes immediately locked onto hers in a tense gaze. He approached their table determinedly, switching his focus to Patrick as he got closer. Roman's vampire sixth sense was bristling, and he knew without a doubt that this was the intruder he had been tracking.

59

"Celeste, hello, introduce me to your new friend," he said brusquely. Celeste could feel the tension emanating from Roman as he stared threateningly at Patrick. Something about his stance reminded her of a snarling dog ready to pounce. She wasn't the only who had noticed, the entire crowd at Ralph's had gone silent.

Awkwardly, she managed, "This is Patrick. We just met him here and Patrick this is Roman, my, uh, friend's brother. And Roman this is Natalie; I don't think you have ever met her either."

Roman nodded to Natalie without taking his eyes off of Patrick, who finally broke the uncomfortable silence. "Hello Roman. I think I've heard about you actually. You are Nico's brother, right?" he asked coolly.

At the mention of Nico, Roman's face tensed up again. "Yes I am. And how is it that you know my brother?"

"I don't really know him, but we were at the same party the other night, and I overheard some people talking. I guess being new in town, we all have something in common," Patrick said grinning, as if it was a private joke that only he was in on.

Roman was still standing at the edge of the table, every muscle tense. Celeste reached out for his hand hoping to coax him into sitting down. The electricity sparked like a live wire when their hands touched and for a split second he relented.

"Sit down with us," she said sweetly.

He considered for a moment and then slid into the booth next to Celeste. Having Roman so close to her sent a tingling chill down her spine. Natalie tried to get the casual conversation going again, but there was no denying the tension in the air. Celeste had an overwhelming urge to get up and make a run for the girls' bathroom with Natalie, but she was worried about what would happen if she left the two men alone.

Natalie began chatting with Patrick again, which gave Celeste the chance to give Roman a questioning look. He looked anxiously back at her, but would give no sign as to what made him so upset. The conversation carried on awkwardly when to Celeste's relief, she saw Nico's smiling face enter the diner. He came straight over and greeted everyone amicably as he pulled up a chair at the end of the table.

"Well good evening all – and you are?"

"Patrick. You're Nico right?"

"Exactly," he replied, grasping Patrick's hand tightly, causing him to wince.

Celeste hoped that Nico's appearance would brighten the mood, and after a few minutes she could see that Roman had visibly relaxed. With the drama seemingly concluded peacefully, everyone in the diner had returned to their normal conversations.

"So tell us something about yourself," said Nico.

Roman eyed Patrick suspiciously as he searched for a response.

"Before you two got here I was telling the girls that I just started at the community college," replied Patrick.

"Interesting, that's where I go as well, and yet I've never seen you. What's your major?"

"I'm still undecided."

"And what made you come to Oak Bluffs?"

"Nico, stop giving him the third degree!" interjected Natalie.

"I'm sorry, I hope I wasn't rude. I simply wanted to get to know the guy vying for my ladies' attentions."

Celeste felt her cheeks reddening and took the opportunity to head to the ladies room. Besides, after two beers she couldn't put it off any longer.

What a bizarre night this is turning out to be!

When she stepped out of the bathroom, Roman was standing outside waiting for her. His posture was tense, his hands clenched at this sides. "Celeste, listen to me, you need to stay away from Patrick. He is not what he seems to be, and you could get hurt..." he said, his eyes full of concern.

"What are you talking about Roman? Do you even know Patrick? Why would he hurt me? You have been acting so weird ever since you walked in here. Just tell me what is going on," pleaded Celeste.

"I can't, but please—you just have to trust me," he begged, his voice rough with emotion.

"Trust you? I barely know you Roman," and she turned to walk away, but he caught her by the arm and pulled her firmly towards him.

"Please Celeste, I promise I will explain everything to you, I just can't right now," he whispered, his eyes locking onto hers, just inches from her face. As strange as all of this seemed, the intense connection that she felt with Roman compelled her to listen to him.

"Take Natalie and go home and let Nico and me deal with Patrick. Trust me," he said as he looked into her worried eyes.

There was something about that look and those mesmerizing blue eyes that were so hauntingly familiar and made Celeste do exactly as he asked.

Once the girls left the diner, Roman and Nico wasted no time escorting Patrick into the back alley.

"What are you really doing here, Patrick?" Nico asked forcefully.

"Whoa, guys, I think we got off on the wrong foot here or something. I didn't know those girls were with you, okay? I just came in here looking for a bite," he said facetiously. "I'm sure there are plenty of humans to go around, right?"

"That's not what my brother asked. Now answer us: what are you doing here in Oak Bluffs?" growled Roman as he shoved him up against the wall. A cat jumped out of the adjacent dumpster with a *clang* startling the three of them. Patrick tried to break free of Roman's grasp, but he held strong. Tightening his grip around his throat, Roman hissed, "Answer me."

"Nothing, I swear. A couple of weeks ago I was just a normal guy, and then one day I wake up, and I'm a vampire. All I wanted to do was sink my teeth into my little sister, so I freaked out and left town. Oak Bluffs seemed as good a place as any to start my new life so I stopped here," he explained. "You two are the only other vampires I've ever met. I'm just trying to figure it all out."

"What were you doing outside of Celeste's house the other night?" questioned Nico, still unconvinced by his story.

"I was out flying around looking for a willing donor, and I saw someone walking by themselves so I stopped for a closer look. Geez, what is it about this girl that has you two so worked up?"

"That's our business, not yours. This is my suggestion to you Patrick: go home, pack your stuff, leave Oak Bluffs and never come back," threatened Roman.

Patrick looked over at Nico who was glaring at him. Patrick seemed to weigh his options and soon realized he would be no match for these two vampires who were obviously much older and stronger than he was. "Okay, okay, there's no need to get violent. This place wasn't that great anyway, I'm outta here."

Roman and Nico watched as Patrick got into his car and drove off, and both let out a sigh of relief.

"That was easy," said Nico.

"Too easy," retorted Roman.

"That guy didn't know anything; he was a new vampire and obviously didn't have the brains to be behind any sort of plot against Celeste. He probably really was at the wrong place at the wrong time," Nico said as he began walking towards the car.

"I'm not convinced little brother. It's all too much of a coincidence. I'm going to keep watch over Celeste tonight just in case. We can't risk anything happening to her."

"I can go," offered Nico. "When was the last time you got a full night's sleep?"

"I'm fine, I can handle it," said Roman. The air glimmered all around him and every molecule in his body vibrated for a split second. And Roman was no longer Roman, instead, a majestic black falcon with piercing blue eyes stood in his place. He flapped his powerful wings and took off into the dark sky. Nico watched as his looming silhouette faded against the bright moon and disappeared into the night.

As Celeste and Natalie drove home from the diner, they couldn't stop talking about their peculiar evening.

"What in the world was up with Roman?" asked Natalie. "Is he always so intense?"

"I guess he kind of is, but this was way beyond normal," Celeste replied as she mulled over the entire series of events in her head.

"Patrick seemed like a nice enough guy, so I just don't get why Roman went all crazy when he saw us with him," Natalie continued.

"Me either. He came into the diner acting like he didn't know him, but the way they stared each other down, you'd think they had been mortal enemies or something."

"Maybe he was jealous because you were talking to another guy," offered Natalie with a devious smile.

"Ha, funny, but it really felt like something much more serious than that. I mean I can't say I know Roman well at all, but there was a genuine desperation in his voice when he told me to leave. It actually scared me..."

"All I know is that he better have a pretty good explanation. After all, I was having fun!"

Celeste dropped Natalie off at her house, and headed back home. She suddenly felt exhausted. The bizarre evening had really drained her emotionally, and she couldn't stop thinking about it.

What did Roman mean when he said Patrick could hurt me and that he wasn't what he seemed to be?

Celeste's head reeled with questions as she got into bed and turned off the lights. She thought she would never get any rest, but moments after her head hit the pillow she fell into a deep sleep with Rocky snuggled up next to her. Meanwhile, outside her window a dark falcon perched in the oak tree, keeping watch over her until daylight.

C hapter 5

When Celeste headed out to school the next morning, she found Brian sitting on her front steps.

"Walk with me to school?" he asked as he held out his arm for her.

Celeste hooked her arm in his and recounted yesterday's events (as was the norm when they hadn't seen each other for a day), the warm sun shining down on them as they walked. She decided to exclude the part about Roman's strange behavior and focused instead on the shopping and prom portion of her evening.

"Natalie's costume is great. She is going to look so cute in it!" she said. "What are you going to wear?"

"I don't know. I haven't really thought about it that much. I mean, a suit is a suit, whether it's the 20's or the 80's, right?" he asked with a sidelong glance.

Celeste laughed, and said, "You better come up with something good. Natalie is really excited about prom, and she's put so much time and effort into it. Actually, I was supposed to ask you if you'd help out with decorating the gym on Thursday night. Natalie already dragged me into it, so I think it's only fair that you help too."

"Sure, Cel, anything for you," said Brian.

As they were walking under the familiar archway of St. Alice High School, Celeste's phone rang. She signaled for Brian to keep going and stopped to answer it when she saw the caller I.D. read Nico.

"Good morning beautiful!" said Nico as she picked up the phone.

"Unless you are calling with an explanation, I don't really have time to talk, I'm about to walk into first period," she said curtly.

"I know, I'm sorry Celeste. I just wanted to check up on you and see how you were doing. Can we grab a coffee or something this afternoon?"

"Sure, I guess we could do that."

"Okay great, I'll pick you up from school then. See you later."

Celeste tried to focus on Mr. Wilson's lecture about the Vietnam War, but her mind just kept wandering. She couldn't believe that this was her last week in high school. Prom was in just a couple of days, then final exams, her birthday, graduation, and her life as a high school student would be over. She really wished that her dad could be here to see her graduate and head off to college. He had gone to NYU too, and she was sure that he would be thrilled that she was following in his footsteps.

Celeste was interrupted from her thoughts by the shrill ringing of the fire alarm echoing through the building. All of the students filed out of their classrooms like they had practiced hundreds of times during mandatory fire drills. As they marched outside and met in their designated areas awaiting further instructions, something at the edge of the woods behind the school caught her attention. She squinted to try to focus better, and could have sworn she saw Patrick. His bright auburn hair stood out against the dark foliage of evergreens, and he was wearing the same tan leather jacket from the night before. He was staring in her direction. She looked around searching for Natalie to confirm her suspicions, but when she looked back at the woods Patrick (or whoever it was) was gone.

When the final bell rang, Celeste grabbed her backpack and found Nico in his fire engine red BMW M5, waiting for her with a gleaming smile and radio blaring. It was hard for her to stay mad at him; he just had such a way about him. As she got in the car, he gave her a swift kiss on the cheek, and they sped off to the café.

The café was filled with the pungent aroma of freshly roasted coffee beans, and Celeste's stomach gurgled in anticipation. After the barista handed them their frothy cappuccinos, they retreated to a comfy sofa in the corner to talk.

"So about last night," began Nico uncomfortably, "I'm sorry Roman overreacted the way he did. He can be a little overprotective at times. I guess it's a side effect of being the big brother-slash-father figure of the family."

Celeste blew on her steaming mocha latte and took a careful sip. "That seemed like something way more than simple overprotectiveness. Does he know Patrick or something?"

"Not exactly...but he knows guys like Patrick. The type who would come into a small town diner and prey on innocent high school girls with alcohol," he stammered.

"I know we're pretty sheltered in Oak Bluffs, but that's what Roman meant when he said that Patrick could hurt me?" asked Celeste incredulously.

"Yes, exactly," he answered without looking up from his cappuccino.

"It seemed much more personal than that."

"I'm really sorry if he frightened you. My brother does have a flair for the dramatic at times."

Celeste looked at Nico, still unconvinced. "I think his paranoia is rubbing off on me because I thought I saw Patrick today at school."

"What?" he asked, almost choking on his hot coffee.

"I'm not one hundred percent sure it was him, because he was pretty far away. I must have been imagining things. Why would he be at my school?"

"That is strange. I know you girls are hot and all, but – "

"Oh stop!" said Celeste as she threw a sugar packet at Nico's face.

As Nico drove Celeste home, she thought about last night and the desperate look in Roman's face when he had told her to leave, and somehow Nico's explanation just didn't ring true. She decided to let it go for now, but she resolved to find out what was really going on one way or another.

***

"Celeste thinks she saw Patrick at her school today," announced Nico as he walked in the house.

"What?" asked Roman, dropping the book he had been reading. "Damn it - he should be long gone by now." He stood abruptly, clenching his fist tensely.

"She wasn't sure it was him, but to be safe, we better keep an eye on her."

"I always do," Roman murmured.

"I hate lying to her, Roman."

"I know that, but it's better for her not to know anything yet. The less she knows the safer she will be for now. Besides, Stellan said her eighteenth birthday is next week, and once we find out if she has been chosen as the next Guardian, nothing will be the same for her ever again."

Chapter 6

Celeste, Brian and a handful of classmates from the prom committee were scattered around the gym hanging decorations and candle-lit chandeliers while setting up poker tables and vintage slot machines. Natalie directed all of the activity, hastily twirling a feather boa while determining the exact location of the DJ booth in relation to the dance floor. By the time they were finished they had succeeded in transforming the gym into an extravagant Roaring 20's Casino.

"Nat, you really went all out, this place looks amazing!" said Celeste, taking a step back to take it all in.

"I couldn't have done it without the two of you. Thank you so much!" she said as she hugged Celeste and Brian. A sneaky look crossed Natalie's face. "I just have one more favor to ask of you Celeste."

"Sure, anything."

"Will you take Nico to prom with you?"

Celeste shot a quick glance at Brian and caught a surprised look in his sea-green eyes, then she turned back to Natalie. "Why Nico?"

"Why not? He's new in town, and Dani Lynn said that he had mentioned to her how he had never gone to his own prom, and how much fun it would have been to come to ours," Natalie explained. "And anyway, I promised you I'd make sure you had the perfect date to match your outfit."

"Isn't he like twenty-something?" interjected Brian. "Why would he want to go to a senior prom?"

"Brian, you obviously are underestimating my talents in creating this epic night. I've heard that all of Oak Bluffs is talking about it, so it totally makes sense that he would want to come," Natalie interjected.

"Right..." he said, shaking his head.

"Come on Celeste, why wouldn't you take him? He's fun and super hot! Imagine how amazing your prom pictures will turn out? I see it as a win-win for all," finished Natalie.

Celeste could feel Brian's eyes on her, awaiting her decision. There was no way she was getting out of this one. "As always I feel like there is no point in trying to argue, so I guess I'll just save us all some time and give in now."

"Yes! This is going to be the best prom ever!" squealed Natalie.

"Celeste, you look so beautiful!" her mom exclaimed as she finished curling her bouncy golden hair. "Sometimes I wish I still had long hair," she said wistfully as she looked at her own tired reflection.

Celeste examined herself in the mirror and smiled. Her hair was curling just right, and the dress that Natalie had picked out was quite flattering on her. Even her boring hazel eyes seemed to stand out with the smoky eye shadow Natalie had convinced her to buy.

"And you were right; my pearls are the perfect match for your dress." Mrs. Wilder placed the necklace on her daughter and reaching under her hair closed the clasp tightly. "I'm so happy I got to see you all dressed up before your senior prom. I can't believe how quickly time has passed; it seems like just yesterday your father and I were bringing you home from the hospital."

"Mom, don't do it, please don't cry or else I will start to and then I'll have to redo my makeup all over again."

"Okay, okay I'll stop. I just can't get over how grown up you are. I still can't believe you're going to be eighteen next week," she said.

"Me neither, I can't wait!"

"You know, eighteen is a pretty big deal. You're going to be an adult now. You may find yourself having to make some important decisions soon."

"I know that Mom, and anyway I already decided where I'm going to college so I think I'm pretty set."

"Right, of course. So when is this date of yours going to be here? I am looking forward to meeting him!" she said, changing the subject. "Although I am very surprised Brian didn't ask you to go with him."

"Oh Mom, I already told you Natalie talked me into taking Nico. He's new in town and needed a date to the dance, that's all. And as for Brian, we'll have to go into that another day." Celeste looked at herself in the mirror one more time before heading downstairs.

As the elegant white limo pulled up in the driveway, Brian walked over as Celeste was saying goodnight to her mother on the front porch.

"Brian you look so handsome! Hold on let me get a picture of the two of you," she said as she snapped away a couple of shots.

"Do you like the suit? Natalie picked it out," he said as he struck a modeling pose.

"Let me guess – you two are going as Bonnie and Clyde?" she chuckled.

As they posed for the camera, Natalie and Nico came up the walkway to join them.

"Good! Now I can take pictures of all of you together!" Celeste's mom exclaimed.

"Don't mind my mom guys, she's a little snap-happy tonight," announced Celeste.

"Good evening Mrs. Wilder, I wanted to introduce myself. My name is Nico Constantin," he said, extending his hand with his usual charm and sophistication. "And it is my pleasure to escort your daughter to the dance this evening." He was impeccably dressed with a black and white pinstriped three-piece suit and red rose in his lapel. Even Mrs. Wilder couldn't help but succumb to his charms as she grinned from ear to ear shaking his outstretched hand. She followed with a not-too-discreet wink and a thumbs-up to Celeste. "Very nice to meet you, Nico. You kids have fun tonight, and don't stay out too late!"

Nico held the door open for Celeste as Natalie and Brian climbed over their friends trying to find a spot inside the limo. She peeked inside and saw her rowdy classmates, drinks in hand, and found she needed a deep breath to steady herself. Nico, sensing her hesitation, flashed her a smile and placed a reassuring hand on her back and she climbed in.

Celeste truly felt like she had stepped back in time to a casino in the 1920's as Nico led her into the candle-lit gym. She looked around in fascination, taking in all of the sights and sounds. The poker tables were filled with gangsters and flappers in colorful roaring 20's attire. Even the DJ was decked out in a vintage mobster suit complete with fedora and black and white wing tipped shoes. There was something magical in the air. "Can I get you some moonshine, doll?" asked Nico.

"Okay daddy-o, that would be just swell," she responded in her best 1920's slang.

Nico and Brian went off in search of beverages, leaving Natalie and Celeste to admire the crowd.

"Doesn't Brian look so hot in his suit?"

Celeste noticed that Natalie's face had lit up with a huge smile. "Oh yes, he looks quite dapper! And I love your beret!" she said. "I'll even admit that you were right. Bringing Nico was a really good idea. I think this is going to be an amazing night."

"I think you're totally right!" she said. "So was it me or did I see you flirting with Nico in the limo?"

"You're so bad Natalie!"

"What? I was just curious. You two looked pretty friendly."

"I don't know. I like Nico, I really do, but there is something about Roman that I just can't explain."

Natalie rolled her eyes in mock disapproval. "Maybe it's his incredible looks and the intense way he stares at you."

"I think it's more than that," she laughed. In all honesty Celeste had no clue what it was about Roman that had her so smitten.

Nico and Brian returned with a vibrant red punch, and with a quick glance around the room Nico pulled a flask out of his jacket pocket and poured a touch of vodka into each of their cups.

"Cheers!"

As Celeste had suspected, Nico was a natural born dancer. He was the perfect partner, twirling her, dipping her, and even picking her up off of her feet once or twice. Celeste laughed breathlessly as Nico led her around the dance floor like a pro. Time flew by as the DJ played hit after hit. During one of her twirls, she glanced around the room and caught sight of Brian sitting by himself on the bleachers staring at her.

"Hey Nico, let's take a break for a second, I need to catch my breath," she said.

"Of course, do you want me to get you something to drink?"

"No, I'm okay. I'll get it. Here comes Natalie, why don't you dance with her for a bit?"

As Natalie happily accepted Nico's extended hand, Celeste walked over to Brian, asking, "Hey, how's it going? Why aren't you dancing?"

"I just needed a break. Natalie had to make her rounds so I snuck off to sit down for a bit," he said. "But I'm all good. You still owe me that dance."

Celeste nodded and they made their way back to the dance floor. A slow song had come on, the lights had been dimmed and a romantic mood pervaded as dozens of couples swayed slowly to the music. Celeste always felt so comfortable dancing with Brian. It was like slipping into a warm snuggly blanket on a cool winter's night. Brian was quiet at first, and she enjoyed the comfortable silence that comes from a long-established friendship.

"You look like you're having a lot of fun out there."

"Yeah, I really am actually," Celeste said contentedly.

"I'm really happy to see you like this. I don't remember the last time I saw you having so much fun."

She paused when she noticed a dismal tone in his voice. "Then why don't you look happy?"

"Huh? I don't?"

She looked up at him questioningly with big brown eyes.

"I don't know Cel, I guess I just always thought that I would be the one to make you feel like that again."

Celeste felt like someone had just poured a large bucket of ice water on her head. She waited for a few seconds to collect her thoughts before answering.

"Brian, you know that you are the one that has gotten me through some of the worst years of my life. I never would have survived losing my dad without you. What we have is so special to me, and I never want to lose you as my best friend."

"You'll never lose me Cel. I'll always be here for you, I promise," he said and pulled her close to him.

Celeste felt tears welling up and her throat began to tighten. She pulled away quickly and excused herself to make a run to the ladies room.

Celeste dabbed at her eyes in the mirror, and reapplied some lip-gloss. As much as she tried to deny it, it seemed that Natalie had been right.

Does Brian really have feelings for me?

She shrugged off the thought, pulled herself together, and headed back to the dance. As she walked through the quiet hallway, she heard footsteps behind her. She turned around quickly, and found herself face to face with Patrick.

"Oh geez, you scared me," she said. "What are you doing here?"

"Sorry about that. I've been wanting to talk to you all night, but I didn't want to get beaten up by your boyfriend," said Patrick caustically. The bright smile from the other night was gone, replaced instead by dark circles under his bloodshot eyes that stood out in contrast to his pale ivory skin.

Patrick lurking in the shadows waiting for her to come out of the bathroom just didn't seem right to her. She tried to remain calm, and keep the conversation casual hoping that she could make her way back to a more public area.

"So what did you want to talk to me about?" asked Celeste.

"It was actually something I wanted to show you. It's in my car -- let's go," he said as he reached forcefully for her arm.

"No, I don't think so," Celeste said equally forcefully as she wriggled away from his grasp. "I have to get back to Nico. He must be wondering where I went."

"It's about your father's death, Celeste. You may want to reconsider."

Celeste's heart froze at the mention of her father. "How do you know my dad?" she asked and the calmness in her voice had disappeared.

"I guess you'll never know unless you come with me."

Visions of Roman warning her about Patrick danced through her head, but if he knew something about her father, she had to find out what it was. Against her better judgment, she followed Patrick out to his car. She kept hoping to pass someone on the way, but the parking lot was deserted. She could hear the echoing of Roman's desperate voice warning her to go back, but she trudged on determinedly.

"I guess meeting you at Ralph's the other night wasn't a coincidence?"

"Not exactly," Patrick confirmed.

"You came looking for me?" asked Celeste desperate to put the pieces together.

"You could say that."

Celeste looked around nervously, but there was no one in sight. "Do you know Roman and Nico? Is that why you were all acting so weird?"

"Not personally, but I know of them."

"What does that mean?" she asked, walking more slowly and trying to stall.

"There are things you don't know about them. But more importantly there are things about your father that you need to know, Celeste," he said as he walked up to the trunk of his car and opened it.

Faster than she thought humanly possible, he picked her up and forced her into the trunk. Celeste screamed and kicked frantically when she realized what was happening. Suddenly everything began to move very slowly. She stretched out her arms, pushing against the trunk door as hard as she could. She struggled to get her legs under her as Patrick reached up to close the lid down on her. Before it slammed down, Roman appeared out of nowhere.

"Roman!" she screamed.

Patrick spun around and met with Roman's stone cold fist and crumpled to the ground. Celeste was petrified with fear, completely numb. She stared in shock at Patrick's limp body stretched out on the black top. Roman reached in and scooped her out of the trunk, cradling her tenderly.

"You're all right. Everything is going to be fine," he whispered to her.

Celeste could feel the edges of her vision blurring as she struggled not to faint. Suddenly, Nico appeared running from the direction of the gym.

"Is she okay?" Nico asked, eyes wide with panic.

"Why weren't you watching her?" Roman growled. "If I hadn't been here..." and he broke off suddenly remembering Celeste's presence.

"Take her back into the gym little brother. I'll take care of Patrick," Roman said, carefully placing Celeste into Nico's arms.

Celeste was in shock and hadn't been able to bring herself to speak yet, but as she looked up at Nico's worried face, she finally asked, "What just happened? We need to call the police! That guy just threw me in the trunk of his car!" Her voice was shaking and she noticed she was trembling.

"Don't worry Celeste, Roman will take care of it," he assured her.

Celeste convinced Nico that she was capable of walking and felt better once she was on solid ground. She began peppering him with questions: "Can you please tell me why in the world Patrick just tried to abduct me? And I don't want to hear some lame excuse like the one you gave me the other day. And how does he know my father? And how does he know you two? And why was Roman here anyway?"

"Celeste, slow down. Can we go back into the gym please? It may not be safe out here, and I'd feel much better if we were inside," he said, surveying the parking lot nervously. "And perhaps we shouldn't tell anyone about what happened just yet, we don't want to cause a panic."

"Fine, but then you are answering *all* of my questions Nico."

As Celeste and Nico walked back into the dance, Natalie came running toward them.

"Where have you two been? I've been looking everywhere for you! They're about to announce the Senior Prom King and Queen." Natalie, so consumed with the news of the announcement, didn't even notice Celeste's disheveled appearance.

Nico gave Celeste an apologetic look and followed Natalie up to the front of the dance floor where Brian was waiting with the gathering students. As they weaved through the crowd, Celeste whispered to Nico, "You are not getting away with this. As soon as they announce the winner, we are going to talk about what just happened."

"And this year's St. Alice's Senior Prom King and Queen are... Natalie Meadows and Brian Kennedy!" exclaimed the announcer. Natalie's face lit up, and she took Brian's hand as they made their way to the stage.

"Nico, you get over here and talk to me right now," Celeste said during the crowning ceremony.

"Celeste, you don't want to miss out on this very special moment for your friends. Come on, get your camera out! Natalie is going to kill you if you don't take some good pictures," he said, purposely avoiding her. The truth was that he had no idea how he was going to explain this.

"You are exasperating!" Celeste shook her head and took her iPhone out so that she could capture the momentous occasion. *Never mind the fact that I almost got abducted by a stranger in the parking lot of my senior prom.*

As Celeste contemplated all the ways she was going to torture Nico into explaining himself, Roman marched into the room. His usual cool demeanor was gone. He looked like he had been in a fight - his shirt was crumpled and his messy hair hung carelessly over his eyes.

"It's taken care of. Do you think you can handle getting her home safely little brother?" he hissed at Nico.

"Roman, you owe me an explanation," Celeste interjected, poking a finger into his firm chest.

"A simple thank you for saving your life would have sufficed," said Roman, batting away her finger.

"And now it's time for the last dance," the DJ announced.

Nico looked at Roman and then at Celeste, both were fuming. "I know what will make everyone feel better, a nice calming slow dance," and he pushed the two of them together and disappeared into the crowd.

Celeste glared at Roman, reluctant to give in so easily, but what with being only inches away from him she was quickly losing her resolve. Roman let out a frustrated breath and closed the distance between them. When he put his hands on her hips, she couldn't help but feel the familiar sensation of electricity where he touched her. Their eyes met as she rested her arms loosely around his neck, and as she gazed into them, the fear and anger began to drift away.

"Thanks for saving my life tonight, Roman," she said breathlessly.

"It was my honor and my duty," he responded formally. "And I apologize for not being honest with you about Patrick from the beginning. I know that I owe you an explanation, and I wasn't lying when I said I would give you one. I was just hoping that all of this wouldn't have started so soon."

"All of what?" she asked.

"We have a lot to talk about Celeste, but this is neither the time nor the place." And with one quick move, he skillfully dipped her in time with the music leaving Celeste breathless once more and entranced by his deep blue eyes.

"Are you sure you don't want to ride back with us in the limo?" asked Natalie, poking her head out of the sunroof. "We are going to grab a snack at Ralph's on the way."

Before Celeste could respond, Roman interjected, "Don't worry about her Natalie, I have my car so we can drop her off on the way home."

"How are the three of you going to fit in his Porsche?" she asked Celeste. "Oh I get it… You'll have to sit on Nico's lap – how cozy!"

Roman looked nauseated and Celeste just shook her head with a weary smile. She waved goodnight to a despondent Brian, and they pulled away in the limo.

As soon as they had situated themselves in the Porsche (and yes, Celeste indeed had to sit on Nico's lap, to her chagrin), she asked, "So did the police come and arrest that creep Patrick?"

Nico looked to Roman for insight, and he finally answered, "Well, no, not exactly."

"Roman, stop the car! I am not going anywhere with the two of you if you don't start explaining yourselves immediately," threatened Celeste. "Maybe it's completely normal to get thrown into the trunk of a car by a complete stranger from wherever you came from, but this doesn't happen in Oak Bluffs, and it definitely doesn't happen to me!"

Roman pulled over to the side of the road, and Celeste jumped out of the car.

"Celeste, please get back in the car. It's the middle of the night and you can't be walking in the road," said Nico, trying to reason with her.

At that, Celeste spun around and slipped on the uneven pavement. Still wearing her beautiful high heels, she was unable to regain her balance, and she began to fall. In a flash both Nico and Roman were at her side, but they weren't fast enough to catch her. Her head hit the pavement with a *thunk* and she passed out from the impact.

"Quick, do something Roman!" Nico said in a panic. "She may have a concussion from the fall."

Roman picked up her head and saw that there was blood where she hit the concrete. He had to look away, as he felt his canines extending at the sight of the fresh blood. He took a moment to steady himself, and with a quick bite to his own wrist, he positioned it delicately on Celeste's mouth and forced her to drink his blood.

"Come on, let's take her home. We can watch over her there until she wakes up," said Roman, picking up her limp body and gently placing her on Nico's lap in the car.

At the apartment Nico carried a still-unconscious Celeste into the spare bedroom and laid her carefully on the bed.

"What are we going to do?" asked Nico. "She's going to be awake soon, and we can't keep dodging her questions – unless you want to keep her knocked out for a few more days."

"I know," said Roman exasperated. "I was just hoping we could put this off until after her birthday, but I don't think there is any way around this."

"Can't we compel her to forget everything that happened tonight?"

"You know that doesn't work with other supernatural beings," he replied.

"But she hasn't come into her powers yet, so maybe it would work," Nico continued.

"No, it won't work Nico. I tried the other night when I was outside her window to reach into her mind, and it was useless. I had no influence over her." Roman hovered over her still body, and gently brushed a stray golden curl away from her face.

Nico was surprised at his brother's confession. He rarely used any of his powers, and he wondered what had made him do so with Celeste. "So what are we going to do then?" he asked.

"I suppose we are just going to have to tell her the truth."

"We can't! Stellan warned us about interfering!"

"I'll deal with Stellan. And anyway, she would have found out eventually."

"Not if she isn't chosen," Nico reminded him.

"Look, you said it yourself; you feel her power already, her attraction. So do I, so did Patrick. I don't think there is really any doubt about what she is," he finished, shaking his head wearily.

As Celeste floated in a state of half consciousness, she had another dream. But this one, unlike all the prior terrible ones, was a pleasant dream. Her father was alive again, and he was teaching her, no training her really, how to fight and to use weapons and to develop her powers. He told her that all of the stories of frightening monsters that he had often read to her as a child weren't fairy tales at all, but in fact were real. "Celeste, it's going to be your duty, just as it was mine, to protect the world against these horrific creatures," her dad said.

As terrifying as it sounded to Celeste, there was something inside her that seemed to understand and take it in stride. It was almost as if she had subconsciously known all along.

"I'm very proud of you Celeste, and I know that you are going to be an incredible force of good in the world. I will always watch over you and keep you safe."

As he said goodbye to her, Celeste pulled her dad close for a hug and cried as he disappeared before her eyes.

Celeste awoke with a start and could feel tears rolling down her cheeks. As she looked around the room disconcertedly, she recognized Nico sitting at the foot of the bed, and Roman pacing nervously behind him.

"What happened? My ankle hurts..." murmured Celeste.

"You fell when you were trying to run away from us," explained Nico. "Do you remember that?"

"I remember that I'm mad at you two," she said as she tried to sit up.

"Be careful, we don't want you to pass out again," said Roman, approaching her cautiously.

"I'm fine," she said as she felt her head and her hand came away sticky, "Was I bleeding? I don't even have a bump."

"Yes you were, but we cleaned it up for you," said Nico. "Roman's a great nurse."

"But I don't even feel a cut on my head –"

"Remember that talk I kept promising you?" Roman interjected, "I think it's about time we had it."

Chapter 7

Roman's dark brows furrowed as he tried to decide where to begin. Celeste noticed how uncomfortable he looked (a look she had never seen before), and almost felt sorry for him as he squirmed in the black leather armchair across from her. She waited for him to start as she situated herself in the bed under the warm comforter, while Nico remained silent at the foot of the bed.

"I suppose we should start from the beginning," he said, fidgeting with a pen in his hands. "Our father, Luka, descended from a wealthy family out of what is now Eastern Europe. Our grandparents had a large estate, and their son was handsome, noble and well-to-do and thus could have had any woman he desired. When he met our mother, Lilliana, it was love at first sight." A faint smile slide across his face, and then he continued. "At first she did not wish to be courted by him, which of course made him want her all the more. He knew that she felt something for him, but he simply could not understand what was holding her back. It was only with time after Lilliana could no longer fight her feelings for him that she told him the truth."

Roman paused to take a breath.

"Lilliana came from a family of great witches, and she had been destined to marry Fabian, a powerful sorcerer."

"I'm sorry, did you just say witches and sorcerer?" Celeste interjected.

"Celeste, please let me finish. I know this sounds insane, but before you stop me, I need to tell you everything."

She nodded silently.

"Lilliana's betrothal to Fabian had all been arranged even before she was born. She could not go against her family's wishes, and she dared not cross Fabian, as he was known for his immense power and cruelty. But none of that mattered to father—he loved her and could not bear to live without her. The very night that she revealed who she was, he convinced her that in order to be free, they must escape together. They married in secret and spent the next twenty years on the run. During that time, Nico and I were born, but any time we felt comfortable in one particular place, we were forced to move on, constantly worried that Fabian would one day find us. Over the years, Fabian grew in power as well as in his hatred for our father for stealing his betrothed all those years ago."

With a reassuring glance, Nico urged him to continue.

"As Fabian's thirst for revenge intensified, he devised a punishment worse than death for our family. He created a curse that would make us immortal, forcing us to run from him for the rest of time, taking away our mother's power as a witch, and condemning us to an eternity as vampires. Since we were turned through a spell, and had not suffered death, we, unlike other vampires, kept our humanity. It was our mother who found the strength to fight against our most terrible predatory instincts, and she found ways for us to survive without killing humans."

Realizing that the story had come to a close, Celeste stared at Roman, wide-eyed in disbelief. His eyes bore into hers, anxiously awaiting a response.

"So you're telling me that you and Nico are vampires? And that your mom was a witch, and there has been an evil sorcerer chasing you around the world for years?" she repeated.

"For 116 years, to be exact," said Nico.

"Either you guys are crazy, or I really did hit my head too hard on the side of the road," she said, pushing away the comforter and sitting up.

"I know it's a lot to take in Celeste, but sadly I promise it is all true," confirmed Nico. "And it's not just vampires and witches, there's a whole supernatural world out there that humans have no idea exists."

As insane as it all sounded, she couldn't help but remember the dream she had just had about her father.

But that was just a dream; it wasn't real...Or was it?

"Prove it."

"Prove what?" asked Roman.

"That the crazy story you just told me is true. How do you expect me to believe any of this?" she asked, her voice rising.

Roman looked to Nico, but he shrugged his shoulders in bewilderment.

"Fine, but just remember, you asked for this."

Roman focused on Celeste's neck. He could feel the rhythmic thumping of blood pulsing through her carotid artery, and his fangs popped out instinctively. Celeste stared in horror. Before she could cry out, he used his vamp speed to dash out of the room and return with a glass of water for her.

"I figured you'd need this," he said as Celeste sat slack-jawed.

"You really are a vampire?" she asked, struggling to form the words. Abruptly she stood up, getting ready to make a run for it if necessary.

"Yes."

Celeste's mind began to race and was flooded with images of all the recent events. "What about Patrick? Is he a vampire? Was that why he tried to kidnap me – so he could drink my blood?" she asked incredulously.

"Well yes, he was a vampire, but there is more to that story than just blood lust. But you don't have to worry about him anymore. I took care of it," Roman said.

"What do you mean 'you took care of it'?"

"Don't worry about it," Roman said dismissively.

"Roman, you said you would tell me everything," she said staring at him point blank.

"Fine, I killed him, and buried his body in the woods behind the school," he admitted coldly.

All the color drained out of Celeste's face, and she looked at Roman horrified.

"You killed him?"

"Celeste, he was already dead. And anyway, we are vampires and that is what we do. My brother and I are different than most, but the majority are evil beings with no sense of morality and a blinding predatory nature. I did what I had to do to keep you safe."

"I need to get out of here," said Celeste.

"I'll take you home," offered Nico.

"No, I can't even look at either one of you right now. I just need to leave," she said as she pushed past Nico and rushed out.

The warm sun was just starting to come up, and as Celeste walked determinedly her head was spinning with everything Roman and Nico had just told her. It couldn't be true. As her mind fought to make sense of the inexplicable, she thought of the dream and her father's words.

No, it can't be. There are no such things as vampires and witches and sorcerers...

She reached into her purse to call the only person she really wanted to see right now.

Brian pulled up in his Mustang just minutes after hanging up with Celeste. She could tell from his bloodshot eyes and tousled hair that he must have been out late last night.

"What are you doing walking way out here at this time of the morning?" asked Brian.

"I ended up spending the night at Nico's last night," she explained. "Don't look at me like that Brian, nothing happened. After the dance, we were hungry so they brought me back to their place to eat, and I passed out in their spare bedroom."

Celeste hated lying to Brian, but there was no way she was going to tell him about the crazy night she had.

"So why are you walking home by yourself at this hour?" he asked with a sidelong glance.

"I wanted to get home before my mom did, but I didn't want to wake Nico up. So I snuck out thinking I could walk home, but it ended up being a lot further than I thought. Thanks for coming to get me."

Brian looked skeptical and asked, "Are you sure you're okay?"

"Yeah, I'm fine, just a little tired and hung over," she confessed.

They drove back the rest of the way in a comfortable silence. With the top down, the fresh morning air blowing through Celeste's curls was just what she needed to clear her head. As they pulled into Brian's driveway, she leaned over and gave him a kiss on the cheek.

"Thank you for always being there for me, Brian."

"Always," he said.

"Well that went well," said Nico caustically as he slammed the door. "Brian picked her up just down the street, in case you were wondering."

"She just needs some time to process it all," said Roman. "Just imagine what a shock this must be to her. Yesterday morning she woke up a normal high school girl, excited about going to her senior prom, and by the end of the night she had been kidnapped, knocked out, and told of the existence of vampires, witches, sorcerers and everything in between."

"I understand all that, I just wish we could have found a better way to tell her so that she wouldn't have run scared. We had each other and our family when this happened to us. She doesn't have anyone to talk to about it."

"We'll be there for her Nico; remember, we only just told her half of the story. Right now we need to figure out who sent Patrick after Celeste. He certainly wasn't putting her in the trunk of his car for an afternoon snack, and I definitely don't believe he was acting alone," finished Roman.

"Why did you have to kill him?" asked Nico. "We needed him alive to question. How are we going to find anything out now?"

Roman came back with an exasperated, "Don't you think I know that?"

"So why did you do it?" Nico retorted.

"I lost it; I was so furious, I completely lost control," said Roman angrily.

"You do feel something for her," said Nico with a puzzled expression. Roman cut him off with a growl and stomped off to his room, slamming the door shut behind him.

Roman sat in his room brooding as he gulped down a bottle of blood. He wasn't even sure why he had gotten so mad at Nico and that bothered him. He was never like this. He was always in control. Roman didn't understand what had come over him, and he certainly didn't like it. Why did Celeste have such power over him? She drove him crazy. Now was not the time to fight with his brother. They needed to work together to determine what they could about Patrick's appearance in Oak Bluffs. As much as Roman dreaded it, he decided it was time to let Stellan in on last night's events.

"You did what?" yelled Stellan over the speakerphone. Stellan, normally so calm and collected, shouted as though he might come through the phone and strangle Roman with his bare hands.

"How could you tell her about the supernatural world? What were you two thinking?"

"There was no other choice, Stellan. How were we going to explain Patrick's attempt to abduct her? And if this is her destiny, what is the point of lying to her? She is going to have to learn about it all soon enough. I thought maybe if it came from us, she would handle it better. I was obviously mistaken," said Roman.

"Roman, it wasn't your place to tell her. Guardians are chosen at the age of eighteen, and when they are, the truth is revealed to them in the appropriate manner," continued Stellan.

"But she doesn't have her father," insisted Roman, "so who will teach her and guide her in the ways of a hunter?"

Nico could see that this conversation was going nowhere and interjected, "Stellan, what is done is done, we cannot take back what we told her. What's important now is to try to find out who sent Patrick, and if more will be coming for Celeste."

Stellan exhaled and tried to calm himself, and Roman stopped pacing like a caged animal.

"I've been doing some research since you boys paid me a visit, and it seems as though there has been a large amount of dark magic in use in the area," said Stellan. "I can't be sure of the exact location or source, but there is something in the air that has the supernatural community in a commotion."

"What does that mean exactly?" asked Nico.

"I'm not sure yet. Sometimes when a new guardian is chosen, it disturbs the balance between good and evil. An oversimplified explanation would be that evil could be trying to compensate for it," explained Stellan.

"And could Fabian be the cause of this?" asked Roman.

"It is certainly possible."

"So what do we do now?" asked Nico.

"I have contacted a few of my more powerful and well-connected friends to see if they can give us more information. Until then we have to wait. If Fabian did send Patrick to find Celeste, and he knows who she is, I'm afraid that we will all be in serious peril."

Celeste awoke the next morning to a rough slobbery tongue on her face. "Hi Rocky," she said with a smile. As she wiped the drool off her face, images from last night came rushing back. She was absolutely positive that everything had been a bad dream. Sluggishly, she pushed the covers aside and slipped her aching feet into her fuzzy slippers. Strewn on the floor was her beautiful prom dress. She picked it up for closer examination only to find bloodstains and frayed material all along the back from her fall on the rough asphalt. The dress was ruined.

How could this be happening? Nico and Roman are vampires. They drink blood and kill people?

Celeste rubbed her throbbing head. This was too much for her to wrap her head around without at least a cup of coffee. She went downstairs and was surprised to find her mother in the kitchen reading the paper in her pink scrubs.

"Good morning sweetie!" she said cheerily. "How was your night?"

Celeste attempted to plaster a convincing smile on her face. "It was awesome mom! We had a great time, danced, took lots of pictures, and made tons of memories..."

She went on to tell her mother about the highlights of the evening, making sure to leave out her near abduction and the fact that her new friends were vampires (or maybe that she was just going crazy). She suddenly remembered the dream she had about her father while she was unconscious, and felt that this was a bit of truth that she could share with her mother.

"I dreamt about Dad last night," she began, "and it was pretty strange, but it seemed so real."

Mrs. Wilder put down the paper and looked at her expectantly. "Tell me about it, Celeste, I know how rarely you ever dream of him."

Celeste poured herself a big mug of coffee, filled it with sugar and cream and sat down at the table. "It was so great to see him, but what he said, it was all so strange. He told me that I had to learn to be a hunter, to protect humans against bad things. He said that I had been called for a greater purpose to be a force of good against evil in the world. He told me that all the scary monsters we thought were imaginary are actually real." Celeste hadn't taken a breath, but when she finished she looked up to gauge her mom's expression.

Instead of the comforting look Celeste expected, her mother had gone completely pale. She tried to compose herself, but it was too late; Celeste had already seen her reaction.

"What is it Mom?" she asked.

"Oh nothing, don't mind me, I have other things on my mind. I'm sorry sweetie, but I have to get to work," she said, looking at her watch. "It's getting late and I have so many patients to see." She stood up abruptly leaving her unfinished breakfast and darted out the door.

Celeste was perplexed at her mother's strange reaction to the dream. She had never seen her look so upset, not for a very long time anyway. Celeste looked longingly at the picture of her and her parents on the nightstand. She wished that her father were here right now. She needed to talk to him about all of the crazy things that had been going on in her life for the past few weeks. He would know exactly what to say to comfort her. Instead, she felt more alone than ever.

Celeste's buzzing phone interrupted her thoughts, and she saw Nico was calling again. This was the fourth time this morning, but she wasn't ready to talk to him yet. She still hadn't been able to accept the notion that he and Roman were vampires, and she couldn't help but wonder how the dream about her father might tie into all of this. What she did know was that it was all too much of a coincidence for it not to. Roman's story did mention his mother being a witch and some terrible sorcerer cursing their family, but did that mean that everything she had dreamt was true? She didn't want to believe that all of those horrible monsters she saw in her nightmare could actually be real.

As Celeste sat on her bed questioning reality as she knew it, she heard a knock at the door followed by a menacing bark from Rocky. She hurried down the stairs and could just make out a tall shadow at the door. She peeked through the window and was surprised to see Roman pacing on her front porch. A chill went through her at the sight of him.

"Come on Celeste, please open the door. I know you're there, I can hear you breathing," he said from outside.

Celeste unlocked the door and opened it a crack. "What do you want Roman?"

"We need to talk. Please let me in. Or if you don't trust me, you can come out here and we can talk out on the porch where you will be perfectly safe," he said with a scowl.

Celeste thought about it for a moment and reasoned that she had been alone with both Roman and Nico on a couple of occasions, and they had never hurt her before. Also she wanted to make sure that Brian didn't see the two of them talking and decide to come over. It was important to protect Brian, and she didn't want him to have anything to do with this. She opened the door all the way and signaled for Roman to enter, but he just stood there unmoving.

"You have to invite me in," he said.

"Seriously? I thought that was just in the movies," she said, suppressing a chuckle.

"No, it's a real thing, and a very important thing at that. You must always be careful about who you invite into your house, Celeste."

"Once you let a vampire in, can you take back the invitation?" she asked intrigued.

"No, unfortunately not."

"Well then, I'm going to have to think about this."

Roman tapped his foot on the floor impatiently while Celeste considered. He looked so good, she wondered if it was a vampire thing. His black hair was a bit disheveled, but in a sexy way and his strong jaw had a trace of stubble on it. She could almost imagine what it would feel like against her skin. *Stop that!*

"Okay, I invite you in, I guess," she said finally.

As if an invisible barrier had been removed, Roman gracefully crossed the threshold. Celeste led him into the sunlit living room and sat across from him, cautiously keeping her distance.

"I thought vampires couldn't come out in the day time," she said.

"I imagine you must have a lot of questions for me," Roman responded, "but first I want to apologize about how my brother and I handled everything last night. I never should have told you about us. It really would have been better if I hadn't."

"And what, you two would have just kept lying to me?" Celeste asked.

"Yes, because it would have been safer for you that way."

"Safer? That's doubtful since Patrick came after me even when I didn't know anything about you," she retorted. Then she paused for a second realization setting in, "Is that why he came after me? Because of you?"

With a pained expression on his face, he admitted, "We don't know, but we are trying to find out. We have a friend, Stellan, who is a sorcerer, a good one, and he's helping us."

"Okay, should I be worried or something?" asked Celeste.

"No, don't be. Nico and I will take care of everything. We will watch over you and protect you. If Patrick did come after you because of us, I promise I won't stop until I find the person behind this," he said.

"And kill them?"

"If that's what needs to be done to keep you safe, then yes, unquestionably."

There was something about the intensity in Roman's voice that sent another chill down her spine. The fact that he would go through such lengths to protect her filled her with nervous excitement.

"You think there is someone else behind this? Like someone sent Patrick for me? I just don't understand why anyone would come after me," she said.

Hesitantly, Roman reached across the table and covered her hand with his giving it a gentle squeeze. He whispered, "Everything is going to be fine, Celeste. I won't let anyone hurt you."

Celeste's phone buzzed again. She glanced at it and said, "It's Nico. He's been calling me all morning."

"My little brother is certainly persistent, I'll give him that," he said teasingly.

Celeste finally answered the phone and assured Nico that she was fine. She was surprised that he had no idea that Roman was with her. After a quick chat, she turned back to Roman who was sitting pensively on the couch.

"So a vampire, huh?" she asked.

"For over a hundred years now," he replied. "And the reason that sunlight does not affect me is that I did not become a vampire in the normal way."

"Oh, right the normal way..." Celeste mused.

"What I mean is … weren't you listening to the story?" He looked flustered. "Fabian turned us through a spell, so a lot of the rules that constrain other vampires don't apply to us. Walking in the sun just happens to be one of them."

"But you still drink people's blood?" she asked awkwardly.

"I do, but not from humans directly," he explained. "My brother and I are able to maintain a healthy diet of blood, mostly from donor banks and hospitals."

Celeste took a deep breath and said, "Tell me more about your life, about when you first became a vampire."

"It was very difficult at first. All of the impulses, the surge of power, it was very overwhelming. I've tried very hard to forget that time in my life," he said grimacing.

"I'm sorry. It's okay if you don't want to talk about it."

"It wasn't all bad. As we grew to accept our new lives, I remember a time when we were actually happy. Nico and I were eternal twenty-year-olds, and we spent decades attending universities around the globe. Because of the spell, we weren't condemned to living in the shadows like other vampires are. We were able to walk freely in the sun, so we could assimilate fairly well into the human world, for short periods of time anyway. This was especially true for Nico, as he always seemed right at home wherever he went. He was charmingly relentless with the ladies, popular with the guys and seemed to fit into the human world much more easily than I ever did."

He paused with a sigh and ran his hand through his wavy hair.

"But inevitably every four or five years we were forced to move on, and leave whatever life we had created to conjure up a whole new one, in a new town, with new people. That was what brought us to Oak Bluffs for the first time in the early 1950's. And it was here that our parents were killed."

This time it was Celeste who leaned across the table and gave Roman a comforting touch. "Why would you come back here then?"

Roman chuckled. "I keep asking myself the same question."

Roman and Celeste spent the rest of the morning playing a series of twenty questions. She found herself fascinated by all of his intriguing adventures filled with magic, world travel and encounters with werewolves and monsters, and she began to feel less afraid. She found it incredibly odd how comfortable she now felt around him, thinking *I am sitting with a vampire on my couch in the living room and I am not freaked out.*

"Celeste," Roman interjected seriously, "I don't want to mislead you about my life as a vampire. There have been some very dark times as well. I've been able to move past it, but I am constantly battling my basic instinct. Nico and I, we manage pretty well, but the others, they are not like us. Now that you know about our existence, you have to be careful."

"I will be. I promise, no more picking up cute guys at Ralph's," she said with a smirk.

"Oh, so you thought Patrick was cute?"

"No, not really. I prefer my guys a little older," she said flirtatiously.

"It's after one o'clock—you must be hungry," Roman said by way of changing the subject. "Would you like to go out for lunch?"

"Do you even need to eat?" she asked.

"No, I don't, but after all of these years of trying to live a human life, I've become quite accustomed to adhering to social norms."

"Then sure, I am pretty hungry. Now that I think about it, I didn't even get to eat at my senior prom last night with all the distractions."

"I'm sorry about that," he said. "I am truly sorry that I ruined your prom."

"It's okay, I really wasn't that excited about it in the first place. And I guess since you did save my life, we can call it even."

Roman opened the car door for Celeste, and as she buckled herself into the sporty bucket seat she noticed blood on the headrest. A wave of fear came over her, but she steadied herself and asked as calmly as she could, "Is this blood?"

"Yes, it is. It's your blood actually," he said very matter-of-factly.

Celeste instinctively reached for the back of her head searching for the spot where she hit it when she fell on the road.

"What happened when I fell? Why don't I have a cut or even a bump?" she asked. "My dress has blood all over it."

"It's another one of our vampire perks I guess you could say," he began. "Our blood can heal humans. When you passed out, we were worried you might have a concussion, so I fed you some of my blood and it healed you."

"I drank your blood?" she asked with a nauseated expression.

"You loved it."

She elbowed him teasingly, and he pretended to wince in pain.

"So I know this is probably a stupid question, but am I going to turn into a vampire now?"

Roman laughed and said, "No, it's not that easy."

"Then how?"

"Well for starters you have to be bitten and drained of your blood, and then when you are almost at the point of death you have to drink a large amount of vampire blood. Then you would die, and when you awoke you would no longer be human."

Celeste was so engrossed in the conversation that she hadn't realized they had just pulled up to Ralph's Diner. As they walked in, she saw Natalie waving happily from a booth in the corner. She signaled for them to come over, and as they approached she saw a familiar sandy-brown head turn around.

"Hi you two!" said Natalie cheerily.

Then Brian chimed in, "Why don't you guys come sit with us?"

"I don't believe we've officially met," said Roman politely. "I'm Roman, Nico's brother. You must be Brian."

"Yeah, hey," he said.

Celeste slid into the booth next to Brian and Roman sat across from her next to Natalie. Celeste wondered if they were intruding on a date and tried to communicate with Natalie via facial expressions, but Natalie just looked utterly confused.

"So what are you two doing here together?" Natalie asked.

Celeste's expression blanked as she searched for an explanation.

"Celeste forgot her feathered boa at our apartment last night, and Nico was hung-over so I offered to bring it to her," said Roman smoothly.

"And I was hungry so I convinced him to take me to lunch," Celeste finished.

"So what were you doing at our prom last night, Roman?" asked Brian rather abruptly.

Celeste looked at Roman anxiously, but he easily replied, "I was asked to be a chaperone actually. I am a member of the St. Alice High School Board, and when I found out my little brother was going to the dance, I decided to go so that I could keep an eye on him."

"And dance with his date?" questioned Brian, a hint of jealousy in his tone.

Celeste nudged Brian with her elbow under the table and gave him a sharp look. She didn't think that Brian had seen them dancing; at the time he and Natalie were being crowned Prom King and Queen.

"I asked him to dance with me," interjected Celeste. "He was standing by himself, looking bored, so I dragged him out on the dance floor."

Natalie broke in and started chattering about how much fun the night had been and how honored she was to be chosen Prom Queen. Anything to change the subject.

After lunch, the four of them walked out together. Natalie grabbed Celeste by the arm so they were a couple steps behind the boys, and whispered conspiratorially, "So which brother are you dating?"

"I'm not dating anyone!" Celeste hissed, knowing that Roman's sensitive vampire hearing could undoubtedly hear every word they said.

Turning back towards the whispering girls, Brian asked, "Hey Cel, why don't I take you home so Roman doesn't have to go out of his way to drop you off?"

Celeste glanced over at Roman who gave her a guarded look revealing nothing. "Yeah sure, just give me a second. I need to get something from Roman's car," she answered.

Celeste walked over to Roman who was leaning casually against his car. It astonished her how he could make any ordinary pose look so attractive.

"Thanks for coming over to talk to me today. I appreciate your honesty, and I feel much better about all the vampire stuff," she whispered.

"Of course, Celeste, anything you need," he replied, firmly gripping her by the shoulders. Celeste stood there transfixed for a moment gazing into his deep blue eyes. Roman dropped his hands stepping back as Brian pulled up, his Mustang roaring.

"Be safe," mouthed Roman as they drove off.

As Roman drove home watching the sun set over the trees, he found himself smiling for no particular reason. It was the first time in a very long time.

Chapter 8

Celeste leaned against her bay window with an American history book open in her lap, distractedly chewing at the end of a pen. Finals would start tomorrow and she had been so preoccupied lately that she was behind in her schoolwork. As she gazed out the window, enjoying the balmy morning breeze, she couldn't help but think about Roman and Nico. They had actually been alive during the Great Depression, World War I and II, the Kennedy assassination—all of the eras and events that she was studying now. Then her father's cautionary words from the dream crept into her conscious thought. *You must protect the world from evil creatures.* She hadn't told Roman or Nico about the dream and she felt terribly guilty.

How can I tell them? They'd think I'd gone insane. And how am I supposed to protect anyone? I'm just a normal girl.

"Morning Celeste!" said her mom as she peeked into her room. "How's the studying going?"

"Not so great."

"I brought you an energy-packed breakfast to help," she said as she set the tray next to her bed.

"Thanks, Mom. Have you even been to bed yet?" she asked, noticing she was still wearing her favorite pink scrubs.

"No, I just got home about an hour ago, but I wanted to see how you were doing before I went to sleep," she answered. "Any more nightmares?"

"Luckily, nothing."

"I'm glad to hear that, sweetie. Let me know if you have anymore, okay?"

"Sure, Mom."

Celeste almost stopped her mother before she walked out of the room. She wanted to ask her why she had bolted the other morning when she had mentioned the nightmare. Instead, she buried her nose in her book and forced herself to study. Something told her she wasn't going to get an honest response anyway.

After a couple more hours of studying, Celeste needed a break. She checked her cell phone and saw that Brian had texted.

Come over. I need a study break.

Convincing herself that she had already been pretty productive, Celeste shut her book with a hint of satisfaction and headed over to Brian's.

Maxi came running to the door when she knocked, jumping into Celeste's outstretched arms.

"I missed you Cel!" she said, "You never come over and play with me anymore."

"I know, I'm sorry Maxi, but I've been so busy with the last few weeks of school. I promise we'll have a play date soon," she said putting her back down on the floor and patting her head affectionately.

"Okay Maxi that's enough. Celeste and Brian have to study if they want to graduate," said Mrs. Kennedy as she dragged her out of the living room.

"I miss her," said Celeste.

"That's just because you don't have to live with her."

"Don't be mean to your little sister!" she scolded.

"Anyway, how's the studying going?" asked Brian as they sat down on the couch.

"Not bad. I'm glad we started studying early because the past week has been a total loss. How about you?" she asked.

"I'm just having a hard time concentrating, but I'll pull it together," Brian answered. He looked away, pulling out his cell phone from his jeans pocket.

Celeste came back with, "Why? What's going on?" She could tell he was avoiding her gaze as he played around with his phone.

"Just stuff," he answered vaguely.

"I know how you feel. I've felt like my life has been a whirlwind the past few weeks. You know, it's my eighteenth birthday on Friday, and I haven't even given it much of a thought," she said.

"Of course I know. I would never forget your birthday. This will be our fifteenth time celebrating it together," he said, finally glancing up at her.

"You've been keeping track?" she asked surprised.

"It's not that hard to figure out. My family moved in next door when we were both three years old, and we've spent every birthday together since then."

"How about that year that you were at basketball sleep-away camp?"

111

"You mean the year that I ran away from sleep-away camp?"

Celeste let out a laugh. "That's right! Your parents and all the camp counselors were freaking out because they thought they had lost you and you turned up at my house."

"I guess I just couldn't stand the thought of missing your birthday." Brian smiled at the memory. "And since it's a pretty important birthday, I have a feeling that someone might be planning a little something special for you."

"Seriously? Natalie better not be throwing me some huge party."

"You didn't hear anything from me, I'm not a snitch," he said. "But you may want to talk to her about the guest list unless you want all of Oak Bluffs invited."

Celeste just laughed.

"So are you and Roman dating or something?" Brian asked abruptly.

"Whoa, where did that come from?"

"Well I know you've been hanging out with him, and at first I thought you liked his brother, but now I'm not sure anymore," he said rapidly, as if he had been holding his breath the entire time.

"No, I'm not *dating* anyone. I like them, though. They are so different, 'ya know? Not the average guys you'd meet around Oak Bluffs. They're fun."

"Good, I'm glad you're not dating either of them," said Brian. "I think there is something weird about both of those guys."

Celeste rolled her eyes. "I sensed that when you gave Roman the third degree at the diner yesterday. What was up with that?" she asked.

"I don't know. I just don't like the way he looks at you. Honestly, I don't like it when any other guy looks at you," said Brian. Impulsively, he leaned in and stunned Celeste with a soft kiss.

Celeste was so surprised that she didn't even move at first, but as her brain slowly realized what was happening she put her hand on Brian's chest to stop him. She pulled away awkwardly.

Brian looked at her face and saw confusion in her eyes. His heart sank. "I'm sorry," he said immediately.

"No, it's okay," she said uncomfortably, "You just really surprised me."

"I've been wanting to do that since the sixth grade, Cel."

"You have?"

Brian nodded and said, "I just figured if I didn't do it now, I may never have the chance again."

How could I have been so clueless?

"Please say something."

"I don't know what to say, Brian," she said, fidgeting with her necklace nervously. "You know I care about you so much; you are my very best friend. I'm just not sure I feel the same way that you do."

"Okay," he said. "Let's just pretend this never happened." He stood up abruptly, trying to hide his embarrassment.

"Are you sure?"

"Yeah, it's no big deal."

Celeste felt overwhelmed with emotions. She struggled to find a comforting word, anything to take away the misery that was written all over her best friend's face. When nothing came to mind, she pulled him into a hug instead. She gave him a hasty kiss on the cheek and ran out the door.

As Celeste sprinted across the lawn to her house, tears began streaming down her face. She felt terribly guilty for hurting Brian. That was the last thing she wanted to do. On some level, she wished that she felt the same way about him as he did about her; then things would be so much easier. Instead she felt this incredibly intense connection to a vampire? What was wrong with her? She plopped down on her bed, miserable, as she contemplated what an awful person she was.

So much for my perfect first kiss...

Celeste had imagined what her first kiss would be like at least a thousand times. She knew very well that most of the girls her age had already been kissed if not done much more than that. But Celeste had always been different. She had seen countless movies where the pretty girl finally gets the hot guy of her dreams – a tear-jerking goodbye scene at an airport, a passionate moment of realization under dire circumstances or a classic kiss in the pouring rain with a montage of romantic music playing in the background. And hers had been nothing like that. She supposed it was rather appropriate that her first kiss be with Brian, since he was "the guy" who had been there for her through it all, but it just wasn't the epic moment that she had been envisioning for so many years.

Celeste must have dozed off at some point because she found herself in a vivid dream. She was in front of the old Oak Bluffs Library, and a horde of vampires was inexorably marching towards her. She looked in her hand and saw that she was clutching a sword with an elaborate engraving on the hilt, and she had an array of other weapons concealed in various parts of her clothing. She looked up as they grew closer, noticing that she was absurdly unafraid.   With a powerful lunge, she threw herself into the advancing mob with her sword raised. Celeste suddenly felt someone at her side and spun around to see her father. He was in full fighting gear, sweat glistening on his forehead, his hazel eyes blazing as he slashed his way through the vampires. She followed him, and they fought side by side for what seemed like hours. Her sword became an extension of her arm, so that with every slice she took down an enemy with brutal force. There was blood everywhere, causing a wave of nausea, but she took a deep breath and drew on a new found strength to continue on. When all of the vampires had been killed, Celeste's father turned to face her, putting his hand on her shoulder. "Well done, Celeste. You are going to be a powerful hunter, and you will make an excellent Guardian."

Celeste awoke as Rocky licked her face enthusiastically with his warm, rough tongue. She glanced drowsily out the window and saw the sun was already setting; she had been dreaming for hours. Out of the corner of her eye, she caught a slight movement in the oak tree and again saw the majestic black falcon watching her. It was perched on a thick branch closest to her window, its powerful talons clenched around the limb. Its piercing blue eyes locked with hers. "Roman?" she said aloud, taking a step towards the window. The bird unfolded its black feathered wings and took off into the night.

***

Fabian sat in front of the fireplace, his long silver hair radiant in the firelight; impatiently he twisted the gold ring around his finger. "It has been three days, and I have heard nothing from that incompetent vampire Patrick. How difficult could it be to find one girl and bring her to me?" he asked Alek angrily.

"I hate to say I told you so, but you should have sent me. A newly turned vampire is hardly reliable even on his best day," said Alek, smoothing his slick platinum hair back.

"You know very well why I couldn't send you. As youthful as you appear, you would not have been able to blend in with a group of high school teenagers, which is why I needed Patrick. I thought that he would be capable of a simple task, but apparently I was mistaken."

"Shall I go to Oak Bluffs to see if I can find him, or will you send another one of your minions?" asked Alek contemptuously.

"No, I still cannot risk Stellan recognizing you. He has always involved himself in matters that do not concern him when it comes to the Constantins. I will send someone else, but this time I will not leave anything up to chance."

"Who can you trust with such an important task?"

"I will send Magnus," Fabian responded with an evil twinkle in his eye.

As Roman strode through the front door he was greeted by a tense looking Nico.

"How is she?" he asked.

"Fine for now, I think she is coping pretty well all things considered. And I believe that her powers are starting to kick in. She saw me in the tree tonight, and I think she recognized me. She's starting to sense things beyond her normal human world," Roman explained.

"So you neglected to tell her that we can transform into falcons?"

"I think we can inform her of that minor detail a little later," he responded.

"You just don't want her to know that you've been spying on her for weeks," admonished Nico.

"I'll tell her when the time is right."

"Well we have some news from Stellan," said Nico gravely. "He asked that we contact him as soon as you got home."

"So you are sure that it was Fabian that sent Patrick?" asked Nico.

Stellan's non-corporeal form had appeared in the middle of their living room, and he was pacing animatedly.

"I am afraid so. I spoke to a colleague who confirmed that Patrick had been turned with the sole purpose of coming to Oak Bluffs to track the two of you," Stellan said solemnly. "Since the selection of the next Guardian is almost upon us, the

Council has been keeping a close eye on Celeste. When they discovered that Patrick, a new vampire, had appeared in town they became suspicious and found what we had feared all along."

"Why didn't they warn you that he was here?" asked Roman clenching his fists.

"Well technically, I am no longer a member of the Council, Roman. I have been officially retired for some time, so they have no obligation to inform me of anything. Additionally, when Patrick first appeared, they were operating under the assumption that he had come for you and Nico. They did not believe that Celeste was in any danger."

"So it *is* our fault that Patrick went after her?" Nico asked as he took the seriousness of the situation in.

"I imagine that he thought it would be the quickest way to get to the two of you," said Stellan, shaking his head.

"But why after all of these years would he suddenly come looking for us?" asked Roman. "Certainly he has had countless opportunities to kill us before now. Why now, and why involve Celeste?" Roman marched restlessly from window to window as Stellan continued.

"As to the timing, I have no clue. As for Celeste, my guess would be that when Patrick discovered the special attachment you both feel for her (he paused and looked accusatorially at them both), he shared this fact with Fabian. He must have been extremely curious to find out more about her which is why he had Patrick try to capture her," said Stellan. "But these are merely suppositions boys…"

"So is the Council going to do something to protect her?" asked Nico.

"Unfortunately, they cannot intervene directly, not without Fabian making an overt move. They will be keeping an eye on things as they develop. Celeste's birthday is only a few days away, and once she comes into her powers she will be able to protect herself," said Stellan.

"Against Fabian? Alone?" snarled Roman, "Are they insane? He is a thousand- year-old sorcerer with more power than the devil himself. If he has found out what she is, there will be nothing to stop him from getting to her. Celeste is a force of good, and he will do anything to destroy her, just like he did our parents."

"Roman, we will protect her," said Nico, putting his hand on his brother's chest to calm the mounting rage.

"No, you don't understand Nico, you never will," he said, pushing his brother aside. "You didn't see what Fabian did to our parents. Our parents were strong and powerful vampires and they were nothing up against him. Celeste is just a girl. She is not ready for any of this." He looked from Nico to Stellan, his eyes filled with fury.

Then Stellan broke in, "We will help her. She will not fight alone, I promise you Roman. I will do everything in my power to keep her safe."

"So how do you think you did on the final?" asked Brian as he caught up with Celeste walking out toward the school parking lot.

"Pretty well, actually, it looks like all that cramming paid off," she answered. "How about you?"

"I think I did okay. One down and only four more to go."

They walked towards their cars together in an uncomfortable silence, when finally Brian said, "Look I'm really sorry about last night. I don't want things to be weird between us; I should have never kissed you."

"Brian, don't be sorry," she said, turning to him with a genuine smile. "And things won't be weird unless we let them."

"Hi guys!" said Natalie as she came bounding towards them. "Thank God at least one final exam is over. I never want to think about American history again!"

"Agreed," they said together.

"Let's go for a celebratory lunch at Ralph's. I'm sure everyone will be there, and I could totally use the sugar high from a chocolate milkshake before going home to study again," said Natalie.

"Sounds good to me," said Celeste.

Celeste wished she could talk to Natalie about what had happened with Brian, but she knew Natalie liked him. Now that she and Natalie were becoming so close, she really didn't want to ruin things. And she *really* wanted to tell her everything about Roman and Nico, but Celeste had been sworn to secrecy. She understood well that it was safer for Natalie *not* to know. It was just so hard to carry all of these secrets alone.

Nico came home to find Roman pacing nervously in front of the fireplace. He couldn't remember the last time he had seen his brother in such a state, and it was very unsettling. Roman was always so calm and collected. Nico shuddered at the thought of the few times when Roman had lost control; it was not something he liked to think about.

"You're going to wear a path into the rug if you keep that up," said Nico jokingly.

Roman glared at him and continued pacing.

Nico pulled out two ornate invitations from his backpack. "We have been cordially invited to attend Celeste's eighteenth birthday on Friday. It will be at Natalie's house. Apparently her family is out of town for the weekend."

"Great," said Roman, "I'll make sure to send my tux to the dry cleaners."

"Now that's the spirit brother! A little humor is exactly what we need in this situation."

"I know your main concern is this party, but there are some more pressing matters we need to discuss."

Nico dropped his backpack and settled in on the massive leather couch. "Please proceed," he said dramatically.

Roman let out a breath. "I have been debating whether or not we should tell Celeste about Fabian. On one hand, I believe she deserves to know that her life could be at risk. On the other, I don't want her to be concerned about something that she has no control over," he said.

Nico paused to consider. "I don't think we should tell her. We really don't know much for certain, and I agree that having her worry isn't going to help anything. She has enough going on right now with final exams and graduation. Let's let her enjoy her last few days of normalcy."

"Fine, we will keep this information from her until we know more, and in the meantime I will keep her safe," Roman said.

"What are you going to do, follow her everywhere she goes?" asked Nico.

"Yes, if that's what it takes."

"Okay, well, that's not creepy," countered Nico sarcastically.

"Be careful, little brother, you are starting to sound like her," Roman said with a smirk.

"You are the one that needs to be careful Roman. *You are falling in love with her.*"

***

Ralph's Diner was packed with rowdy students celebrating the end of the first day of final exams. No one was giving a second thought to tomorrow's exam or the next day's; that could wait until later this evening. Celeste, Natalie and Brian sat at the end of a large communal table with half of their senior class happily eating, drinking and chatting away.

"Okay, we need to talk details for your birthday on Friday!" said Natalie excitedly.

"Let's not go too overboard, okay? I just want a low key get together with my dearest friends," said Celeste.

"But it's your eighteenth birthday! That's a really special year, and who knows where we will all be next year. This could be our last year celebrating together." Natalie crinkled her nose and furrowed her eyebrows looking as determined as ever.

"Okay, okay, so what were you thinking?" she asked afraid to hear the answer.

"I was thinking a costume ball would be fun!"

"What? That's not low key, Natalie. That's the total opposite of low key!"

"Come on, it will be so much fun to get all dressed up in costumes. I already know what I want to be – Cat Woman – meow!" said Natalie. "And anyway, the invitations already went out so there's really nothing we can do now."

Celeste just shook her head and laughed. Natalie was absolutely incorrigible.

"Hello there beautiful ladies—and Brian," said Nico as he sauntered up to the table and pulled up a chair. His short dark hair was gelled perfectly in place (as usual) and his designer sunglasses rested casually on his head.

"Hi Nico!" the girls replied, as the entire female population of the table turned to stare at him. Even the cute young waitress in the poodle skirt who had been ignoring their table for most of the afternoon appeared out of nowhere, flashing a smile.

"I don't want to be a bad influence, but can you bring me your finest pitcher of beer please?" asked Nico playfully.

"Bad influence... only if you don't share!" said Natalie with a flirty wink.

As the chatter ensued, Nico took a second to send Roman a text message.

I'm with Celeste at the diner. Don't worry she'll be safe with me.

Surely his brother would relax a bit knowing she was with him at a crowded restaurant filled with eye witnesses.

Later that evening Celeste attempted to study for her calculus exam, but she kept glancing out the window into the oak tree hoping to see the falcon. She unlatched the lock and pushed open the window, peering into the dark branches of the tree. As unnerving as it had been when it first appeared, she had started to feel curiously comforted by its presence lately. Nearly every night before she went to bed, Celeste saw it perched on a limb watching her. There was something almost human about the way it looked at her. And those eyes - she had never seen a bird with blue eyes. It was the strangest thing. It was those familiar blue eyes that had caused her to unconsciously shout out Roman's name the other night. A part of her knew she was crazy even thinking it, but after everything she had discovered in the past few days, nothing seemed impossible anymore.

"Celeste, are you still awake?" whispered her mother as she noiselessly came up the stairs.

"Yup, still studying," she responded. "What are you doing home?"

"It was a slow night, and I feel so guilty about how I've abandoned you lately. We haven't had a night together in weeks, and I miss you!" said Mrs. Wilder as she sat down on the bed next to her daughter.

"I miss you too, Mom," she said as she hugged her tightly.

"You seem so preoccupied lately. Is everything okay?" she asked, her eyebrows furrowed in concern.

Celeste wished she could tell her mother about Roman and Nico and all of the wild thoughts that were running through her head. After her reaction the last time, she had a feeling it wouldn't be wise.

"I guess so, except for the fact that Brian kissed me yesterday."

Her mother's eyes lit up. "He did?"

"Yup."

"Well, I can't say that comes to me as a total surprise," she said. "He's been crazy for you since you were little kids."

"How come I'm the only one who didn't know that?" Celeste pondered aloud.

"Sometimes it's harder to see when you're the one in the situation."

"I guess so."

"How do you feel about it?"

"I kind of freaked out when it happened. It was a total surprise to *me*. Brian and I have been best friends forever, but I had no clue he felt that way about me."

"What are you going to do?"

"Pretend like it never happened!" said Celeste, closing her book.

"Celeste," scolded her mom, "you know Brian is a wonderful boy, and I know he cares about you so much. Maybe you shouldn't be so quick to dismiss his feelings for you, or your feelings for him."

"But that's the thing, Mom, I just don't feel that way about him. I almost wish I did."

"Not the way you feel about Nico, you mean?"

Celeste smiled and said, "Well, yes and no. I really like Nico, he's sweet, and super hot and a lot of fun—"

"But?"

"When I first met him I thought maybe there could be something there, but there's someone else."

"Oh really? Spill young lady!" said Mom excitedly.

"It's Nico's older brother, Roman."

125

Chapter 9

"I can't believe we're done!" Natalie exclaimed as she, Celeste and Brian walked under the archway of St. Alice's for the last time.

Celeste looked back at all the swinging classroom doors, seniors spilling out from every which way. She suddenly felt a pang of nostalgia remembering her first day of high school. Mrs. Kennedy had driven her and Brian, and Celeste had been so nervous, wondering if she would make new friends, if she would like her teachers, meet a cute boy. The last four years had flown by, and she felt that she had missed out on some of the best parts of high school because she had felt so empty inside. But now everything was changing. She could somehow feel it: deep inside, she knew that nothing was ever going to be the same.

"Cel, are you coming to the bonfire on Parker Hill tonight?" asked Brian as he threw his backpack into his car.

"She needs to get her beauty sleep tonight," interjected Natalie. "She has to be well rested for her eighteenth birthday costume bash tomorrow!"

"Actually, I was thinking of going for a little while."

Both Natalie and Brian paused dramatically.

"I never thought I would see the day when Celeste Wilder actually wanted to go to a party – two days in a row, even!" said Natalie.

"This is the new Celeste Wilder," she said with a smile.

"Great, do you want to go together Cel?" Brian asked.

"You can pick us both up," said Natalie. "I'll be at Celeste's making sure her costume is appropriate for the birthday extravaganza I have planned."

"So what do you think?" Celeste asked Natalie as she did a little twirl in her costume.

"I love it! That black mini dress is super sexy with that chiffon cape, and is that a bat on your belt? Amazing! Let's see the fangs!"

"I don't want to put them in yet. I sound funny when I talk," said Celeste, holding out the pointy white fangs in demonstration.

"This is going to be the best party ever! I am so excited."

"I am too, Nat. I don't think I ever thanked you for planning this amazing birthday party or for being such a good friend. I know I was the one that pushed you away when we were younger, and I really appreciate you giving me a second chance."

"Don't be silly Celeste, I love you! You are one of my best friends and always will be," she said, putting an arm around her friend.

Celeste felt tears welling in her eyes, but Natalie interjected, "No, no, none of that tonight. We are going to our last bonfire as seniors, exams are over and we are done with high school!"

When they reached Parker Hill, there was hardly a place to park Brian's Mustang. It seemed like all of St. Alice High School along with some of the recent grads now attending the community college had shown up. The clearing was teeming with students drinking, laughing and enjoying their first night of freedom after exams. Natalie bounded ahead toward a group of girls, leaving Brian and Celeste struggling to keep up.

"I'm going to grab a beer. Do you want one too?" asked Brian over the blaring music coming from a nearby parked car.

"I thought you were our designated driver," she said with hands on her hips.

"I said I'd bring you girls here, but I never promised a ride back," he said.

Now Celeste really frowned.

"Relax, I'm kidding, Cel. The Oak Bluffs taxi company is giving free rides for graduating seniors all night so I'm planning on leaving the 'Stang here for the night."

"Then yes, I will have a beer!" she said with a grin.

Brian had gone off in search of Natalie, and Celeste sat sipping her beer gazing at the flickering flames of the fire. As she stared, the flames appeared to change and transform, taking on ominous figures – first a skeleton, then a monster, next a demon. It seemed like they were dancing in the firelight. She gasped and quickly turned away, but when she looked back they were gone. As Celeste rubbed her eyes in disbelief, she felt a cold hand on her shoulder and almost jumped out of her skin.

"It's okay Celeste, it's just me, Roman. Are you alright?"

She leapt into his arms without thinking. "Oh Roman, yeah, I'm okay." Feeling suddenly awkward she quickly released him and took a step back. "What are you doing here?"

"Nico forced me to come along so that I would get out of the house and have fun, *and* serve as his designated driver, no doubt." The look on his face made her think he didn't mind it as much as he was pretending to. She laughed and slid over on the bench to make room for him.

"What were you thinking about when I walked over? You seemed to be deep in thought when I startled you," he said.

"If I tell you, do you promise not to think I'm crazy?"

Roman nodded.

"I've been having these dreams, and they are filled with horrible creatures coming for me. And my father is in the dreams with me sometimes, training me to fight so that I can protect the human world from these monsters. I don't even know how to explain it. You must think I've totally lost it."

"Of course I don't Celeste. Of all people, I know what kind of monsters this world is filled with." He gave her an encouraging smile.

"When I was looking at the fire just a minute ago, I had another dream – or more of a vision, I guess. It was terrifying."

"Do you want to tell me about it?"

"No, not really. I don't know what's wrong with me. I'm dreaming about my dead father, I'm having supernatural visions. I'm pretty sure I'm going crazy."

"You're not going crazy," Roman began.

"Do you believe in ghosts Roman? I mean, are they real?" She looked up at him anxiously, her hazel eyes lit up by the glowing fire.

"With everything that you've learned in the past few days, do you really find it that hard to believe that they could be?"

"I don't know what to believe anymore."

"Why are you asking?"

"Well, these dreams that I've been having about my dad – I guess I've never really told you much about him."

"Nico mentioned he passed away when you were young."

"I was ten. He was a private investigator so he worked late and traveled a lot. He had gone out to meet a client on a rainy night, and he was killed in a terrible car crash. I never got to say goodbye."

"I'm sorry, Celeste." He reached out for her hand, squeezing it reassuringly.

"So do you think he could be a ghost?"

"I'm not sure, but if he's only appearing to you in your dreams, I would think not," Roman assured her.

"You're probably right. It's just that the things he says to me, they seem so real."

"Like what?"

Again Celeste considered telling Roman all the details of her dreams, but something stopped her. How could she tell him that she dreamt about killing vampires?

"I don't really want to talk about it. I just hope all the bad dreams or visions or whatever they are go away soon."

Roman searched for words to comfort her, but anything he said would have been a lie. He wanted to tell her that it was just a dream, to assure her that everything was going to be all right, but he couldn't be certain of that. So instead he put his strong arm around her shoulders and let the warmth of the fire soothe both their worried minds.

"There you guys are," said Natalie as she and Nico stumbled to an adjacent bench by the crackling fire pit.

"You two look like you've been making the most out of the keg," said Celeste.

"Well, it looks like the two of *you* have been making the most out of the romantic firelight," countered Natalie. "And I am perfectly fine, Celeste, see – I can touch my nose while walking in a straight line – no problem!"

Nico caught Natalie just in time as she stumbled trying to keep her balance.

Celeste laughed and asked, "Where's Brian?"

"We thought he was with you," she replied.

"No, he went off a while ago looking for you, and we haven't seen him since."

"I'm sure he found a cute blonde to hit on or something," said Nico.

Both Natalie and Celeste shot him a look.

"Should we all go look for him then?" suggested Roman.

They split up to cover more ground: Natalie and Nico went toward the center of the bonfire and Celeste and Roman took the outer perimeter. It was a brisk night for May and Celeste wrapped her jeans jacket tightly around herself as they searched. She tried to keep up with Roman, but her stride was no match for his. He stopped suddenly, surveying a tall tree ahead. It was obvious that his keen vampire sight had seen something that she did not.

"What is it?" she asked.

"Nothing. Come on, this way," he said with a worried look in his eye.

As they walked deeper into the woods, all of the festive sounds of the bonfire dissipated and the darkness enveloped them.

Brian, with a red Solo cup in hand, had been wandering around Parker Hill looking for Natalie. With as much as he had been drinking, he knew he needed to stay safely away from Celeste, and Natalie could prove a useful distraction. He had walked up to countless groups of pretty brunettes, but Natalie was nowhere in sight. Tired and losing focus on his mission, he plopped down on the ground. Leaning against a tree, Brian pulled out his cell phone and noticed missed calls and texts from both Natalie and Celeste. He started to type out a reply when a tall man came out of the shadows.

"Geez, I guess they don't have an age limit at the community college these days," mumbled Brian.

The mysterious man said nothing, inexorably marching towards him. Before Brian could utter a word, the man grabbed his head and forced him to look into his fearsome black eyes. Brian felt like the whole world was spinning for a moment, and then he felt nothing.

"Are you Celeste Wilder's best friend Brian?" he asked.

"Yes."

"Where is she?"

"She's here somewhere, but I don't know where," he replied with a vacant stare.

"Do you know Roman and Nico Constantin?"

"Yes."

"Are they here too?" the stranger questioned.

"I don't know," Brian managed. "I haven't seen them."

"Do you know what the Constantins want with Celeste?"

"Want with her? I don't know, I guess they are into her," said Brian.

The strange man continued to assault Brian with questions never dropping his dark gaze until he heard voices approaching. He quickly turned back to him saying, "Brian, you will remember nothing that just happened," and he disappeared into the dark forest.

"Brian, where have you been? We've been looking everywhere for you," said Celeste.

"Oh sorry, I think I passed out. Too much beer and not enough sleep I guess," he said shaking his head drowsily.

Roman offered him his hand and hauled him up onto his feet. "Come on it's getting late, why don't I get you kids home?"

Walking back to the bonfire, they reconnected with Natalie and Nico, and all piled into Nico's car with Roman at the steering wheel and Celeste riding shotgun. As Roman drove, Celeste looked over at him and he caught her eye. She silently mouthed "thank you" and he shot her a quick smile before turning his focus back on the road.

When they pulled into Celeste's driveway, Brian mumbled his goodnights and walked unsteadily home while

Nico snored in the back seat. Roman escorted Celeste to the front door.

"Is your mom home?" he asked, looking at her intently.

"No, she's working the overnight shift again."

"Are you going to be all right by yourself?"

"I'll be fine. I do it all the time," Celeste reassured him.

Roman looked at her for a long moment, and she could see the inner struggle flash through his eyes. Finally he said, "I can stay with you if you want, so you don't have to be alone."

Celeste felt her face flush at the thought of spending the night with Roman in any capacity. "I'd really like that, as long as we get you out of here before my mom gets back in the morning," she said, trying to hide the beaming smile on her face.

Roman returned to the car to wake Nico and let him know he'd be staying for the night. Even in his inebriated state, Nico had to question this decision.

"You're going to spend the night inside her house, just the two of you? Do you really think that's wise?"

"I'm doing it to protect her," he responded. "It's the night before her birthday. According to Stellan if we are right about her, it will happen tonight. Someone needs to be there for her."

Nico shook his head, but knew there was no arguing with his brother on the matter. "Have you fed today, Roman?" he asked.

"No, but I'll be fine."

"Are you sure about that?"

"Yes," he said resolutely.

Celeste had put on her cutest pajamas, and was brushing her teeth looking at her reflection in the mirror contemplating how much her life had changed in a matter of weeks. Just a few short weeks ago she knew nothing about the existence of vampires, and now she was fairly sure she was falling in love with one. She felt an intense excitement building inside of her as she giddily thought about a night alone with Roman.

Am I crazy to think he could possibly feel the same way about me? He must have dated hundreds of girls...literally! The sound of Roman's footsteps coming up the stairs snapped her out of her musings.

"Hi," she said as she popped her head out of her bedroom door, "come on in."

"You don't have to invite me into every room in the house individually," said Roman, eyes twinkling.

As he walked around the room admiring her pictures, Celeste suddenly felt uncomfortable being alone in her bedroom with him. Her heart was racing and her palms were getting sweaty.

"Everything okay?" he asked as he sat down on the foot of her bed.

She was a bit thrown by his observation. She wasn't entirely sure he *wasn't* reading her mind. She wondered if he felt the intimate connection as strongly as she did.

"Yeah, sure, I was just thinking about how my mom would totally freak out if she knew I had a guy in my room in the middle of the night when she wasn't home."

"Am I making you uncomfortable? Do you want me to leave?" he asked sounding a little hurt.

"Of course not. I'm really happy that you are here. But maybe we can go sit in the den instead?"

"After you," said Roman and he let her lead the way back downstairs.

Once they were settled in on the couch with the television tuned into a late night talk show, Celeste felt much more at ease. Roman had taken off his jacket to reveal a cozy black Henley shirt underneath, paired with dark, stylish jeans. She tried not to stare at him, but her eyes kept wandering in his direction. His dark, wavy hair rested right above his brow, drawing attention to his beautiful deep cobalt blue eyes. His hand rested casually next to her thigh, almost touching it. The attraction that she felt towards him was uncanny, but as striking as he was to look at, she knew it was much more than just his good looks drawing her in. She had felt something similar when she had first met Nico, but it was nothing as powerful as this. Looking up she realized he was staring at her too.

"It's almost midnight," said Roman, dispelling the building tension.

"Yup! You know, when I was little I used to have to beg my parents to let me stay up until midnight on the night before my birthday," she said. "Then after my dad passed away, Mom was hardly ever home at night so I kept the tradition going; only it was always just me."

Roman placed his hand on her leg and gave her a comforting smile.

"Thank you for staying with me tonight. It really means a lot to me," she said. Slowly, she leaned in and planted a lingering kiss on his cheek.

Roman, giving in to a brief moment of abandon pulled her face toward his. When he was only inches from her lips, he felt an agonizing pang in the pit of his stomach and his fangs began extending. Before Celeste could process what had happened, Roman had leapt off the sofa and had pinned himself up against the far wall. She glanced up to see his face, and he looked utterly mortified.

"I am so sorry, Celeste," he said, turning towards the door. "This was a bad idea, I never should have stayed. I must leave."

"No, please Roman, don't go. I'm fine, you didn't hurt me, I promise," she said as she walked towards him.

He backed further away from her. "No, but I could have," he said with such sorrow in his beautiful eyes.

"But you didn't," she insisted as she took a step closer.

"Please Celeste, don't..."

"Why not?"

"I don't know if I can control myself around you."

Celeste just stared at him, not knowing what to say. The thought of him leaving was worse than what she imagined he could ever do to her. She wasn't scared of him.

"Do you remember when I was telling you about our mother, and how she helped us when we were first turned into vampires?"

She nodded.

"What I didn't tell you was how bad it was at first. We couldn't control our newly found thirst for blood. With every life taken, we suffered horribly with the guilt and remorse because we still possessed our humanity. We promised our mother we would never be those monsters again, but it's not easy Celeste."

"You're   not   a   monster."

Bong! Bong! Bong!

The old grandfather clock in the dining room struck midnight.

"Well happy birthday to me," she said miserably, turning away from him.

The sadness Roman heard in her voice resonated throughout him. He summoned up all his self-control then cautiously approached Celeste. Ever so gently, he leaned down and placed a tender kiss on her forehead whispering, "Happy birthday Celeste."

***

Olivia Wilder stared at the glowing computer screen in her small office in the hospital. It was the eve of her daughter's eighteenth birthday, and she knew it was time. She put on her reading glasses and pulled the crumpled piece of yellowing paper from her pocket, staring fondly at the familiar handwriting. She copied the email address exactly, then typed a short message. She hesitated for a moment and then she clicked send.

***

With quite a bit of persuading, Celeste was finally able to convince Roman to sit with her on the couch again. All of a sudden, she was feeling very sleepy, and as hard as she tried to fight it, within minutes her head had dropped on Roman's shoulder. He watched her sleep for a while, as he had done so many nights before from outside of her bedroom, before nodding off himself.

Roman awoke abruptly with Celeste thrashing wildly in his arms. "Celeste, wake up, you're having a nightmare," he said, while gently trying to rouse her.

She tossed and turned and screamed and cried, but no matter how hard he tried, he couldn't wake her up. It was as if she were in a trance, transported somewhere far away from him.

Celeste remembered falling asleep in Roman's warm arms, when suddenly she was harshly torn away from him. She found herself in a large circular room with no windows or doors. The curved walls were a stark white and the scant furniture cold, metallic silver. As she scanned the room Celeste realized she was seated in front of a tribunal of sorts. There were five somber-faced individuals in dark robes seated on a bench in front of her, scrutinizing her every move.

"Where am I? Who are you people?" she asked unable to keep her voice steady.

She could hear her voice echoing off the walls, and there was a long pause before anyone answered her. They seemed to be examining her, maybe even probing around in her mind.

Finally, the portly man with the stern face seated in the elevated middle chair spoke.

"Celeste Wilder, you have been chosen to be the next Guardian. It is your duty to train as a hunter and to protect the human world from all the evil of the supernatural one."

Celeste's mouth dropped, and she stared into nothingness unable to comprehend what was happening. She shut her eyes tightly. *This is all a dream. I'm just having another bad dream. This isn't real. I want to wake up, please wake up!*

When she opened her eyes again, she had hoped she would find herself safe and sound in her bed, but to her disappointment she was still in front of the panel of scrutinizing faces.

"I don't understand what you want from me," she said. "I'm not a guardian or a hunter or whatever you said. I'm just a normal girl, and I want to go home."

Celeste's voice was bordering on hysterics now, though she tried to remain calm, she knew she was quickly losing the battle. A silver-haired woman with thick purple-framed glasses at the end of the bench spoke to the others saying, "Perhaps we should call on Kristof."

At the mention of her father's name, Celeste looked up anxiously. And just like that, he appeared before her.

"Daddy," she said, tears streaming down her face. He knelt down in front of her and wiped the tears from her cheeks.

Holding her hands tightly he said, "Celeste, you must be strong. You have been chosen to fulfill your destiny. This is our family legacy. You will learn just like I did what it truly means to be a Wilder – a hunter. You are an extraordinary young lady, and you have been given special powers to be used for good. Without guardians like us, the world as we know it would not continue to exist, it would be consumed by evil."

Celeste could do nothing but stare in wonderment as she clutched onto his hands desperately.

"I wish that I could be here for you, to help you and train you as my father trained me. But I promise you this; I will do everything in my power to help you as much as I can. I love you Celeste, and I know that you can do this."

Then he was gone.

Celeste choked down a sob and tried to process what her father had said. All of a sudden, a series of visions flashed through her head; a sequence of vampires, zombies, phantoms, witches, and warlocks, death and destruction was everywhere. She cried out, feeling as though her head would explode from the onrush. Everything that she had seen in her dreams had been real. She understood that now, and magically was able to accept it. It was as if some part of her brain that had been dormant for all of these years had suddenly been unlocked.

The portly man spoke again. "Now that you understand your duties, you must begin training."

"Understand my duties? I don't understand anything about this."

He seemed to ignore her, continuing with, "Your powers will begin to reveal themselves now that you are eighteen, and they will get stronger as you do."

"What powers? And how am I supposed to train? I don't know what to do," said Celeste. She looked up at the strangers before her, eyes desperate.

"Everything will be revealed to you in time. Let your instinct guide you. It will lead you on the right path."

Well that's not the least bit cryptic...

"Good luck, Celeste Wilder, and may good always triumph over evil."

"But wait –"

Celeste opened her eyes warily, and saw Roman's anxious face hovering over her. Startled, she looked around and saw that she was back in her cozy den on the couch with a blanket wrapped tightly around her.

"Are you all right?"

"I think so," she said trying to sit up. Roman took her hand to help her up, and she felt the oddest sensation when his hand touched hers. It wasn't the same exciting spark that she had felt before; instead it felt darkly ominous. She jerked her hand away from his touch. He looked at her, and she could see the flash of hurt in his expressive eyes and then it was gone.

"Was it another bad dream?" he asked, clearing his throat.

"I think it was much more than a bad dream," Celeste retorted.

"Do you want to tell me about it?"

"I don't know if I can," she responded. A large part of her wanted nothing more than to tell Roman everything, but a little voice inside of her fought against it. *Aren't vampires one of the evil beings that I am supposed to protect the world against? But Roman isn't evil. He is a good person...uh...vampire.* Celeste felt so conflicted. It was as if she were being pulled apart by two opposing forces – her brain and her heart.

"If you want someone to talk to I'm here," he said coolly. "But I should leave soon. It's almost dawn, and I'm sure your mother will be home shortly."

"Please don't leave yet."

Celeste caught his hand and pulled him down on the sofa, forcing him to sit close to her. As if conducting a science experiment, she ran her hand down his arm and felt that dark feeling in her core, but along with it she also felt the familiar exciting pull. It was slight, but it was still there. It was like the opposing forces of a magnet equally pulling her towards and pushing her away from him. Roman sat perfectly still, watching her tensely as she inched closer to him. Abruptly, Roman shot up, "Your mom! I hear her car pulling up in the driveway."

Celeste was still caught up in the moment, slightly breathless and her senses on high alert.

"I can leave out the back door," he said.

She could only nod and follow him towards the door. As he opened it to let himself out, he paused and turned back for a moment. She could tell he was wrestling with his feelings just as much as she was. With a quick turn he gave her a hurried kiss on the cheek and disappeared before she could say a word.

Celeste heard the click of a key sliding into the lock, but after all that had happened, she couldn't bring herself to face her mom. She slipped quickly up the stairs and crawled into bed. Celeste hoped that she would be able to sleep, at least a few hours, before having to deal with the realities of her destiny and the new life that would undoubtedly come along with it.

Chapter 10

Celeste could hear the buzzing from her phone on her nightstand, but she couldn't muster the strength to pick it up in time. Rubbing her eyes, she looked at the clock and saw that it was already past noon. She really must have been exhausted. Her phone indicated that she had three missed calls from Natalie, a text from Brian, and another from Nico.

"Good, you're finally awake birthday girl!" said her mom as she poked her head in the doorway.

"I am!" she said as cheerfully as possible. With everything that had happened last night, she had momentarily forgotten that today was her birthday.

"Happy birthday to you, happy birthday to you..." Her mom entered her room singing and holding a tray full of Celeste's favorite breakfast treats – French toast with powdered sugar, crispy bacon and fried eggs with fresh orange juice.

"I made you a special birthday breakfast, and it's been waiting for you for hours. I hope it didn't get too cold. Did you kids stay out late last night at the bonfire?"

"Yeah, I guess it was pretty late, and then I didn't sleep very well last night," she answered while nibbling on some bacon.

Celeste looked up to see her mother's eyes fixed on her. Celeste found it oddly unnerving and almost said something, but shook it off attributing it to her frayed nerves.

"You finish up your breakfast, and then get ready. I have a special day planned for us. It's not every day that you turn eighteen."

That's the understatement of the century.

As Celeste got dressed, she kept replaying the vision in her head. She remembered the guardians telling her that she would soon get her powers. She wondered what sorts of powers she would possess, and how would she train to become a hunter. She had never been the athletic type growing up, and now she was expected to battle supernatural creatures? She had seen how strong and fast Roman was when he had knocked out Patrick at prom. How could she be expected to compete with that?

"Are you almost ready sweetie?" shouted her mom.

"Coming!"

Celeste couldn't help but laugh when she and her mother pulled into the Oak Bluff's Children's Zoo.

"I hope you don't think this is too silly?"

"No mom, this is great!" Celeste said giggling.

"I remember how much fun we used to have here when you were little. You loved feeding the goats at the petting zoo and you'd spend hours watching the howler monkeys swinging from the trees."

"I remember. I used to want to be a monkey!" Celeste admitted.

Just spending time with her mother was a treat, and spending a relaxing, supernatural-free day at the zoo was exactly what she needed.

The sun was warm on Celeste's shoulders, and if she focused solely on the soothing sound of the ducks paddling in the pond, she could almost forget everything that had happened last night. Celeste and her mother sat on the lush grass overlooking the pond at the zoo and enjoyed a picnic lunch together. She began recounting all the details of the extravagant birthday party that Natalie had planned for her.

"That sounds like it's going to be quite the party! I'm sure it will be the social event of the year, if Natalie has anything to say about it."

"That's what I'm thinking too."

"Well, I am so happy that you will be spending your eighteenth birthday with all your friends. And how about Nico and Roman—will they be there too?"

The thought of facing them after what happened last night made Celeste slightly nauseas. She didn't know how her relationship with them was going to fit into her new life as a Guardian – whatever that meant.

"Yes, they're both coming," she answered.

"Maybe you'll get a kiss on your birthday."

"Mom, stop please, you're so embarrassing!" said Celeste blushing.

When they got back home, Celeste happily headed up to her bedroom with a stuffed monkey her mother had bought her as a souvenir to commemorate her eighteenth birthday.

"Follow me sweetie," said her mom taking her hand.

"Why are we going up into the attic?" asked Celeste.

"I have another birthday surprise for you."

Mrs. Wilder led the way to the back corner of the attic. Celeste hadn't been up here in years. She walked by the dusty boxes and old furniture causing her nose to twitch, reminding her why she typically avoided the attic at all costs. After her mom moved a couple of boxes and lifted a worn sheet, Celeste saw a bulky wooden trunk that she had never noticed.

Her mom paused in front of it. "This was your dad's, and I thought it would be fun to go through it together. There is something that he wanted you to have."

Celeste examined the old rusty lock on the trunk, and when she jiggled it, it sprung open. She lifted the lid to see stacks of letters, photos, a couple of books, and some clothing, among other things. The trunk was deep, and it would take some digging to get to the bottom of it. They started with the pictures on top. Celeste began to flip through dozens of them with her and her father, with her mom when she was pregnant, with her as a baby, and with all three of them together smiling happily. Celeste set aside some of her favorites to take with her back to her room. As her mom was sorting through the photos, Celeste came across some books – *Myths and Legends, Stories of the Occult, The Underworld*, along with other foreboding titles.

"You remember that your dad always had such an active imagination. He always loved reading all of those scary stories." Celeste just smiled, and secretly set one aside to read later.

"And this is for you," her mom said as she handed her a worn leather pouch.

"What is it?" Celeste asked inquisitively.

"It's from your father. He told me to give it to you when you turned eighteen if anything ever happened to him. I don't know why he would have worried about that, but I guess it's fortunate for us that he did."

Celeste untied the knot and opened the pouch which held an antique key on a black leather cord. The key was an ornate gold with a sparkling blue sapphire encrusted in the head.

"That key has been passed down for generations, Celeste. I have no idea what it may open, but I know that it's been in the Wilder family for centuries, and it was important to your father that you have it," she said, handing it to her with a wistful smile.

Celeste looked thoughtfully at the ancient key as she felt its weight in her hand. "It's beautiful Mom. Thank you," she said clutching it tightly.

"Celeste! Where have you been all day?" said Natalie excitedly over the phone. "I've been calling you for hours!"

"Sorry, Nat, I got up late and then was out with my mom. We just got home." As she listened to Natalie, she took the stuffed monkey out of the plastic bag and placed it on her bookshelf next to a picture from her first birthday at the zoo. She couldn't help but smile.

"Okay, well I guess I'll forgive you since you are the birthday girl. Don't forget to be at my house in full costume by eight o'clock."

"Right, got it," she said, her mind focusing back on the present. "Do you need me to bring anything?"

"Nope, just you and your *fang*tastic self!"

"Oh man, I'm really rethinking my costume now."

"Don't you dare!"

She glanced down at her watch. "Okay, okay. Brian is picking me up in an hour so I'll see you soon."

***

Roman had gotten home, woken Nico up and called Stellan immediately to update him on the latest developments. Stellan's hologram was currently pacing in their living room, listening intently.

"But she didn't tell you what happened exactly?" he asked.

"No, she was too upset to talk about it, and then her mom arrived so I had to make an impromptu exit," explained Roman.

"But you're sure that she had the vision? Celeste was definitely chosen?"

A look of sadness infiltrated his perfectly chiseled features. "Yes, I am sure. When she woke up, I touched her and she flinched."

"Are you sure that wasn't just you?" asked Nico snickering.

With a nasty glance at Nico, Roman continued, "She definitely felt something when I touched her, and it frightened her. It has to be her powers starting to emerge."

"Yes, that does sound right," said Stellan, a mixture of concern and awe in his tone.

"And it was certainly no ordinary dream that she was having because I repeatedly tried to wake her, but there was nothing I could do. She was in some sort of a trance."

"Right, so we have to assume that Celeste is now a Guardian. You should start to notice when her powers come about. The only thing we can do is continue to keep an eye on her. Roman, you seem to be pretty close to her; try to get her to open up to you."

"I will gladly try, but I think that she is holding back now because of what I am. Something has changed." He turned his back to them, looking away sullenly.

Stellan discontinued his anxious pacing and turned to face the brothers head on. His voice took on an ominous tone as he warned, "Both of you must remember that as Celeste's powers become stronger, her natural instinct will be to kill you. It has been ingrained in her that all vampires are evil. This may prove to be difficult considering the current situation."

"Celeste wouldn't hurt us. We are her friends," said Nico.

"Though that may be true, as she is transitioning into a Guardian, her emotions will be on high gear. Until she gets a handle on them, I caution you both to be careful," Stellan finished.

"Well, that should make for a fun party tonight," said Nico glancing at Roman.

As Celeste put the finishing touches on her makeup, she suddenly felt ridiculous dressed up as a vampire, especially after everything that had happened last night. She wished she had enough time to get a new costume, but she knew Natalie would kill her if she showed up in her plain clothes. She looked at herself in the mirror and didn't recognize the girl standing before her. The elaborate black eyeliner, bright red lipstick, fake fangs protruding from her upper lip and the blood dribbling down her chin was all too much. *I can't believe I'm doing this.*

"Celeste! I'm downstairs. Come on out!" yelled Brian through the walkie-talkie on her dresser.

Here goes nothing...

"Wow Brian, you look great!" He was wearing a white oxford shirt with buttons ripped open to reveal the classic red and yellow Superman emblem underneath. The black-rimmed glasses drew attention to his bright green eyes and were sparkling with excitement.

"Do you have your retainer on or something? You're talking funny."

"It's the fangs! They give me a lisp. It's actually getting better; at first my mom couldn't even understand what I was saying. Maybe I should take them off?"

"No, it definitely completes the costume. The lisp is kinda sexy," he said laughing.

"Very funny, Brian. I love the Clark Kent transforming into Superman look you've got going."

"Thanks, I really didn't think I could pull off the tights," he said grinning.

"Aww, and I was so looking forward to that."

"You have a little something on your chin..." he said reaching for her.

She quickly darted out of his reach. "It's blood Brian, and it's supposed to be there! I'm a blood-sucking vampire, remember?"

As they drove up to Natalie's house, Celeste took one look at the number of cars parked on the street and almost made Brian turn the car around. They could hear the music booming from down the block!

"Natalie must have invited all of St. Alice's *and* the community college," she said, shaking her head.

"Well, we knew she was going to go all out for this," said Brian walking in amazed.

The house had been flawlessly decorated in a black and white motif with candles, sparkling streamers, and eighteenth birthday banners.

"Celeste, you're here!" said Natalie as she came bounding down the stairs in a skintight cat woman costume. "What do you think?"

Celeste looked around, taking in all the shiny decorations and hoards of people. "It's amazing Natalie, thank you so much for doing all of this for me. Just one question – who are all of these people?"

"Oh come on, you know everyone here, and who cares anyway! All that matters is that they are all here to celebrate your eighteenth birthday!"

"I'm going to find a drink," said Brian.

Celeste turned to follow him.

"Oh wait, I have something for you. Stay right here," directed Natalie, as she pointed at Celeste. Seconds later she was back with a black sash, marked with sparkling gold lettering that read "Birthday Girl".

"Oh Natalie, you shouldn't have..." But it was too late. Natalie had already flung the sash over Celeste's head and was meticulously adjusting it. "There, we want to make sure it doesn't cover that cute little bat belt!"

Natalie led the way with Celeste in tow, steering her around the crowd as she received countless birthday wishes from perfect strangers. The pair made their way out to the backyard, which had been decorated with hundreds of string lights and colorful Chinese lanterns dangling from the trees. The dance floor had been set up over the pool and the DJ was spinning high-energy dance music in the corner. Everyone was dancing and laughing and having a great time. This was exactly what Celeste needed to forget all about last night. She and Natalie worked through the crowd to the middle of the dance floor, and all Celeste thought about was the pounding rhythm of the music and keeping her body moving to the beat.

Celeste was completely entranced by the pulsating music when she felt a strange sensation that snapped her into awareness. She turned around and saw the crowd parting and girls staring as Roman and Nico walked towards her. At the sight of Roman, her heart sped up a bit, but she willed it to return to normal as he approached. He and Nico were wearing one-shouldered white togas with half of their bronzed chests exposed (to all the girls' excitement) with a crown of laurels resting on their heads.

"Let me guess, you two are Greek gods?" asked Natalie with a witty smile as they approached.

"It was just something we had lying around," said Nico with a wink as he pulled Natalie to dance.

Roman inched closer to Celeste, and whispered, "nice costume," in her ear. "A little ironic, don't you think?"

A shiver went down her spine as his hands made contact with her waist. She wrapped her arms around his neck and began swaying to the music. As their bodies got closer, she felt that threatening sensation again, like every nerve in her body was on edge, telling her that something was wrong. She tried to ignore it and fight against it, but it was too overwhelming. As if Roman also sensed there was something wrong, he looked down at her questioningly.

"Sorry, I have to go check on something. I'll be back soon," she said pulling abruptly away from him and disappearing into the crowd.

This can't be happening... Why am I feeling this way around Roman?

Celeste darted back to the house as a wave of misery washed over her. If being the Guardian meant feeling this terrible repulsion towards Roman, then she didn't want to be one. Roman was the first guy that she had ever felt so strongly about, and she didn't want to lose him. She pulled the fake fangs out of her mouth and tucked them into her purse as she waited impatiently outside of the occupied bathroom. Suddenly, an intensely ominous feeling similar to the one she felt around Roman but highly magnified overtook her. She looked around, half expecting to see Roman or Nico, but instead saw a tall man with a blood red mask walking towards her. As he approached, the terrifying feeling intensified, and every nerve in her body compelled her to run, so she did.

Celeste sprinted outside to the crowded pool deck and spotted Nico.

"Are you okay?" he asked. She looked as pale as the sheet wrapped around his waist.

"No. I don't know. There was someone inside, and I just got a really bad feeling about him so I ran."

"Where is he? What did he look like?"

"He was tall, dressed in black with a red mask, and jet black hair with a crazy white streak down the middle and an ugly scar above his eyebrow. I think he might have been a vampire," she said finally.

Roman appeared out of nowhere as if he had heard the "v word" from afar. "Celeste, go stay with Brian," said Roman, taking her arm and nudging her back out toward the party. "We'll go check it out."

"I want to come," she said determinedly.

"No, it's not safe Celeste. You're not ready yet," said Roman looking at her sternly.

"What do you mean, I'm not ready *yet*?" she asked.

"Celeste please, let us go and see if we can find this guy. Brian's on the dance floor looking lonely. Go keep him company. We'll be right back," said Nico. And they turned and stalked away.

As soon as they were out of sight, Celeste doubled back toward the house.

"Do you sense anything?" asked Nico as they crept inside the quiet house.

"No, nothing. Which means he's either very old and powerful enough to conceal himself or there's just a strange human lurking around the party."

"I'm going to get an aerial view while you check in here," said Nico and he took off.

The house was practically empty; everyone was outside enjoying the DJ and music. Roman tiptoed around the kitchen, into the den, through the living room, but found no one. He tried to focus in on his keen hearing and heard a muffled noise from upstairs. He bolted up the stairs using his vamp-speed, and found himself face to face with Celeste at the top landing. The vampire had his powerful arm clenched tightly around her neck, his fangs inches from her flesh. Roman stopped dead in his tracks and looked helplessly at her frightened face. The monster took a few steps back, dragging Celeste into an open bedroom. She was fighting to get away from him, but it was no use; he was too strong for her.

"Let her go," roared Roman, "or you won't leave this house alive."

The vampire's dark eyes peered at him through the crimson mask. "I would guess by your unnatural affection for this young lady in a rather naughty vampire costume that you must be Roman Constantin."

"I am. And you are?" he asked, his voice unwavering.

"Obviously not as stealthy as I thought I was since you have found me. And what in God's name are you wearing?"

Ignoring his snide question Roman continued, "I am going to ask you again, who are you and what do you want here?" He was putting on a false bravado, inside he knew very well that this vampire was much older and stronger than he was, but that was not going to stop him from saving Celeste.

"I am actually here for you and your brother."

"Fine, here I am and I assure you that my brother is not far behind. Let her go. She has nothing to do with this." Celeste's eyes caught Roman's momentarily, his blue eyes blazing with intensity.

"I'm not so sure about that," he said. "You seem to be very attached to this pretty human. That could prove useful to me. And I simply can't get over the irony of her choice of costume. Does she know what you are?" A flash of a smile crossed his sinister face.

"That is none of your concern."

Celeste continued squirming, but she couldn't break his iron grip on her neck. Behind her, Roman caught a glance at a snowy white falcon in the window; it was Nico, still in his bird form assessing the severity of the situation. Roman knew his only hope was to catch this vampire by surprise; otherwise, they would be no match for him.

As if on cue, a drunken sorority girl stumbled into the room, teetering on her high heels. "Nice costume man. You look really scary," she said, waving her drink at the stranger. "Does anyone know where the bathroom is?"

The vampire whirled towards the girl, revealing Celeste's panicked face straining against her captor.

"Hey, you're the birthday girl, aren't you?" she said, pointing at Celeste. "Are you okay?"

157

"No! Quick run! Get help!" screamed Celeste.

"Get out of here!" echoed Roman.

The poor girl's reactions were horribly slowed by the alcohol in her system. She turned to run, but was stopped dead in her tracks. The vampire had caught her in his dark gaze, and was mouthing something that only she could hear. She stood frozen in place.

This was Celeste's chance. She gathered her strength and flung her head back as hard as she could. The impact of Celeste's skull against the vampire's nose made a sickening crunch. He released his grip, dazed, and in that moment, Nico flew through the window speeding towards the vampire. The screeching falcon's talons ripped into the vampire's face mercilessly. The distraction was just enough to give Roman a split second to yank Celeste out of his grasp. Finding himself without a valuable hostage and at a disadvantage, the uninvited guest transformed into a bat, whizzing out the window in a blur. Nico darted after him, but it was no use. He was gone.

Celeste had collapsed in Roman's arms and was trying to pull herself together so that she could stand up unassisted. The girl, too, seemed to have passed out when she was released from the monster's gaze and was lying on the ground unconscious.

"It's fine. I'm okay," said Celeste, rubbing the back of her head.

"Why don't you come sit down for a minute?" said Nico, who had reappeared in human form.

Reluctantly, Celeste sat down on the bed so Nico could examine her head and neck for bruises. When he was satisfied that there wasn't any permanent damage, he looked up at Roman who was scowling, lost in thought.

"Okay, so is anyone going to say anything?" asked Nico.

"I told you to stay outside," said Roman to Celeste.

She ignored him. "What did you mean when you said I wasn't ready *yet*, Roman?" she asked accusingly.

"I don't know Celeste, it just came out in the heat of the moment. It didn't mean anything," he said avoiding her eye contact.

"So the fact that I just head-butted that vampire seems totally normal to you?" she asked standing up and looking pointedly at both of them.

"Points for style," said Nico with a smirk.

"Roman, answer me. I know that you know something that you're not telling me."

"That *I'm* not telling *you* something? I think you've got it backwards," and he stormed out of the room.

"Whoa, what's going on with the two of you?" asked Nico.

"I have to go talk to him," she said and rushed out.

Celeste ran down the stairs to try to catch up with Roman, which was hardly fair since he was using vamp-speed.

"Hey, where have you been?" asked Brian coming out of the bathroom underneath the stairs.

"Just taking a quick break from the dancing," she said trying to sound as normal as possible. "Have you seen Roman?"

"Yeah, I think he left. I saw him go out the front door."

Without even responding, Celeste took off toward the entryway. As she hurdled through the front door, she practically tripped over Roman who was sitting on the steps brooding. Somehow her heightened reflexes kicked in and she was able to maintain her balance, somehow avoiding further embarrassment by falling on top of him.

"I thought you left," she said as she attempted to pull herself together.

"I was leaving, but then I stopped. I was worried that whoever that vampire was would come back, and I thought it would be irresponsible of me to do so," he answered without looking up.

Celeste sat down next to him on the steps, and the two of them remained in silence staring blankly ahead refusing to look at each other. Finally it was Celeste who broke the silence, "Do you know what I am?"

Roman hesitated for a moment, and then with a sigh said, "Yes."

"So you knew all along?"

"Yes, but it's not that simple..."

Celeste's blood was boiling.

I could kill him for lying to me! What is going on with me? Why am I so angry?

She took a deep breath and tried to calm down. Her nerves were fried and being so close to Roman was not helping. A part of her brain was screaming at her to rip his head off. She struggled to shut off the voice in her mind.

Roman was looking worriedly at her. He couldn't help but think about Stellan's warning about her emotional state. "I

160

didn't tell you because we didn't know for sure," he finally said keeping his voice calm and controlled.

"But last night, when you were at my house, you knew what was happening to me?"

"No, not exactly. I've never seen someone get chosen to become the next Guardian, I had only heard about it. I knew it would happen on your eighteenth birthday, but that was all."

"So that's why you stayed?" She heard the disappointment in her own tone and chided herself for it.

"Not entirely, but yes that was one reason."

The adrenaline had stopped pounding through her veins, and Celeste was starting to feel normal again. She took another deep breath, saying sarcastically, "It was a great birthday gift."

Roman had been eyeing her nervously, but seemed to notice the change in her immediately. "When you came out of the vision, I wanted to talk to you about it, but it certainly didn't seem like you wanted to talk to me."

"I did want to, Roman, but every fiber in my being was telling me not to."

"I figured as much."

Celeste turned towards him, looked deep into his beautiful blue eyes that now held a twinge of sadness. "We'll get through this, I know we will."

"I'm not so sure Celeste. That vampire that came after you today was ancient and extremely powerful, and if he's after Nico and me and he's using you to get to us, I don't know if I can protect you."

"But you did today, and that's all that matters. And anyway I'm going to be an invincible Guardian right? I must have some cool powers or something."

Roman grinned. "Well I will admit that move you pulled back there was pretty cool."

Celeste was starting to feel like herself again finally. "I know, right! I have no idea where that came from by the way. It was like I wasn't even in control of my body. And it's weird, but I think I feel stronger and more agile already."

"That certainly sounds like your special abilities are kicking in."

Celeste took another deep breath and noticed that all the rage she had been feeling just moments ago was gone.

"I almost forgot: what are we going to do about that girl upstairs?"

"Don't worry about it. Nico will take care of it."

"No Roman! He can't kill her!"

"Relax! He's just going to compel her. She won't remember anything that happened."

"Oh okay, good."

"More importantly, what are we going to do about the fact that you've essentially been programmed to hate and kill Nico and me?"

"I could never hate you, Roman," she said as she put her hand on his hesitantly. Roman squeezed her hand watching her, waiting expectantly for a reaction. "What do you feel?"

Celeste inhaled deeply and said, "It's hard to explain. It's kind of like when you have a really bad feeling that something terrible is about to happen and just when you think you're going to have to run or do anything to get away, something pulls you back."

"Sounds pleasant..."

"It's not *that* bad, and I think I'm getting a better handle on it already. I noticed that when I'm around you or Nico the bad feeling isn't as bad as the vibe I got around that scary vampire who tried to take my head off."

"You must feel varying degrees of evil. I'm glad we're only evil lite..."

"Stop it, Roman. What's important is that I think I can learn to control it," she said hopefully.

"I'm sure you will," he said standing up and pulling out a small gift box tucked away in the folds of his toga. "This is for you."

"You got me a present?"

"I know I'm old, but I still know that an eighteenth birthday is a special occasion for a young woman, and a gift is appropriate. I found this, and I thought of you," he said with a shy look.

Celeste untied the pretty red bow and opened the box carefully. Inside was an antique gold ring with a dazzling blue sapphire.

"It's beautiful, Roman!" she said as she slipped it on her finger.

"It was my mother's," he admitted.

"This is so special. I can't believe you would give this to me. I am truly honored."

"I thought you could use it," he said. "It was my mother's birthstone and she said it always gave her strength."

"I love it!" she said as she pulled him into an embrace. They remained locked in each other's arms for a few moments, but then Celeste was forced to pull away.

"You know my mother had been part of the Council, but when she was turned vampire her official duty had been terminated. However, she had never been fully able or wanted to escape her duties. She always kept an eye on special guardian families throughout the years, particularly the Wilders."

"Wow, really?"

"Yes. And that's why I know that she would want you to have it."

Celeste gave him a big smile as she admired the sparkling ring.

"Celeste! I have been looking everywhere for you!" said Natalie as she came barging outside. "It's time to cut the cake!"

What seemed like hundreds of people gathered around Celeste in the middle of the dance floor waiting for her to blow out the eighteen candles on her beautifully decorated cake. She paused for a moment thinking about what to wish for. A part of her wanted to wish that none of this had ever happened—that she had never met Nico or Roman or learned about the supernatural world. She especially wished that she had never become a Guardian. As she reflected on the past day, a bigger part of her felt that somehow everything was finally as it should be. So she closed her eyes, wished that she would become the greatest Guardian that ever lived, and blew out the candles.

Chapter 11

The next morning, Celeste awoke feeling much better about the prospect of her life as a Guardian. In fact, she may even have felt cheery. She performed a quick scan of her emotions and everything seemed in check – no intense anger, no burning desire to kill vampires, no supernatural alarm in the pit of her stomach. She decided she could be the Guardian and still live a normal, or at least semi-normal life. Graduation day was the day after tomorrow, and all she wanted to do was enjoy the momentous occasion with her friends and family.

"Good morning day-after-birthday girl," said her mom. Her mother's face looked weary and something else too. She couldn't quite put a finger on it – was it anxiety, fear? "How was the party?" she asked, forcing a cheery smile.

Celeste decided to do the same. "It was so great, Mom! Natalie did an amazing job with all the planning, and the decorations were over the top as usual. I have a bunch of pictures on my phone that I'll show you."

"Great, I can't wait to see them!" she said. "So what's your plan for today sweetie?"

"I want to go through more of dad's stuff in the attic. I didn't even get halfway through it the other day."

165

As soon as Celeste heard her mother's car pull out of the driveway, she climbed up the creaking stairs to the musty attic. She sorted through more pictures, miscellaneous knick-knacks and yellowing newspaper clippings, among other things. One old newspaper in particular caught her attention; it was from eight years ago, just a month or so before her father died. The headline read "Mysterious Death Blamed on Wild Animal Attack." She went on to read the editorial, which explained that a woman had been found with bite marks on her neck and had bled to death on the side of the road. A shiver went down Celeste's spine as she imagined another creature that could have caused that horrific death. She put the article aside, and continued digging in the trunk. She finally reached the bottom, and when she pushed aside a heavy photo album, she noticed a small keyhole and what looked like a hidden compartment.

Celeste dashed down to her room to retrieve the old key that her mother had just given her and ran quickly back upstairs. She knelt down, breathless, in front of the trunk and examined the keyhole. She inserted the key and gave it a twist and was awarded with a *click*. The lid popped open and in the small compartment she discovered an old VHS tape and an envelope. Celeste's heart was racing as she looked at the envelope and recognized the familiar writing. It was from her father and it was addressed to her. She opened it carefully, scanning the note in her dad's meticulous penmanship.

My Dear Celeste,
I have no idea how old you will be when you read this, but I can only hope that you are a grown woman

with children of your own and that you have led a long and happy life – a life that I was a part of. If not, that means that I have met an untimely death and unfortunately you've had to bear the burden of my passing. I'm sorry. Although I am gone, please know that I will always be with you in spirit especially now with all that awaits you. There is so much that I want to tell you and yet I cannot seem to find the words. Many years ago when you were just a baby I made a video for you, and I hope that it will bring you comfort during this difficult time.

I love you Celeste, and I know that you will become the exceptional woman that you were destined to be. Take care of your mother, and above all things trust your instincts.

Love, Dad

P.S. I have a few items that may be of use to you, I have included the address below:

U-Save Self Storage
Unit# 99
125 Willowbend Road

A lone tear rolled down Celeste's cheek as she clutched the note against her chest. She allowed herself a moment of grief to remember her father then pulled herself together. Celeste had a mission. She picked up the tape and wondered where in the world she would find a VHS player.

"Well that was a huge revelation yesterday," said Nico barging into the living room.

"Which revelation was that little brother, the fact that an ancient vampire is looking for us or that Celeste is pre-programmed to hate and possibly kill us?" asked Roman, the turmoil evident in his troubled eyes.

"When you put it that way, you make things sound so depressing..."

"We need to find out who that was and why he's looking for us. I'd bet my life on the fact that this has something to do with Fabian."

"Yes, I tend to agree with you," Nico admitted.

Roman slumped down on the couch and buried his head in his hands.

"How's Celeste?" asked Nico.

"She seemed to be okay when we left the party."

"And how are you holding up?" he questioned.

"Me? I'm fine."

"You don't think that this aversion that Celeste has developed will affect your...uh...relationship?" Nico asked.

"What are you getting at brother?" he asked, irritation ringing in his voice.

"Nothing, never mind. But I think it's necessary that we figure out this new 'evil radar' that she has magically been gifted with."

"She will learn how to control it." Roman paused tentatively, "But yes perhaps we could use some help."

"I think it's time we pay another visit to Stellan. And maybe this time, we take Celeste with us," said Nico.

Celeste made a quick call to the Oak Bluffs Library, and just as she had guessed, they still had VHS players in their children's movie room. Picking up her purse and car keys, she headed towards the door. Suddenly, the prospect of facing such an important discovery alone made her stop in her tracks. She picked up the phone to call Brian; he would go with her anywhere. Then she hesitated: Celeste didn't want Brian to know anything about this. Without realizing it, she found herself dialing Roman's number instead.

"Thanks for coming to get me," she said to Roman as she hopped in his car.

"Of course, it's my pleasure," he said formally.

Every so often when Roman spoke, Celeste was reminded that he wasn't your average twenty-three year old; in fact he was well over one hundred years old. The thought that he had been alive for more than a century was too overwhelming at times, so she tried not to think about it often.

"Roman, I'm sorry I didn't tell you about my visit with the Council right away. I've just been struggling with all of these new feelings that come along with being the Guardian," she blurted out.

"You don't have to apologize to me. I know that you will tell me when the time is right."

"I want to tell you about everything." Celeste began to describe her vision of the Council in detail, including the appearance of her father. As she spoke the words aloud, it all became much more real and being able to share it with Roman also made it much more bearable.

"I just have so many questions for them. And they wouldn't tell me anything!"

"From what I've heard, the process of becoming a Guardian is shrouded in mystery."

"Can't they just give me a guidebook or something?" Celeste asked, only half-kidding.

"Celeste, it's not that easy. But remember that you were born into this, everything will come naturally to you," Roman reassured her.

"Now you're starting to sound like them with their vague advice."

"I'm serious. Don't you remember how well you took the news about me and Nico being vampires?"

"You're joking right?" she asked with a sidelong glance.

"Okay, well I meant after you ran off," he said with a smile pulling at the edge of his lips. "As unbelievable as all of this may seem, there is something inside of you that is taking it in stride, right?"

"Yeah, I guess."

"It's innate Celeste. And it's that something that will lead you to become the next Guardian – without a guidebook." He gave her a smirk.

Roman and Celeste walked through the silent library, their footsteps echoing on the marble floor. The children's room was empty luckily, with the exception of a few colorful children's books strewn on the bright yellow carpet. Celeste had no idea what the video contained, but she figured the least amount of prying eyes the better. She tried to steady her trembling hands as she inserted the videotape into the VCR and pressed "Play." First a few lines of static flashed across the screen, and then her father's face appeared. It was nothing like she remembered it though. She was astonished at how young he looked. His hazel eyes were vibrant and his wavy shoulder-length brown hair was tousled, and he seemed excited yet anxious.

"He must have recorded this video a long time ago," she whispered to Roman. "I remember seeing pictures of him looking like this when I was a baby."

Hi Celeste! Well, I don't know really know where to begin... It's hard for me to picture the future you watching this video since I just left the present you in your crib moments ago. This is all so surreal. But now that I am a father, I feel that it is important to document our family history so that one day you can fully understand it. I hope that we will be able to watch this together on your eighteenth birthday, but if for some reason I am no longer with you, I hope that this will help. I will give your mother very specific instructions to give you our family key on the day of your eighteenth birthday. At that time, you will have had the vision if you were chosen. The key is charmed as is the trunk, and the secret compartment will only reveal itself to those who have been chosen. Perhaps this will clear up a few things for you.

You have been born into a very special family – the Wilders are a long line of hunters that have been protecting the human world from evil for centuries. In fact, the name Wilder comes from an ancient language meaning "hunter"- you are a hunter, my dear Celeste. It's hard for me to imagine that when I see your sweet innocent face. When I turned eighteen, I had a vision in which I was chosen by the Council of Guardians to be the next Guardian, and I was trained by my father. And my father was trained by my grandfather and so on. Not all Wilders in a family line are chosen, and no one really knows why some are passed over. If you are watching this video, I can only assume that you have been selected. This is a very special honor Celeste, but I am not going to lie to you and say that it is an easy task that you are poised to take on. You will have to make many sacrifices in your life in order to fulfill your duties. But I want you to have as much of a normal life as possible. As you know now, I managed to do so. I got married to a wonderful woman, and I had you, my beautiful daughter. I wish the same happiness for you.

As a Guardian, you have been given special abilities; you should begin feeling them shortly after your birthday if you haven't already. You will become stronger and faster, and you will begin to sense the supernatural world around you. Your emotions will be heightened and your survival instinct will intensify. You must learn to trust that instinct, as it is in place to protect you. If I am no longer here to train you, I will make sure to designate someone in my place. The Council will guide you, so turn to them if you need anything. They have been sworn to protect all guardians, and will keep our family secret safe.

There are so many things I want to tell you my darling daughter. Be strong and be brave, and know that I will always be with you. I love you.

At some point during the story Roman had taken her trembling hand in his. As Celeste sat in silence attempting to process what her father had said in the video, she felt a reassuring squeeze.

"So he knew all along," she said her voice small and shaky as the weight of her father's message sunk in. "He knew that it was very likely that I would become a Guardian like he was. All those years he lied to us. I thought he was a private investigator, and meanwhile he had been fighting the forces of evil?"

"I know it's a lot to take in Celeste," said Roman.

"I don't think you do. I feel like everything I knew about my father was a lie, all he did was keep secrets and live this double life," said Celeste sadly.

"But he did it to protect you and your mother, to keep you safe," he said turning towards her.

"And how am I ever going to be safe now? If he had just told me when I was younger, at least I would have been prepared."

"It's not going to be easy Celeste, but you'll get through this. We will help you." He cupped her face in his hands tenderly.

"And who is this someone that is supposed to train me? Don't you think I would have met them by now?"

Roman hated feeling powerless. Seeing Celeste so upset and not being able to do anything to comfort her was killing him.

"My dad was supposed to train me, and he's gone. How am I supposed to do this alone?" Celeste wailed.

"You're not alone Celeste. You have me and Nico, and we can train you. We have both done our fair share of fighting, and who better to teach you than the enemy," he said with a smirk.

She couldn't help but feel a little better any time Roman flashed that million-dollar smile. As draining as it was for her to fight the push and pull inside of her whenever she was around Roman, she felt it was somehow worth it.

"Yeah, I guess," she said sounding slightly less miserable.

"Come on, there's still one more place we have to go today," he said, taking her hand.

Roman led Celeste through the gray sterile hallways of the storage facility as the fluorescent motion-sensor lights flicked on upon their approach. The feeling of desolation that Celeste felt inside mirrored the empty walkways.

"Well this is it, storage number 99," Celeste said as she unlocked the door.

When the door swung open, Celeste's mouth dropped in shock. Roman stood stiffly behind her taking it all in. The small storage unit looked like a military arsenal from medieval times. As she surveyed the room, she saw swords, crossbows, knives, spears and even wooden stakes lining the walls. Even Roman was taken aback by the magnitude of weapons. He reached up and removed an iron broadsword from the hook on the wall to take a closer look.

"This sword is quite old. Judging from the etchings in the hilt my guess would be sometime in the eighteenth century."

Celeste picked up a couple of knives and said, "Look they all have the same symbol engraved on them."

"Do you recognize it?" he asked.

"No, should I?"

"I think it might be the Wilder family symbol. I've heard stories that every hunter family has a unique one."

"Wait a minute," she said examining the symbol more closely, "it does look kind of familiar. Yes! I think I saw it in my dream." It was the first dream she had in which her father was training her. She had been holding a sword with the exact same symbol on it.

"All of these weapons must have been passed down through the generations," he said.

"That's pretty crazy, huh? This sword could have belonged to my great-great grandfather," she said inspecting it.

Roman looked at the symbol more closely. "I believe this is from the Phoenician alphabet – that looks like the letter W."

"And what are those? Swords and a sun?"

"Yes, those are common elements in hunter symbols."

Roman continued walking around the room to more closely admire the archaic weapons. As strange as this had all seemed to Celeste when she first walked in, she began to feel more at ease as she familiarized herself with her families' treasures. There was something about being here that made her feel closer to her father and to all of her ancestors. She felt a surge of power springing from inside of her as she picked up a small sword with a gilded handle and the now familiar engraving. As if by instinct, she began swinging it around ever so gracefully.

"Look at you, you're quite a natural," said Roman.

"It's weird, but I felt something when I picked up the sword – like it was supposed to be mine."

"Well then, I think you should take it with you," suggested Roman.

"Where am I going to keep it, under my bed? What if my mom finds it?"

"Celeste, I think it's time you had a talk with your mother. From what your father said, it seemed like she may know a little more than what we think she does."

***

"Where have you been all day?" asked Nico looking up from his laptop as Roman shut the door behind him.

"Researching some family history with Celeste," he said evasively.

"So is everything alright with the two of you now? She didn't try to kill you or anything?" Nico asked.

"She's getting a handle on her urges, yes."

"And how about your urges, Roman?" He gave his brother a sidelong glance.

"I'm fine," he retorted.

Nico looked at him doubtfully.

"I'm keeping my distance, okay?" Roman tried to assure his brother.

Nico chuckled. "Are you really? If this is keeping your distance, I can't imagine what dating would be like for the two of you."

"Dating? Nico, don't be absurd. I don't date, and even if I wanted to be *with* Celeste, we both know that's impossible." He turned away from Nico, shielding the tortured expression in his eye.

"Why is it so impossible? You can deny it all you want, but I've never seen you act this way with anyone before. You obviously care about her, so why can't you just admit it?"

"To what end, Nico? So that I can torture myself with something that I can never have? She's a hunter and I'm a vampire. The universe certainly likes to play its dirty tricks, doesn't it?"

"So that's it? You're just going to "protect" her and be her friend?"

"Exactly. And I don't want to talk about this anymore," said Roman, slumping down on the couch. "On another note, I was thinking about what you said about bringing Celeste to meet Stellan. You were right, and I think we should go tomorrow."

***

"Hey Mom, do you have a sec to talk?"

"Oh sure sweetie, I'm just going to pop this lasagna in the oven for you for dinner tonight, and I'm all yours." Celeste often wondered how her mother found the time to still cook dinners for her while pulling twelve-hour shifts at the hospital.

177

Celeste went into the living room to wait for her mother. She considered what would be the best way to tell her that she had been chosen to be the next Guardian and that she would be responsible for saving the world from all things evil. *Why don't they make a Hallmark card for that?*

"So what's up?" her mother asked as she sat down beside her.

Celeste steeled her nerves. "Mom, remember that key you gave me for my birthday from dad?"

"Yes, sure."

"Well the other day, I was looking through the trunk, and I found a secret compartment on the bottom."

Celeste paused to read her Mom's face to gauge a reaction, but so far it was blank.

"And the key was a perfect fit. I found a note from dad. It was more than a note; there were actually instructions and a video tape."

Her mom's cool façade began to crumble as Celeste continued. She stood up and walked back and forth in front of the window.

"I watched the video, and it was of dad when he was much younger, and he told me about our family...uh... legacy."

At that, her mother broke down and turned to her, angry tears streaming down her face. "Oh no Celeste, I never wanted any of this for you. I was hoping that I could protect you from it all."

"So you knew? Why didn't you tell me? I've been going crazy for the past few weeks having the strangest nightmares and visions, and worrying about what I was going to tell you." Celeste was up pacing now too.

"I'm sorry sweetie, but I had hoped with all my heart that you wouldn't be chosen. That you wouldn't have to bear the responsibility that your father had to."

"Well, I was chosen and I do have to. How could you keep that from me?"

"You have to understand that when I first met your father, he kept everything a secret from me, but as time went on, it was a secret too difficult to keep hidden. We tried to protect you from it, to let you lead a normal life, but when your father was killed..."

A sudden realization hit Celeste like a speeding freight train. "Wait, Mom – Dad wasn't killed in a car accident was he? Oh my God, he was killed fighting, wasn't he?"

"I'm so sorry, Celeste," said her mom between sobs.

Celeste felt a horrible tightening in her chest, and a terrible anger building. "Who killed him Mom?" She was gripping her mom by the shoulders now and she was shaking her roughly.

Her mother didn't answer, purposely averting her grief-filled eyes from her daughter's as angry tears continued to spill.

"Mom, who killed dad? Tell me, I deserve to know."

She choked back a sob, looking at her daughter's determined face. "I don't know exactly. All I know is that there had been a series of supposed 'animal attacks' in the area and your father had been hunting a vampire."

Celeste took off out of the house with her mother chasing after her, but it was no use she was much too quick for her. The streets whizzed by in a blur. Celeste ran and ran until the pain in her chest had subsided, only to be replaced by the burning fatigue in her legs. She stopped where she was and flung herself on the grass, staring blankly into the sky as dark clouds rolled in overhead.

"Cel, are you okay?"

"Brian? What are you doing here?" she asked in a daze. A tidal wave of emotions hit her at the sight of her best friend. Impulsively, she jumped into the comfort of his arms.

"Whoa, nice to see you too. Your mom called me in a panic about a half an hour ago saying you had a fight, so I've been driving around looking for you." He held onto her for a minute longer before finally letting go.

"Thanks for coming, I'm sorry she freaked out."

"What happened?"

Celeste wanted more than anything to tell Brian what had happened over the past few weeks. She had always told him everything, and yet now it was like an invisible wall had been built between them.

Celeste took a deep cleansing breath, expelling all the pent up hurt and anger. "Nothing, I just overreacted and ran out of the house. I've been feeling really emotional lately with graduation coming and everything."

Brian raised an eyebrow at her skeptically.

"Well it didn't seem like nothing to me. Your mom was hysterical, and seemed really scared for you. And I know you've been crying," he said, as he reached to tenderly wipe smudged mascara under her eye. He held up her chin examining her face worriedly.

"I want to tell you, Brian, but I just can't right now. There have been some things that I've recently found out about my family and my dad. I'm just trying to work through them."

He dropped his hand from her face. "But why do you have to do it by yourself? I'm here for you, and maybe I can help you get through whatever it is."

She just shook her head.

"Why are you shutting me out? We've been through so much together. What makes you think that you can't let me in on this? I love you, Celeste."

Something happened to Celeste when she heard those three little words that every girl dreams about. She felt a huge weight lifted and stopped fighting the emotional battle that had been surging inside of her for days. So when Brian leaned in to kiss her, she let him. There was something so comfortable and safe about being in Brian's arms, and the kissing wasn't bad either. After a couple seconds of allowing herself to get lost in the moment, she pulled away, back to reality.

"I should probably get back home. I'm sure my mom must be worried," she stammered.

"Sure, whatever you want Cel," said Brian.

As they drove back in silence, Celeste tried not to think about the repercussions of the stolen kiss. On one hand, she wished it would be enough that Brian loved her, and she could be a normal teenager with a normal boyfriend. On the other hand, she knew it would never be.

Why did I let Brian kiss me again?

She certainly couldn't deal with this right now, not with everything else going on. She had to focus on becoming a

Guardian, training, becoming a skilled hunter and avenging her father's death. She would find the vampire who killed him, and she would make him pay for taking him away from her.

Celeste felt strange as she opened the door to her house: everything seemed to be tainted by lies. Everyone in her family had kept secrets from her. She looked at her mother's tear-stained face and felt a slight pang of guilt. Her mother wrapped her arms around her tightly.

"We need to talk about this," said her mother.

"Not now. Everything's going to be fine, Mom. I just need some time," she said numbly and went up to her room.

She had left the house in such a frenzy that she hadn't even bothered to take her phone with her. As she glanced down at it now, she noticed three missed calls from Roman and one from Nico. Celeste felt torn between the desire to talk to Roman and tell him about her father's death, and the terrible anger growing inside of her that a vampire had killed him—a *vampire just like what Roman is.*

Celeste pulled the small sword from its hiding place under the bed and clutched it in her hands. She knew it wasn't rational, but she was angry with Roman for being a vampire, and most of all she was angry with herself for letting Brian kiss her. She had an overwhelming urge to stab something with her sword. Instead, she attempted to channel her energy and swung the sword in a few arcs around her bedroom. Her phone rang again, and seeing that it was Roman, she sent it to voicemail, continuing her swordplay against an imaginary foe.

***

182

"How could you have let her escape again?" asked Fabian furiously, his towering figure looming over Magnus.

"I've already explained it to you. Roman and Nico appeared, and as you had forbidden me to kill them or her, it was unlikely I would have been able to get her out of a crowded party without drawing unnecessary attention," said Magnus.

"He's incompetent just like the rest of them," said Alek contemptuously.

Magnus leapt at Alek with his fangs bared and rage in his wild eyes, "I could snap your neck like a twig, boy. Don't tempt me."

Though Magnus was a full head taller than Alek, he casually stepped away from him completely unflustered. Then with a voice dripping in sarcasm asked, "What are you going to do to remedy this situation?"

"I will go back for her, and bring her to you as promised."

"That may be easier said than done," said Fabian, "especially now that they will be more cautious after your last failed attempt."

"I have a much less subtle tactic in mind this time," Magnus said, black eyes blazing.

***

Celeste, sweaty after her impromptu workout, sat at the bay window taking in the warm summer breeze as dusk began to set in. As she gazed out into the darkening sky, she felt that newly familiar, ominous sensation come over her and saw a winged creature alighting in the oak tree outside. Another question that she had been meaning to clarify with Roman was becoming clearer now. The falcon peered intently at her, blue eyes questioning. Celeste stood up and feeling rather silly, signaled for the creature to come in. It flew in, and in the blink of an eye had transformed back into his human form. Celeste plopped down on her bed taking a moment; imagining a bird turning into a man and seeing it were two entirely different things.

"I'm sorry to stop by unannounced, but you didn't answer any of my calls," Roman said.

"Sorry, but I was busy," she said haughtily. "So it's been you in the tree for weeks?"

"Yes," he admitted.

"But that was before we had even met."

"Celeste, there's a bit more to the story than what I have told you so far," he said nervously. "The truth is that one of the reasons that Nico and I moved back to Oak Bluffs was you, well the Guardian, I mean. One of our oldest family friends, Stellan, he used to be on the Council, and he knew that the new Guardian was to be chosen. As I told you, my mother, before being turned into a vampire, had also been part of the Council and had always kept an eye on the hunter families. When you first met Nico, and he told you that he had met some Wilders years ago, he wasn't kidding. As your father said, you come from a very long line of hunters."

Celeste nodded and let him continue.

"Stellan had been in the habit of letting us know whenever a new Guardian was to be chosen, and we would generally stay away. But this time it was different. When he told me about you and your father, something clicked in my memory, and I had to come here to see you."

"So..."

"Please, Celeste, let me finish," he said pacing anxiously in front of her. "About fifteen years ago, Nico and I were living in New York City, and I was in a rather dark period of my life. As I've told you before, it's not easy being what we are. I have to fight the dark urges constantly. I had fought with Nico and taken off on the road only to find myself here in Oak Bluffs. I was hunting, and I came across a stunning woman walking in the streets alone at night. I descended upon her. As I was about to feed on her, I saw the most beautiful little girl with blonde ringlets come ambling out on the front porch calling out for her 'Mama.' Moments later, a Guardian came running from the house, stake in hand. When he saw that I had spared his wife and child, a look of astonishment crossed his face, and he put down his weapon. A part of me wanted to die. I wanted him to end my life once and for all, but he didn't kill me. He gathered his child into his arms and helped his wife into the house. He let me live."

Celeste couldn't believe what she was hearing.

"I was that little girl? And they were my mom and dad?"

"Yes. Your father saved me. He may not have known it, but he did. I'll never forget the look he gave me that night. He made me feel like I was worth saving. He gave me a second chance, when many others would not have done the same. He made me realize that I could be redeemed, and that I could start again and be better." His normally bright blue eyes were clouded with remorse.

185

"So you came back to Oak Bluffs to see if I was going to become the next Guardian?"

"Correct. When Stellan told me that the new Guardian was to be chosen, I did a little calculating and some research, and I found out that your father had been killed. As soon as I got back into town, I came to your house to see if it really was you."

"And you stalked me through the window," she said.

"I was just trying to protect you," he countered.

"Just when I feel like my life couldn't possibly get any more insane, you tell me this. I can't believe you almost attacked my mom, my dad almost killed you, and you met me as a toddler!"

Roman slid down to the floor and kneeled in front of her, taking her delicate hands in his. "Celeste, I'm sorry I didn't tell you sooner, but there has been so much for you to bear lately! I didn't want to add *another* piece of the puzzle until the time was right."

"It's kind of an important bit of history, Roman. Did you ever see my dad again? Did you know that he was killed by a vampire?"

"No, I never saw him again. I never came back to Oak Bluffs until a few months ago. I only found out recently that your father had been killed, and I have no idea who did it. You must believe that I would tell you if I did." His stormy blue eyes gazed into hers pleading her to trust him.

"I don't know what to believe anymore. Every time I blink I find out something new and terrible. I feel like my life is spinning out of control," complained Celeste.

"I'm so sorry, Celeste."

"You know, my mom knew all along. She knew what my dad was and that I could be the next one. She wanted to keep me from it all. She doesn't want me to be the Guardian."

"She's your mom, of course she doesn't want that life for you. She, above all people, wants to protect you."

"What if I don't want this? What if I can't be a Guardian?"

"I'm afraid that that is a decision that only you can make, Celeste. But remember, guardians are designated after much consideration; it is not a selection that is taken lightly. They chose you for a reason, because they saw something in you, the same thing that I see," he said, a serious expression crossing his handsome face.

"And what's that?"

Roman sat down beside her, and reached out to cradle her face in his hands. "A beautiful, courageous young woman with an extraordinary heart and the capacity for immeasurable greatness."

She smiled, and looked into the blue depths of his eyes. "I don't feel like any of those things."

"You will, Celeste, I know it. I want you to come somewhere with me tomorrow. I want you to meet Stellan."

C hapter 12

Celeste reached under the bed, retrieving her sword from its hiding spot to place it carefully into her oversized backpack. Oddly, Celeste now found its presence comforting, and she wondered if it had some sort of magical, calming powers. She swung the backpack onto her shoulder and looked anxiously out the window, hoping to see the black Porsche. If Roman was correct, Stellan would be able to answer many of Celeste's questions about the guardians, the Council and the entire supernatural world. She felt nervous and excited all at the same time.

Celeste felt strangely relieved to see the bright red BMW and Nico's smiling face pulling into her driveway. The tension between her and Roman had gotten a bit intense lately, and Nico's presence was a welcome distraction.

"Well, hello beautiful," Nico said kissing her on the cheek.

She and Roman exchanged brief pleasantries, and the threesome set out on the road as the sun crept higher in the sky.

"And you must be the famous Celeste Wilder," said Stellan, welcoming them into his home.

"I don't know about that," she said blushing, "but I have heard many things about you, and I really appreciate you meeting with me."

Celeste surveyed the entryway as she walked in. There were rows of shelves lining the walls filled with old books in ancient languages. She stared up in awe at the high vaulted ceiling with mahogany rafters stretching from end to end. As expansive as the home was, there was a certain cozy feeling about it, like it had been thoroughly lived in. Celeste took a breath and noticed a peculiar smell too, a mixture between mothballs and incense. She felt strangely reassured.

"Well of course, it's my extreme pleasure. It's not every day that I have a Guardian in my humble home," responded Stellan graciously.

"Stop kissing up to her, Stellan, it's not like she's going to try to kill *you*," Nico teased.

"You on the other hand, Nico, are not so safe," she said with a wink.

In truth, after the four-hour car ride with two vampires, Celeste was feeling antsy. It took all of her strength to fight her budding murderous urges.

"Roman, Nico, why don't you make yourselves useful and get started on lunch. I'd like to speak to Celeste alone for a bit."

Roman looked at Celeste for approval, and when she nodded, the brothers headed toward the kitchen.

"Why don't we go sit outside? It's much more pleasant," Stellan said.

...And out of vampire earshot.

Stellan led Celeste out to the rustic back porch overlooking the woods and sat beside her on the wooden bench. The air smelled so pure in the countryside, and Celeste filled her lungs with it, reveling in the refreshing sensation.

"Let's get right down to it then," he said with a pleasant smile. Celeste let go of the breath she had been holding. "I'm sure it's of no surprise to you that Roman and Nico have kept me apprised of your situation."

"No, they told me that you were the one who told them about me in the first place."

"Very true, my dear. You see, after all this time, I still keep in touch with Guardian affairs, and I've been in the habit of informing the boys over the years. I care deeply about both of them, as I did their parents. I try to keep them safe and up to date with supernatural matters that may concern them."

Celeste nodded, her inquisitive eyes urging him to continue.

"When I found out about you, I informed them as well, simply because of their proximity to you. I had no idea that Roman would want to come back to Oak Bluffs, and it wasn't until yesterday that he finally admitted why, as he did to you."

"Right, because he knew my dad."

"Yes, and to be perfectly honest, Roman is not the only one that has been keeping secrets. I haven't told the boys this, but I also knew your father. I knew him very well. In fact, I was on the Council when he was made a Guardian so many years ago."

It took every ounce of Celeste's self-control not to burst into tears or hysterical laughter – she wasn't sure which was in order. Everything was a lie: her father had lied to her, her mother lied to her and now she was meeting one of her father's oldest friends whom she had never even heard of.

"So you knew my grandfather and my great-grandfather too? I just found out I come from a whole line of guardians apparently."

"Yes, I have met many generations of Wilders during my time on the Council. You come from a special family, and I'm honored to have the opportunity to train you and help you to become what you were born to be."

"*You* are going to train me? You're the one my dad was talking about in the video..." Celeste eyed his slim wiry frame skeptically. She didn't think he was capable of teaching anyone to fight.

"Yes, Celeste. Many years ago, I made a promise to your father that if anything ever happened to him, I would step in and help you in whatever way I could. As a matter of fact, I received an email from your mother just a few days ago. She of course had no knowledge of who the recipient was, but it was your father who had instructed her to contact me."

"But my dad died almost eight years ago. Why didn't you come to me before this?" Celeste demanded.

"I'm sorry Celeste, but your father was very clear that he didn't want you exposed to anything in the supernatural realm unless you were chosen. Once Roman told me you had been selected, I was going to come find you and tell you everything. Before I could, they suggested you come here, so I let them think it was their idea."

"Why didn't you want them to know the truth?"

"I was curious about their attachment to you, and I didn't want them to be influenced by me. Of course, at the time

I didn't know about Roman's personal history with your father. I had warned them to stay away from you, Celeste. It was my fault for telling them. They should never have come into your life. I've now put your life at risk because I was trying to protect them. Fabian is not someone with whom we should trifle, and he has been after the Constantin clan for decades. I'm afraid I've given him a way to get to them now." Stellan looked away for a moment, but not before Celeste caught the flash of worry in his kind grey eyes.

"But Roman and Nico are strong, and I'm going to be the Guardian so I can protect them too."

"Celeste, you remind me so much of your father – that enormous heart and eternal optimism. The best thing for you, my dear, is to stay as far away as possible from both Roman and Nico. It hurts me to say that to you because I know how much they care for you, but a hunter cannot be friends with vampires, let alone vampires who are being pursued by Fabian. I promised your father many years ago that I would protect you, and I must keep my word."

"But I need them," she murmured softly.

***

"Paging Nurse Wilder, Nurse Wilder you are needed at the ER front reception a.s.a.p."

Celeste's mom hurried to the Emergency wing of Oak Bluffs Hospital, wondering why they would need her in the ER.

"Nurse Wilder, there is a man here looking for you. He said it was an emergency—something about your daughter," said the ER nurse.

As she approached the man the nurse had pointed out, Olivia noticed a white streak in his hair and an ugly scar across his right eyebrow, and the tiny hairs on the back of her neck shot up as a cold shiver shot down her spine.

***

"Do you have any questions for me, my dear?" asked Stellan.

"How much time do you have?" retorted Celeste.

Stellan chuckled good-naturedly. Looking into his kind grayish eyes, she was reminded of her own grandfather. Perhaps it was this resemblance that allowed Celeste to trust Stellan almost immediately.

"I don't understand how I'm supposed to fight all of these evil creatures. After our encounter with that vampire, I just don't see how I could ever be a match for any of them."

"As I'm sure the Council told you, you will begin to develop special powers. You will become stronger and faster. And you have to train. Some of this will come to you naturally, but there is nothing better than hard work and effort."

"That's what Roman and Nico said," Celeste agreed.

"Yes, well sometimes they do know what they're talking about."

"Did Roman tell you that I see my dad in dreams?" Celeste asked Stellan.

"No, he didn't. That is quite extraordinary. It is not easy for a former Guardian to manifest himself in dreams."

"Really?"

"Yes, it is quite rare. It must be because he loves you so much." Celeste threw him a grateful smile.

"Is there any way to regulate my emotions? I feel like I'm losing control of myself sometimes."

"That's normal and it will get better with time. As you know, your emotions are heightened right now, but there's a reason for it. It allows you to become aware of the supernatural world around you," Stellan counseled her.

"So there's no magical on/off button?"

"No, I'm afraid not."

Celeste bit her lip and spit out the question she had been too scared to ask. "Is there a way to train myself to not want to kill Roman or Nico?"

Stellan glanced at her with a knowing smile. "I'm sure we can figure something out."

Roman and Nico stood on one side of the sunny clearing behind Stellan's home while Celeste and Stellan stood on the other. Celeste wiped her sweaty palms against her jeans and tried to focus on Stellan's calming voice. He was standing behind her, holding her firmly by the shoulders.

"Now the fact that you are able to be in such close proximity to those two without being overwhelmed by your urges means that you are already exerting a high degree of control."

"Uh huh," murmured Celeste, with little confidence.

"Now, I'm going to ask you to completely let go and drop whatever defenses you're using to block those urges."

"Okay."

Roman and Nico looked on anxiously from across the yard.

"Go on, don't be afraid. I've got you," said Stellan, increasing the pressure on her shoulders.

Celeste breathed in and out slowly and closed her eyes in concentration. She searched deep inside her mind and dropped down the wall that she had carefully built up over the past few days. She was immediately pummeled by an onrush of emotions, getting stronger by the minute. Blindly driven by rage, she lunged towards the vampires. Stellan, who was stronger than he looked, held her in check.

"Celeste, keep breathing, slowly, in and out. You can't block the feelings. You must take them in and allow them to become a part of you."

"I can't! It's too much." She wriggled, straining to get away.

Celeste caught sight of Roman's tense expression from across the field. A different kind of emotion flowed through her. She knew she had to try for him. She breathed in again slowly and as she inhaled the air, she let all the intense feelings and emotions circulate through her. When she exhaled, she blew them out as hard as she could. She repeated this exercise a few more times while Stellan murmured encouragingly.

"I think that's enough for today," he said. "How do you feel?"

"Exhausted. But I'm better, I think."

"Good. You will see that it will get easier every day."

Before Stellan released her, she let the wall come back up in her mind. To her pleasant surprise, she found it wasn't necessary to build it quite so high this time.

Celeste sat on the squeaky porch swing staring out into the quiet woods behind Stellan's house. She was thinking about what he had said to her about her father, how he didn't want her to have anything to do with supernaturals.

Well it's a little late for that...

"Penny for your thoughts," said Roman as he came out onto the porch.

"With all the thoughts I have going on in my head right now, you'd need to give me much more than a penny," Celeste joked.

He smiled at her ruefully and joined her on the swing, which creaked in protest at his additional weight. "So did you have a good talk with Stellan earlier?"

"Yeah, I guess you could say that. He knew my father too, Roman."

"I had a feeling he might have. I knew he had been on the Council so I figured he must have crossed paths with him at some point."

"No, but he really knew my dad; he said they were very close. Stellan is going to train me. He's the one my dad was talking about in the video. He promised him that he would."

"That's great news Celeste. Stellan will be a wonderful mentor for you—kind, patient, wise and above all powerful, as you have seen. He will make sure that you are prepared for what's to come."

"Uh huh."

"What's wrong?" he asked, resting his arm around her shoulders.

"So much is wrong! I don't even know where to begin."

"Celeste, everything is going to work out. The fact that you will have Stellan at your side is wonderful news. Between him and Nico and me, you're going to have the best trainers in the world."

"Right."

Celeste couldn't bear the thought of telling Roman that Stellan didn't want them to be a part of her life. She was pretty sure that he wouldn't take it well either. *But is Stellan right?*

"Come on, let's go for a walk. It's really beautiful out there. I love coming out here and getting lost in the woods. It's so peaceful."

"I could definitely use some peace," she said.

As they strolled through the tranquil forest, Celeste did begin to feel more at ease with every step, taking in deep cleansing breaths. She admired the lush green evergreens and focused on the melodic chirping of birds perched in the branches above. Crunching through the fallen leaves, she missed a step and tripped over a fallen branch. Roman reached out for her and thanks to his quick vampire reflexes caught her just before she hit the ground. And this time when his arms came around her, she didn't feel that ominous sensation when they touched. She let herself fall into his strong arms, and she looked up into his intensely smoldering eyes as he held her tightly.

"I got you."

"I know," she said, gazing breathlessly into his bottomless blue eyes.

197

As he helped her stand back up, she got up on her tiptoes and ever so lightly brushed her lips against his. The reaction she got back was more than she had hoped for. Roman pulled her closer to him, arms enveloping her, and kissed her feverishly. She felt his need for her, the hunger burning inside him. The intensity of the moment startled her, and half-consciously she pulled away.

"Sorry," he said looking embarrassed. "I shouldn't have done that."

"No, don't," she said, reaching out to caress his face. "I wanted you to." She looked away feeling the redness creeping up into her face. "I think we should probably head back though."

Walking back in a contented silence their hands clasped together, Celeste couldn't help but smile as she thought about the thrilling, spine-tingling kiss.

Now that is what it's like in the movies!

Chapter 13

"Celeste, your phone has been blowing up," said Nico, as she and Roman came in. Celeste hurried off to find her purse and Roman joined the others in the kitchen.

"You see how I keep up with the slang of my contemporaries?" he said to Stellan with a wink.

"You really are a wonder, little brother," quipped Roman.

All of a sudden Celeste came running into the kitchen with a look of sheer panic on her face. All three men froze.

"It's my mom! The vampire from my birthday—I think he has her!" Celeste's eyes were wide with panic, and her voice had begun to shake.

"What did he say?" asked Roman, rushing to her side.

"He said that if I don't meet him in an hour at the Oak Bluffs cemetery by our family plot, I'll find her buried in it."

"We'll never make it back in time," said Nico.

"Maybe you can't, but I can get you there," said Stellan. "Now before I send you into a trap, we need to take a moment and make a plan."

"Hurry Stellan please, it's my mom," she said, her voice rising in panic.

"Based on what the boys told me, I am quite sure that your mystery vampire is Magnus. He is an ancient and treacherous vampire who is frequently sent as a mercenary to do other's dirty work. He does not have a shred of humanity in him, and he kills for the pure pleasure of it. He is certainly stronger than the two of you, I'm afraid." Stellan had begun pacing and was waving his arms animatedly.

"But he doesn't know about me, right?" asked Celeste.

"I hope not, but in any event Celeste, you are not ready to fight. I am not sending you into a battle that you have no chance in winning," he said.

"Agreed," said Roman and Nico in unison.

"Anyway, it's us he wants, so we will go and trade ourselves for your mother," said Roman.

"No, I won't let you!" said Celeste.

"We'll be fine, don't worry about us," said Nico.

"Good, it's settled. I will open a portal to transport Roman and Nico to the cemetery, and Celeste will stay here with me. We will be able to watch what is happening, and I can track you if necessary."

Celeste walked away with arms folded obstinately across her chest. When Roman approached her she said, "I am not okay with this."

"I promise that no harm will come to your mother. I *will* get her back to you safely, believe me," Roman promised.

"And what about you and Nico? Who's going to get you back to me safely?"

"Nico and I can take care of ourselves. We are a lot tougher than we look, and we defeated him last time so this time should be all the easier."

"What if you are all right and this is about Fabian? Stellan pretty much confirmed that this Magnus is just hired help. He killed your parents – what does he want with the two of you?"

"I don't know Celeste, but I'm tired of spending my life running. It's been over a hundred years, maybe it's time we finally confront him."

"I can't lose you," she said, tugging on his shirt.

"You won't," he said as he pulled her into his arms.

Stellan pulled out a thick leather-bound book with frayed, yellowing pages that reminded Celeste of the spell book the Halliwell sisters used in *Charmed*. After mumbling a few words, the air in front of them began to shimmer and swirl and a portal large enough for a full-grown man to walk through appeared. Celeste stared in awe at it, wondering what it would feel like to pass through. She held out her hand, penetrating the swirling air in front of her and her fingers disappeared right before her eyes. She quickly pulled it back and was relieved to see all of her fingers were still intact.

"Roman, Nico – are you ready?" asked Stellan.

They both nodded in agreement.

"The portal will drop you at the entrance of the cemetery just about one hundred yards from the Wilder family tomb, which will hopefully provide you the element of surprise. Good luck boys!"

Roman squeezed Celeste's hand, and she responded with an encouraging smile. Nico jumped first with a "Whoohoo!" then Roman leapt through the whirling vortex. Before Celeste knew what she was doing, she lunged at

Roman's shirttail and plunged in after them, gleaming sword in hand.

Seconds later, Celeste landed with a thud on the hard gravel entryway of the Oak Bluffs Cemetery. "Ouch!" cried Celeste. She examined her elbow and carefully removed a few pieces of gravel that were encrusted in her skin.

"Celeste! What did you do?" asked Roman angrily.

She got to her feet and brushed the dirt off of her jeans. "I'm not letting you two do this alone. She's my mom and I'm the Guardian, and I should be protecting her," she said resolutely.

"But we can't protect you and fight him," said Nico.

"I don't need to be protected; I brought my sword," she said raising it up as it glimmered in the sunlight.

"Stellan is going to kill us," said Nico.

"We don't have time to argue," said Roman, "it's almost time. Celeste, you stay behind me at all times, and please don't try anything stupid."

The threesome crept up the path, weaving between headstones and flowers for loved ones placed with the utmost of care. The sun was just beginning to set and an eerie stillness blanketed the graveyard. Ahead Celeste could see a tall dark figure huddled over a woman slumped on the ground.

"Mom!" she murmured.

Roman gesticulated for Nico to go around the other side, and he and Celeste approached Magnus head on. This strategy had worked last time, and though it was unlikely it would work twice, it seemed the only possible course of action. As they marched towards Magnus, panic alarms sounded throughout Celeste's body. She tried to do as Stellan had taught her and allowed the feelings to wash over her.

"Ah, well if it isn't the lovely Celeste come to rescue her mother with her handsome vampire boyfriend," said Magnus smugly. "What, no costumes today?"

"Let her go, Magnus. You can take me instead," said Roman.

"Very clever boy, I see you have discovered my name. Let me assure you that everything that people say is true. There is no point trying to fight, since I always win."

"No one is going to put up a fight. I am surrendering to you. My life for hers," said Roman pointing at Mrs. Wilder, who lay unconscious on the grass.

A muffled "No!" came involuntarily out of Celeste's mouth. "My, my, she really does care about you Roman. She should be scared to death, but instead she stands here, willful and defiant. This is no ordinary human." He took a step toward Celeste, his black eyes gleaming.

"Leave her out of this," Roman advised, moving swiftly in between him and Celeste. "I told you from the beginning, it is me that you want, and here I am. Release her mother and let Celeste leave unharmed. I will go with you wherever you want."

Roman recognized a disturbing twinkle in Magnus' eye. He scanned the area looking for Nico, hoping he was nearby.

"This is quite a predicament we are in now isn't it? I was sent here to bring you and your brother back, but now I find this girl to be of more interest to me."

Celeste's heart dropped.

"Why would she be of interest to you? She is nothing, just an ordinary human girl --"

"Whose life you seem to value immensely," Magnus finished.

"No, you are wrong. She means nothing to me," muttered Roman unconvincingly.

Magnus' face glowed bright red, and his black eyes narrowed. "Do you think I'm stupid Roman Constantin? I've lived for over a thousand years, and if there is one thing I am certain of, a vampire would never give up his life for an ordinary girl, even one as beautiful as this one."

"This has nothing to do with her Magnus," growled Roman, his fangs fully extended and a chilling gleam in his eye. "Do you think *I* am stupid? I know exactly who sent you - it was that coward Fabian. He thinks he can hide behind despicable beings like you, but I am tired of hiding, tired of running. Take me to him and let's end this." Roman took a step toward Magnus, daring him to make a move.

Celeste had never seen Roman like this, and it frightened her.

"And what, the second I make a move towards you your brother will plunge a stake into my back?" Magnus countered. "You underestimate me. I know very well that Nico is lurking nearby. No matter, I could easily take you both down if I wanted, but I am far more intrigued by your friend Celeste." Celeste looked at him defiantly.

Addressing her he said, "As a gesture of good will, I will release your mother. All I ask is that you come with me in her place."

"Fine," she said.

"No!" snarled Roman as he lunged at Magnus.

Nico darted out of the foliage and joined the fray, the three vampires rolling into a tangled mess of snarling and biting. Roman and Nico were young and fast, but Magnus had a lifetime of experience on his side. He quickly broke away from them and disappeared into a mausoleum.

The brothers followed him into the foreboding structure. "Are you sure he came in here?" whispered Nico.

"Yes!" hissed Roman as he peered into the dark tomb.

Magnus sprang up from the shadows and with one well-timed punch sent Nico sprawling across the room. Roman reacted quickly, grabbing Magnus by the throat and almost succeeded in snapping his neck, but Magnus was too strong and in seconds had Roman pinned against the wall. Nico, recovering from the blow to his head, rushed to his brother's aid and yanked Magnus off of him.

As the fight ensued in the mausoleum, Celeste ran to her mother's side and picked up her wrist frantically checking for a pulse. She was relieved to see that she was alive and breathing, but still unconscious. She quickly untied the thick ropes around her mom's wrists and ankles and when Celeste realized there was no waking her, she picked her mother up and started running. As she reached the entrance of the cemetery, she saw a glimmer of air, and the portal opened in front of her. Stellan stepped through it appearing in a whirling cloud of matter. With a stern expression on his face, he held out his arms and took her mother's limp body.

"Please Stellan, take her with you. I have to go back," she said with determination in her eyes.

"Celeste, you are going to get yourself killed, and your father will haunt me from the grave for the rest of my days," he said, handing Mrs. Wilder back over to her. "Take your mother through the portal, and I will go help Roman and Nico. We will be right behind you. Now go!" he said, pushing her through the entrance.

Stellan could hear the snarling, vicious animal sounds as he approached the Wilder family tomb. Magnus had Nico in a chokehold, trying to snap his neck, but Roman quickly thrust a fallen tree branch into his back, missing his heart by inches. Although Magnus was easily able to pull it out of his back, it provided enough of a distraction to release Nico from his grasp. Roman and Nico stood in front of a wild-eyed Magnus ready to strike again, pausing only momentarily from the frenzied fighting at the sight of Stellan's approach.

"Enough!" he said. A blast of lightning shot out of his outstretched hand, sending all three vampires scrambling for cover.

"I was wondering when you would show your face," said Magnus picking himself up off the ground.

"You are meddling in affairs that do not concern you Magnus. Believe me, if you choose to come after Celeste again, you will have me to deal with."

"Well, now I am more convinced than ever. There is something special about that girl, and I will find out what it is. Fabian can come after these two himself."

Roman thrust himself at Magnus but he slipped through his grasp and took off into the darkening sky.

Celeste hovered worriedly over her mother as she laid breathing slowly on the worn leather couch in Stellan's living room. She ran her fingers through her mother's fine hair and wiped away a smudge of dirt from her cheek. The deep creases at the corners of her eyes and mouth were smooth now – she looked so peaceful. Suddenly, the room lit up with a bright white flash as the portal opened in the middle of the kitchen and Stellan, Roman and Nico came hurtling through.

"Thank God you're all right!" Celeste said as she jumped up, trying to get her arms around all three of them. "You're covered in blood..."

"We're fine. We're already beginning to heal, see? A nice hot shower and we'll be good as new," assured Nico.

"How is she doing?" asked Roman.

"I don't know. She won't wake up. I've tried everything, but it's no use." "Maybe it's magic?" suggested Roman.

"Yes, that is what I was thinking as well," said Stellan. "Let me take a look at her."

Roman put a comforting arm around Celeste as she watched nervously while Stellan examined her mother.

"It appears that Roman was correct. Mrs. Wilder is in fact under a sleeping spell, but no need to fret my dear. It will wear off soon. And the best part is that she won't remember any of this dreadfulness."

"Thank goodness!" she said, rushing over to hug Stellan. The look of awkwardness on Stellan's blushing face coupled with the tension of the day was more than Nico could handle. He burst into a giggle and his contagious chuckling spread to the entire room as the relief set in.

Roman carried a still sleeping Mrs. Wilder up to her room as Celeste made sure that all the windows and doors of their home were securely locked. When he came back down the stairs, he found her sprawled on the couch.

"So are you ready for your big day tomorrow?" he asked.

Yawning, she answered, "I guess so. Graduation hasn't really been my top priority what with my mom being held hostage and all."

Roman's face with filled with remorse. "I'm so sorry about all of this Celeste. It's all my fault. Nico and I should have never come back to Oak Bluffs. All of this could have been avoided."

"No, it's not true. I was destined for this, I'm the Guardian. I would have had to deal with this whether you had come into my life or not. And I'm so happy you did. I don't think I could have gotten through any of this without you," she said, reaching out her hand to his.

"Of course you would have. You don't need Nico or me. You have Stellan to guide and protect you. We are actually just making it worse for you."

"Don't say that Roman. The best part of all of this has been meeting you." She pulled him down to the couch and kissed him whole-heartedly.

His lips were soft and gentle as they moved over hers, seemingly testing the waters. Celeste waited for that ominous feeling to overwhelm her again, but instead she felt only the lively sparks where his skin touched hers. She relaxed a bit, and could feel Roman becoming more comfortable as the fiery kiss deepened. His hands ran through her long wild hair as she held on tightly to his well-defined arms, gradually letting all of the madness of the day melt away. For a moment, she was able to fully let herself go and think of nothing except enjoying the intense feelings that were spreading over every inch of her body. Finally, breathlessly, she pulled away, all the while maintaining his gaze hoping that he would not back away as he had so often before. He looked guiltily at her as she inched away, but said nothing.

"What are you thinking?" she asked.

"That I don't deserve you," he said, averting his eyes. She took both of his hands in hers, and forced him to look at her.

"How can you say that when you have saved my life so many times already?"

"Your life would never have been in jeopardy in the first place if it wasn't for me."

"Roman, I am not having this conversation with you again. This is my life too, and with or without you in it, it would be dangerous."

"I just couldn't bear the thought of something happening to you because of me, but for the life of me, I just can't walk away from you either. I know that I should. I heard what Stellan said to you at his house, and he's right. It would be best for you to keep away from us – to keep away from me."

"No, he's wrong. He doesn't know what's best for me. He doesn't know me at all. As terrible as this past week has been, I've never felt so alive. Something inside of me has been awoken, and a large part of that is because of you. I've never been so terrified or so happy as when I'm with you."

Roman's blue eyes filled with emotion. "Celeste, in over a hundred years I have never met anyone like you. The feelings that you have stirred in me, I thought had long since disappeared. What I feel for you is indescribable, and it frightens me that I may not be able to control it."

"Everything will be all right, Roman. I know you, and I know how strong you are. You can control it, and you can protect me. We will get through this together."

"Celeste, Celeste sweetie, are you down there?"

At the sound of Mrs. Wilder's voice, Celeste and Roman quickly pulled apart. She ran up the stairs, and when she saw her mother sitting up in her bed, tears of joy began falling from her cheeks.

"Mom, I was so worried about you!"

"What happened? The last thing I remember was getting a page at the hospital, and then I woke up here in my bed."

"Nothing Mom, everything's fine. You're all right and that's all that matters."

"I can't believe I missed out on all the excitement last night."

"Trust me Mom, it's better that you did," said Celeste. She was rummaging through her closet trying to find something suitable to wear under her graduation gown.

"How about this one?" said her mom, holding up a linen powder blue sundress. Celeste crinkled her nose and shook her head.

"So I take it the handsome stranger that was in our home last night was Roman," her mom scolded. "He looks quite a bit older than you Celeste – how old did you say he was?"

"Yeah, I'm sorry Mom. With everything that was going on I totally forgot to introduce you," she responded, purposely avoiding her question.

"I could tell who he was by the way you looked at him. And from how he couldn't keep his gorgeous blue eyes off of you, I imagine he feels the same way."

Celeste blushed, hiding her face in the closet. "I wish it were that easy Mom. Things are pretty complicated between Roman and me."

"Because of our family 'legacy' you mean?"

"Yes, that and he's a vampire," she murmured, burying her face in the closet.

"No Celeste! Please don't tell me that you are in love with a vampire? They are evil cruel creatures that our family has fought against for centuries. And are you forgetting that it was a vampire that took your father away from us?"

Celeste spun around in a rage. "I know that Mom, don't you think I know all of that? But he and Nico are different; they are not like the others. They still have their humanity, and they are good."

"So they don't drink human blood?"

"Well yes they do, but not directly from people! And they've saved my life more than once already."

"Your life has been in danger?" Celeste's mom asked incredulously.

"I don't want to talk about this anymore." There was no way she was going to tell her mother about Patrick, Magnus and especially not about Fabian.

"Just because you're the Guardian now, it doesn't mean that you're not still my daughter. I'm still in charge around here," Mrs. Wilder said, her voice rising.

"I know, Mom."

"I don't like this one bit," she continued.

"Well there's not much that you can do about it."

"Look, I know this is a big day for you, so I'm going to let it go for now, but this discussion is not over."

"Right," said Celeste obstinately.

Her mother took a breath and walked over to her. "Are you all right?"

"It's just graduation. I'm sure I'll survive," whined Celeste.

"You know that's not what I'm talking about."

"Yes, Mom I do, but there is nothing I can do about it. I was chosen, I am the Guardian and now I have to live up to those responsibilities. I was going to tell you after the ceremony today, but I guess there's no time like the present."

"Tell me what?"

"Stellan has offered to let me stay with him for the summer so that he can train me, and I will be safe with him in the meantime. I think it's the best idea for everyone."

"I don't think I like the idea of you spending the summer with a complete stranger."

"He's not a complete stranger. He was dad's trusted friend. And if dad believed in him enough to train me, then you should too."

"Are you sure about this? Is that really how you want to spend your last summer before college?"

"Well, it's not backpacking across Europe, but I don't think that's in my future anytime soon," she countered sarcastically.

"Oh Celeste..."

"Yes Mom, it's what I want, and it will be for the best."

Chapter 14

Hundreds of white folding chairs had been arranged neatly in rows on the green turf of the St. Alice High School football field, all facing a stage with a table covered by stacks of diplomas. The graduating seniors, donning navy blue caps and gowns, were beginning to file in as the A/V guy completed a last-minute sound check. Celeste had left her mother with the Kennedys, and she and Brian went to look for their assigned seats.

"Hey! There you guys are!" shouted Natalie.

"Yup, we made it," said Celeste. "I can hardly believe it."

"This is so exciting! In less than an hour, we will be official graduates, and then we will have the entire summer to enjoy together!"

Celeste thought wistfully about a lazy summer where she could lie out in the backyard reading her books and spend evenings hanging out with Natalie and Brian at Ralph's, maybe even go on a real date with Roman. She knew, though, that wasn't what the future held in store for her.

"Hello beautiful ladies, and Brian of course," said Nico as he sauntered over with two colorful bouquets of flowers.

"They're gorgeous!" said Natalie, giving Nico a kiss on the cheek.

"Yes, they really are. Thank you Nico," said Celeste with a warm embrace.

"Not as gorgeous as you two stunning graduates."

Both girls beamed and Brian rolled his eyes. "Laying it on pretty thick, huh Nico?"

"Why Brian I have no idea what you are talking about," said Nico smirking.

Looking around, Celeste asked, "Where's Roman?"

"I don't think he's coming Celeste, I'm sorry. But he wanted me to congratulate you on his behalf."

"Thanks," she said weakly, her heart plummeting. She thought everything had been all right between her and Roman when he had left last night. "I'm going to go find my seat."

"Celeste don't forget the graduation after party at Dani Lynn's!" Natalie yelled after her.

Celeste sat still, lulled into drowsiness by the warm summer day, watching her classmates pass one by one to receive their diplomas. Suddenly, a throbbing pain pierced through her head. She clenched her teeth and buried her head in her lap to keep from screaming. A flash of pictures raced through her mind, and she struggled to keep conscious. She saw an image of a large group of people at what looked like a party, then she saw Magnus with blood dripping from his fangs, and then Dani Lynn pale with eyes as red as burning coals. A surge of panic gripped Celeste as the images continued to flash through her mind on repeat. Then without warning, just as quickly as they had started, the images stopped. She looked around nervously, hoping that no one had seen her. Apparently there were some benefits to being the last one in the last row, she thought ruefully.

What in the world was that?

215

The rest of the ceremony flew by for Celeste, and before she knew it the majority of her class had received their diploma, making it her turn to walk up on stage. As she marched up to the front, she plastered a fake smile across her face and attempted to enjoy the moment. As she walked, she heard loud whistling coming from the audience and turned back to see Nico jumping up and down, clapping and making a general fool of himself. A real smile pulled at the corner of her lips, and as she spun back around, she caught a glimpse of Roman watching from behind the bleachers.

"What a beautiful ceremony," said Celeste's mom. "I can't believe my little girl is all grown up."

"Oh Mom, don't you start crying on me," Celeste said.

"I can't make any promises," she said with a smile. "What are you kids planning on doing for the rest of the day?"

"Jessica's sister, Dani Lynn is having a graduation party at her place," said Brian, "and we're all invited."

"Sounds like some good normal high school fun," said Mrs. Wilder, shooting Celeste a reproachful look.

"Yes Mom, I'm sure it will be, so no need to worry about me or wait up. I'll be home later."

Her mom gave Brian a hug goodbye and said, "Watch over my girl, okay?"

"I always do."

Dani Lynn cheerfully greeted Brian and Celeste as they walked into the party which was already well under way. They found Natalie and Jessica, talking and laughing flirtatiously, surrounded by a group of freshman boys from Oak Bluffs Community College.

"Come on Celeste, it looks like you could use a drink," said Brian.

"You read my mind - lead the way."

At the keg, they found Nico chatting up one of Natalie's friends from the cheerleading squad. When he saw Celeste approach, he ran up to her with a big smile, abandoning altogether the conversation with one clearly disappointed girl.

"Can I steal you away for a second, Celeste?" Nico asked.

"Sure," she said. "Brian, I'll be back in a few minutes."

Nico led Celeste out to the courtyard of the apartment away from the noise where they could actually hear themselves speak.

"What's up?" she asked.

"I just wanted to make sure you were okay," he said.

"I'm fine, why wouldn't I be? I just graduated high school; I'm at a party with all my friends. I should be ecstatic, right?"

"Look, I know you've been through a lot lately, and Roman told me what Stellan said about keeping away from us, but I don't think he's right. I wanted you to know that you can't get rid of me that easily! Unless you want to of course... I don't want to get on a Guardian's bad side," he said with a grin.

She giggled. "You always know what to say to make me smile."

"It's a natural talent," he said, pinching her cheek teasingly.

"Of course I don't want to stay away from you *or* Roman. This whole Guardian thing is just so new to me, and I don't know what's right and what's wrong anymore."

"You'll figure it out. I have no doubts about you. But do me a favor, don't give up on Roman, okay?"

"Me? He's the one who is giving up on us. Every time I think we are making progress, he pulls back. He thinks he should stay away from me."

"That may be what he says, but I know that's not how he feels. Trust me, I've known my brother for a long time, and I've never seen him like this before. What you two have is worth fighting for."

"I just feel like that is all my life is ever going to be – fighting for Roman, fighting with my mom about being a Guardian, fighting for the good of all mankind against the forces of evil. It's all so overwhelming."

"It won't always be. When I was first turned, I felt the same way. I was constantly fighting my bloodlust, my darkest urges, but our mother helped us through all the bad, so that with time we learned to control it. You will too. Stellan might be wrong about not wanting you around us, but he has your best interests at heart, and he will make an excellent Guardian out of you yet."

"I hope so," she said, not entirely convinced.

"Come on, let's get back to the party. It looks like you could use a refill on that beer." He put his arm around her and gave her a reassuring squeeze and led her back up to join their friends.

"Have you guys seen Dani Lynn?" asked Jessica, popping up next to Brian and Celeste.

"No, not since we first got here," said Brian.

"That's so weird, I can't find her anywhere," she said and hurried away to continue the search.

Brian turned to Celeste, "So, how are you doing Cel?"

"I'm good. Why?"

"I don't know, I mean we kissed again the other day, and now you're acting like nothing ever happened."

Celeste felt her cheeks redden, and she paused to take a sip from her cup hoping it would help. "I'm sorry Brian, I've just had so many things on my mind lately."

"Things that you can't tell me, right?"

"I wish I could, I really do." Brian turned away, but Celeste held onto his arm insistently. "Wait –"

"I don't know if I can do this, Cel. You've always told me everything, and now you're keeping secrets from me and acting all distant. Is this just because I kissed you?"

"You guys kissed?" asked Natalie, barging in on the conversation.

"Shhhh!" said Celeste nervously.

"Oh nice, Cel. Wow, now I get it. Are you embarrassed about this? That kiss obviously meant way more to me than it did to you," said Brian, walking away angrily.

"Brian, don't go!" she shouted after him, but he didn't even turn around.

"Whoa, what was that about?" asked Natalie.

"Ugh! I don't know, Natalie. I guess you were right about how Brian felt about me, and now I don't know what to do."

"Well how do *you* feel about him? Was he a good kisser?" she asked, eyes filled with mischief.

"That's the problem, I just don't know how I feel. Obviously I care about Brian a lot. He's my best friend. I could even say I love him, but I don't think I'm *in* love with him. And I refuse to answer the kissing part."

"Well then you need to tell him that Celeste. He's never going to move on if he thinks he still has a chance with you."

"I know, I just don't want to lose him. I need him in my life."

"I don't think you'd ever lose him, but you should probably set him free," she said.

"That was a pretty wise thing to say, Natalie."

"Thanks! Every once in a while I come up with a good one."

Celeste reached out for her arm, "And Natalie, I'm sorry, I know you kind of liked Brian."

"Nah, no worries, do you see how many cute guys are at this party? There's no point in being tied to just one!"

Celeste knew there was a reason she loved Natalie.

Celeste started weaving through the crowd of inebriated students looking for Brian. She knew that Natalie was right, and as much as she wished she felt the same way about Brian as he did for her, in her heart she knew that she didn't. She had searched the entire apartment and Brian was nowhere to be found. She headed outside, taking the emergency stairwell to avoid the rowdy crowd waiting for the elevator. As she rounded the corner of the second floor, she heard a muffled cry coming from the trash room. Celeste's senses turned on overdrive, and the intense ominous feeling took hold of her like a tidal wave, swallowing her whole. A sharp, metallic odor permeated the air and made her gag. She walked into the trash room, treading lightly trying not to make a sound. In the corner she saw a dark figure huddled over a girl's motionless body. A small gasp escaped from her mouth, and the figure spun around looking straight at her.

"Magnus!" she screamed.

"Oh sorry, I hope you don't mind, but I was so hungry and your friend here was just too delicious."

Suddenly, Roman dashed into the room, appearing out of nowhere, and firmly planted himself between her and Magnus.

"Well, I think that's my cue to leave," said Magnus. "And don't worry about your attractive friend, you'll be seeing her again soon enough." And he shot out the door before Roman could make a move to stop him.

Roman spun around to Celeste, "Are you all right?"

Celeste had run over to Dani Lynn and was assessing the gaping hole in her neck from where Magnus had bitten her.

"Yes, I'm fine, but I don't think she is. Can you give her your blood? Won't that heal her?"

Roman knelt down on the floor and examined her carefully. "I'm sorry Celeste, I don't think there is anything I can do for her now."

"Please try Roman. Give her your blood!"

"Celeste, look at her mouth, it's covered in blood. That's not her blood; it's vampire blood. Magnus was trying to turn her. I don't hear a heartbeat."

221

"No, no! This can't be happening!"

Roman put a comforting arm around Celeste as she crouched down beside Dani staring in shock.

"What are we going to tell Jessica? We have to call the police!"

"We can't call the police. They won't be able to help her. And what's going to happen when the coroner collects her body and a couple of hours later she gets up and walks away?"

Celeste's rational mind was trying to piece together what was happening. She flashed back to the conversation with Roman about turning a human into a vampire, but she still couldn't believe it. She looked at Dani Lynn's mangled body in front of her, and felt the bile rising in her throat.

"So Dani Lynn is really going to become a vampire?"

"Yes, I'm afraid so," he said.

"Uh oh, what happened here?" asked Nico appearing in the stairwell.

"Magnus happened," said Roman.

Nico took in the gruesome scene and turned away, looking at Roman. "By the way, what are you doing here?" he asked.

"I came to keep an eye out on things, and by the look of it, it's a good thing I did." He stood up now, glaring angrily at Nico.

"And by things, you mean Celeste, right?" asked Nico, standing up to his older brother. "Because you don't trust that I can protect her?"

"Obviously I was right."

"That's enough, both of you," she said, squeezing herself between them. "As you can see, it wasn't me that needed protecting."

Roman and Nico looked guiltily at Dani Lynn's crumpled body lying in the corner.

Suddenly, a rush of anger engulfed Celeste and she whirled at Roman. "So you've been here the whole time? Following me?"

"I haven't been following you, just keeping an eye on you from a distance."

"Like at graduation?"

"Yes."

"And during the whole party?"

"Yes." Now Roman was getting angry at the onslaught.

"And when I was talking to Brian?"

"Yes Celeste, and I wish I could say that I hadn't heard your conversation with him, but I did."

Celeste's face flushed at the thought of Roman discovering that she and Brian had kissed, listening into their private conversation.

"Unbelievable!" she said and stormed off.

Nico and Roman carefully wrapped Dani Lynn's body in a crimson bed sheet they found in her apartment, then lifted her into the trunk of the car. Celeste wanted to be there for Dani Lynn when she woke up, no matter what Roman and Nico said. They had told her it wouldn't be safe, and that she wouldn't be the same, and that above all things she would be *hungry*. But Celeste had ignored them and refused to go home. So the three of them piled into Nico's car, Dani Lynn's lifeless body in the trunk, and drove to the brothers' apartment to wait for the inevitable.

"I'm sorry," said Roman. He watched Celeste as she sat on the bed wiping the blood off of Dani Lynn's neck and matted dirty blonde hair. "But you let Brian kiss you?"

"I kissed him back too," she said spitefully. As soon as the words were out of her mouth, she regretted them. She saw the hurt written all over his face, and she felt a stabbing pain in her heart. "I'm sorry, I didn't mean that," she said.

"No, you're right. You have every right to kiss anyone you want to. It's none of my business. I can't give you what you deserve, and maybe he can," he answered icily.

"So that's it? You're just giving up? You're not even going to try and fight for this?"

"Celeste, I've already told you, I am no good for you."

"And I've already told you that you are wrong. This is *my* life Roman, and no matter how crazy it has become, you are the one thing in it that has made it bearable."

"Then why did you kiss him?"

"I don't know. But it was before you and I..." She paused, fidgeting with the beautiful ring Roman had given her for her birthday, not knowing how to continue. "It was a couple days ago after I had found out everything about my dad and how a vampire had killed him and that my mom knew all along. It just seemed like everything in my life that I had known to be true came crashing down on me. I took off in a panic – my emotions raging, and Brian found me. And that's when it happened."

Roman nodded silently, his eyes clouded with sadness.

"It was just comfortable, nice. It was nothing like when you and I kissed," she said searching his eyes.

"He's better for you than I am," he said, the warmth back in his tone.

"But I don't want him the way that I want you."

And faster than Celeste's eyes could follow, Roman's lips were on hers, kissing her desperately. His strong hand gripped her by the back of the neck, pulling her toward him. A surge of heat swelled through her body as the kiss intensified. It was as if their bodies were electrically charged, feeding off of one another. She gasped, struggling to get a breath in between the relentless onslaught of emotions.

"Whoa, whoa, I would say get a room, but I guess technically you are in one," said Nico as he walked into the guest room finding Roman and Celeste in a compromising position.

Celeste could feel her face flush with embarrassment as she untangled herself from Roman's arms.

"So our sleeping beauty hasn't awoken yet, I see."

"It shouldn't be long now," said Roman visibly flustered, "so we should keep watch over her until she does."

"Ah right, so that's what you were doing," said Nico with a wicked grin.

"Oh! With all the vampire craziness, I totally forgot to tell you about my vision," Celeste interrupted.

"What vision?" asked Roman.

"During the graduation ceremony, I got a blinding headache and then I saw images of Magnus and Dani Lynn, and it was pretty much an extended preview of what happened a few hours later."

"So it was a premonition?" asked Nico.

"Yeah, I guess it was. I couldn't make out all the details, but looking back on it, it was definitely a warning, and I totally missed it." She felt horrible all of a sudden. *What kind of a Guardian am I if I couldn't even save my friend?*

"That could be an extremely useful gift," said Roman.

"That must be one of your new Guardian powers," added Nico.

"Next time I will have to pay closer attention to what I see. It was just so hard with the searing pain in my head. I should have done something to save Dani Lynn."

"It's not your fault Celeste. You didn't know what it was," said Roman.

"And at least you found her; if you hadn't who knows what Magnus would have done to her," said Nico.

"You mean besides kill her and turn her into a vampire?" she said sarcastically.

"He could have taken her with him. At least she's here with us, and we can help her," said Nico.

"Speaking of Dani Lynn – look I think she's waking up," she said.

Dani Lynn's eyes were red and bloodshot as she looked painfully around the room trying to recognize her surroundings. Celeste tried to walk over to her, but Roman held her back protectively.

"Dani Lynn, it's me Celeste. How do you feel?"

"I'm so thirsty, my throat feels like it's on fire," she answered. "Where am I and what happened?"

"You're at my place," said Nico. "You had a bit of an accident, and we brought you here to recover."

She sat up, and looked around still squinting from the morning light. "Can you close the blinds? My eyes are killing me and my head is throbbing."

Celeste scooted past her to get to the window, and as she did Dani Lynn's vacant eyes shot up towards her. Like a wild animal pouncing on its prey, she lunged at Celeste, her new fangs in full view. Roman, who was much faster, attacked her in mid-air and pinned her to the bed in an instant.

"Celeste get out of here, it's not safe for you," said Roman as Dani Lynn wriggled underneath him trying to get free.

"No Roman, I need to be here for her. Just hold her down, let me try to talk to her," she insisted. Celeste walked to the opposite end of the room so that her scent would be less appealing to the struggling Dani Lynn.

"What is wrong with me?" Dani asked desperately. "Why do you smell so good?"

"Dani Lynn, I'm so sorry, there's no easy way to say this. You were killed and now you're a vampire."

"I'm a what?"

"A vampire. And that overpowering feeling that you have is the thirst for blood, but you must fight it," said Nico.

"This can't be happening. This must all be a really bad dream. There's no such thing as vampires," she said, rubbing her temples.

"I'm sorry Dani Lynn, but this is real, and you are a vampire just like Roman and Nico," Celeste said taking a step forward.

227

Dani Lynn's nose twitched at the subtle movement, and her incisors sprang out through her gums. She quickly clapped her hand over her mouth.

"Celeste is your friend, and you don't want to eat her, right?" asked Nico.

"No, of course I don't...but I need her blood!" she said jerking savagely. Roman had to use all his strength to keep her down.

"Geez, I had forgotten how strong new vampires were," said Nico.

"I could use some help here little brother, if you're not too busy of course," said Roman.

"Calm down, Dani Lynn," Nico said as he sat on the bed next to her. "Take deep breaths and try not to focus on the hunger."

"I can't help it, it's all I can think about," she said, her canines extended. "Ouch!"

"Be careful, those fangs will take some getting used to," he said. "Roman, grab a bottle of blood from the fridge. I've got her."

Celeste watched in awe as Nico gently fed Dani Lynn the bottle of blood as she gulped it down hungrily.

"More, I need more!"

"No, that's all you get for now," he said. "You have to learn to control the hunger, and there is no time to start like the present."

"Come on, let's leave Nico and his eager new pupil. You are far too delicious of a distraction," Roman advised Celeste.

Celeste was sufficiently convinced that Nico knew what he was doing and that her presence could possibly be causing more harm than good, so she gave in and left them alone.

Celeste sadly pondered the fate of her friend. She couldn't imagine what she must be going through. Then her thoughts went to her poor family; Jessica and her parents were going to be devastated by their loss. All of these thoughts ran through her mind as she considered for the first time what it truly meant to be a vampire. Roman and Nico made it look so easy, always in control, or at least most of the time anyway.

Do they feel that hunger every time they are around me too?

"So what is Nico going to do with her now?" Celeste asked, finding Roman in his bedroom.

"He's going to have to keep her isolated from humans for awhile until he's sure that she can control herself. It's not going to be easy, but if she has strong will power, she might make it."

"Might?"

"Celeste, I don't want to lie to you and give you false hope. It's not easy to control the bloodlust. Nico and I are different because of how we were turned, as I've told you before. We have our humanity, but I'm afraid that Dani Lynn does not."

"So what if she can't control it?"

"Let's not worry about that right now."

"I would have to kill her, wouldn't I? I mean, isn't that what I'm supposed to do as a Guardian? I'm supposed to protect humans from things like her."

"Let me take you home, Celeste. It's well past dawn and your mother will be getting home soon. She's going to be worried if you're not."

As tired as Celeste had been when she passed out on her bed, she still had vivid dreams for the few hours she slept that morning. She didn't mind them though because her father was there. He brought her to the now familiar storage room filled with their family weapons, and after they had selected a few, they were magically transported to a lush open field where they spent the day training in the sunshine.

"Celeste, the sword that you are holding is very special. I see that you have already chosen it as your own," he said.

"It was weird—from the first moment I saw it, I was drawn to it."

"That sword was forged from a mystical metal that is lethal to all supernatural creatures. The Guardian who wields that sword is no longer bound by a wooden stake to kill a vampire, or silver for a werewolf, or iron for mischievous fairies. You are fortunate that it has chosen you."

The grass was soft under Celeste's bare feet and the sun felt warm on her shoulders as she and her father lunged and parried first with swords then on to spears, axes and stakes. After what seemed like hours, her father gave her a parting hug, and she awoke in her bed slightly sweaty and definitely sore, but with a contented smile on her face.

"Good morning sweetie! Late night?"

"Yeah, I stayed at the party pretty late, and then we went to grab some food at Ralph's," she said, pouring a hot cup of coffee.

Celeste didn't know why she lied, but she just couldn't tell her mother about Dani Lynn, not with all the explanations that would have to go along with it. She suddenly began to understand why her father had kept the truth from her for so many years.

"Good, I'm glad you had some normal high school fun with your friends."

Celeste shot her a look. "Don't start Mom."

"Celeste, we have to talk about this."

"No, we don't," Celeste responded, heading for the door.

"Don't walk away from me. I need to tell you something about your father."

It bothered Celeste that her mom could push her buttons so well. She knew exactly what to say to make her stay. "What?"

"Please sit down."

Celeste pulled out the chair at the kitchen table and slumped down on it, defeated.

"Your father was the Guardian when I met him, and as I told you before, he didn't tell me at first. For the longest time, I thought he was seeing someone else," she grinned ruefully. "He would cancel our dates, disappear in the middle of the night, and he was always so secretive."

"Humph."

"Finally, on the day he proposed, he told me everything. He didn't think it was fair for me to agree to marriage before knowing what I was getting into. That's all that I want for you – to be able to make a choice."

"It's not exactly the same thing Mom. You could choose whether or not to marry Dad. It's not that simple for me. I was chosen."

"I don't pretend to know what that responsibility must feel like for you, but I know that in life we always have a choice."

"Well, I don't feel like I do."

"I wanted to talk to your father about this very thing, but whenever I brought it up he would get upset. We had no idea he would be taken away from us when you were still so young. We had hoped there would be time to discuss what to do in this situation."

"I know what he would want me to do. He'd want me to be the Guardian."

"But is that what you want?" her mom asked.

"Yes, I think it is."

Mrs. Wilder put her hand on Celeste's shoulder and squeezed. "You're a very brave girl, and I'll stand by your decision as I stood by your father."

"Thanks, Mom. I appreciate the support."

Her mom started to walk away, and then turned back. "By the way, is everything okay with you and Brian now?"

"Not really. Why?"

"I saw him hanging out in front of his house earlier. It seemed like he was trying to decide whether to come over here or not."

"I have to go talk to him," she said.

"Go easy on him, sweetie."

Celeste stepped out into the warm sunny day and marched across the yard to Brian's house. She dreaded the thought of the awkward conversation that would undoubtedly ensue. She had to tell Brian the truth about how she felt no matter how scared she was of losing him. Natalie was right; she had to set him free.

"Hey," said Celeste as Brian opened the door in his basketball shorts. He was *just* in his basketball shorts, and she found herself staring appreciatively at the smooth definition of his chest and upper arms. "Can we talk?" she said, recovering herself.

"Sure. Let's go for a walk though okay? My parents and Maxi are all home. Let me put a shirt on, and I'll be right out."

Celeste nervously twisted the ring around her finger as she waited for him on the steps. Finally, he came out and by the look on his face, he seemed to know what was coming.

"Brian, I'm so sorry about last night. I shouldn't have avoided talking to you about the kiss, and I want you to know that it wasn't something that I took lightly. I really just needed some time to process it all."

"And?" he asked.

"And, you have to promise me that no matter what I won't lose you."

"That doesn't sound good." Celeste stopped and took his arm, forcing him to turn towards her. "Promise?"

"Yes, I promise, Celeste."

"I have been selfish with you Brian. I love you, but not in the same way that you love me. And I should have told you that, but I was so scared to lose you that I didn't want to. I can't imagine my life without you."

Disappointment flashed across his face. "I feel the same way, but lately I feel like you are pulling away from me more and more each day. I feel like I'm grasping at straws. I understand if you don't feel the same way about me as I do, but don't push me out of your life."

"I'm not Brian, I swear. There are just so many things--"

"I know, that you can't tell me," he said finishing her sentence.

"Well there is something that I need to tell you. I'm going to be gone for the next few weeks."

"Gone where? I thought we were supposed to spend our last summer before college together."

"I know. I wish we could, I really do. I have to go stay with an old friend of my dad's. It's just a few hours out of town in the countryside. It was what my dad wanted."

"And you just found out about this now?"

"Yes, just recently. It's something I have to do, Brian. But I promise you that when I get back we'll hang out, okay? And maybe you can come out and visit me one day. He lives in a beautiful big house at the foot of the woods."

"Yeah sure, I guess."

Celeste got up on her tiptoes and pulled Brian into a heartfelt hug as they approached her front door.

He turned to go, and then hesitantly turned back. "Celeste, if you had never met Roman, would you feel differently about me?"

She felt her throat constrict at the question, deep inside she knew the answer, but she couldn't find the words.

234

Brian saw the answer clearly written on her face. "Never mind," he said and walked away.

Celeste finished loading her last bag into Nico's trunk and looked up at her mother whose eyes were brimming with tears.

"Oh Mom, don't cry. I'm only going to be gone for a few weeks, and it's only a couple hours away. You can even come visit me on your day off."

"I know sweetie, I just can't imagine you not living with me under the same roof. And it's making me dread your move to college at the end of the summer."

Celeste gave her mom a big hug. Clutching the family key she now wore religiously around her neck, Celeste promised she would call her mom everyday. She took one last long look at her childhood home and jumped into the car. As they sped off towards Nico's apartment, Celeste couldn't help but think about Brian. He knew that she was leaving today, and she had asked him to come say goodbye, but he hadn't shown up. Instead, he had texted her with a last-minute excuse about early morning hockey practice. Celeste knew he was avoiding her. Knowing that Brian was in pain and she was the cause of it made her feel utterly miserable.

"Hey beautiful, are you okay?" asked Nico.

"Oh yeah, I'm fine. Just thinking, that's all."

"Staying with Stellan really is the best option, you'll see."

"I know," she said. "Nico, do you think I will actually get to go away to college like I had planned?"

"Of course you will! As a vampire, I've gone to college dozens of times. Why wouldn't a Guardian be able to go?"

"Well, I've been thinking about it lately, and college is the last thing on my mind right now. How am I supposed to concentrate on picking a major, new classes and studying when I'm training and learning how to fight and become a Guardian?"

"Celeste, I have no doubt that you can do both. Look at your father, he had a wife and a child and still managed to keep Oak Bluffs safe from the supernatural."

"Yes, by lying to us all."

"Look, you have the rest of the summer to figure out this Guardian thing. Take it day by day and don't worry about it," he said as he patted her arm in encouragement.

"Speaking of taking it day by day, how is Dani Lynn doing?"

"Not bad. Actually I'd like you to see her today before you and Roman head off to Stellan's."

"I'd like to see her too. Poor Jessica and her family are going crazy trying to find her. They have the entire police department searching, and there are Missing Person signs with her picture plastered all around town. Do you think she will ever be able to go back to her family?"

"It's still too soon to say Celeste. A new vampire's emotions are highly erratic, everything is heightened – as you have experienced. Although she seems fine one moment, she could easily lose control the next."

Standing at the door of the apartment, she could sense Roman on the other side. She had been practicing controlling her new emotions and supernatural urges like Stellan had taught her, and she found it much easier to be around her vampire friends now. When she opened the door, Roman greeted her with a bright smile and dancing blue eyes.

"Are you ready for a little road trip?" he asked her.

"As ready as I'll ever be."

Nico walked in behind her toting a cooler with the Oak Bluffs Hospital logo on it. At Celeste's questioning glance, he said, "Refreshments for Dani."

"I see," she said.

"Don't worry, I left some in the car for you too Roman. But before you go, I'd like to borrow Celeste for a moment."

"For what?" Roman asked defensively.

"I need to test something out with Dani."

"You want to use my g---, Celeste as vampire bait?"

Roman tried to recover from the slip, but Celeste had caught it and casually turned away hiding the huge smile spreading across her lips.

"Oh don't be so dramatic Roman, I can control Dani Lynn," he said.

"Fine, but only if I am there too."

"Of course, oh untrusting one."

"Doesn't anyone care about what I have to say?" asked Celeste. "I'm the 'vampire bait' after all, and I say let's do it."

"Why am I not surprised?" said Roman, rolling his eyes.

Due to the bright sun, which constantly streamed in through the floor to ceiling windows of the apartment, Dani Lynn was forced to spend the day in hiding. Nico had built what Celeste affectionately called the "vampire hidey hole" out of the basement laundry room. He led the way down the stairs with Celeste trailing a few steps behind and Roman bringing up the rear.

"Hi Dani, how are you?" asked Celeste from a safe distance.

"I'm bored and I'm hungry," she answered.

"Now, now Dani, that's no way to talk to your friend who came to visit you," said Nico.

"Sorry Celeste. I'm just going crazy down here. I can't go outside except at night, and I have no one to talk to except these two. And I think Roman hates me," she said as she burst into tears.

"No, Dani Lynn, don't cry. Roman doesn't hate you," Celeste said as she moved towards her to put a comforting arm around her shoulder.

"No!" yelled Roman.

But it was too late. Dani Lynn grabbed Celeste and spun her around, pinning her arm behind her back and poised with fangs at Celeste's neck.

"Stop! Dani, you don't want to bite her," Nico said in a calm soothing voice. "Let her go now."

The tension in the air was palpable. Roman's fangs were bared, and he was primed to strike at the slightest movement. While their attention was focused on Dani Lynn as she struggled between instinct and willpower, Celeste whipped around throwing Dani Lynn off balance. He flipped her over her shoulder and pinned her to the floor with one quick movement. When Dani Lynn opened her eyes in shock, Celeste was on top of her holding a stake menacingly above her chest.

"Wow, impressive Celeste!" said Nico, clapping his hands.

"I told you I wasn't vampire bait!" she said proudly. "Also, I've been having training dreams with my dad."

"Training dreams?" asked Nico.

"I'm not really sure what they are, but they seem to be working."

"I wish I could go with you Celeste, but I don't think we should leave Dani alone while she's still transitioning," said Nico as he hugged her goodbye.

"I know. Just promise you'll come visit me soon!"

"I promise, I will. And Roman, take care of my car," he yelled over the engine.

"Oh please, I should be saying the same to you. You're the lucky one in this deal."

"It's not my fault that your little Porsche has no trunk space."

"But it more than makes up for it in horsepower."

"Okay boys, let's not argue about whose car is better than whose or else we'll never leave," said Celeste climbing into the front seat.

***

Fabian paced restlessly in front of the open window, his long silver hair blowing in the chilly breeze. Outside the snow-covered peaks loomed in the distance, blocking the last rays of the sun. The valley below was finally beginning to return to life after the many harsh months of winter.

"I cannot believe that fool Magnus has double-crossed me!" said Fabian, bringing his fist crashing down on the table.

"I hate to say I told you so--" said Alek.

"Then don't!"

"What does he think he's doing anyway?" asked Alek. "I understand he is still in Oak Bluffs."

"He is after that human girl that is always with the Constantins. He has been making some inquiries about her."

"Inquiries? What kind of inquiries?" asked Alek.

"It seems as though he believes she is not simply some human girl."

"Well, that is interesting."

"Yes, it is. Since he is the only one that has had contact with her and lived to tell about it, it has made me curious as well," said Fabian.

"Magnus has sent word that he will no longer be fulfilling your orders along with return of payment," said Alek.

"This must be a very special girl that our friend has stumbled upon to risk defying me for."

"Yes, it is highly unusual."

"Alek, I think it is finally time that we make our own visit to Oak Bluffs."

Chapter 15

"Welcome my dear," said Stellan with an elaborate bow. "My home is your home."

"Thanks for helping me, Stellan," said Celeste. "I'm sure you have enough going on without having to worry about training a newbie Guardian."

"On the contrary, my dear, this is exactly what I should be doing. I spent so many years on the Council and always felt that we could do more for the guardians, and now I can."

"I really do appreciate it."

"Of course! And to be perfectly honest, before you came into our lives, I was beginning to get a little bored."

Roman chimed in saying, "You certainly won't be bored now that Celeste's around. She's a magnet for trouble." Celeste shot him a sidelong look, but couldn't help but laugh in agreement.

"Roman, please show her up to the guest bedroom at the end of the hall on the second floor. It's the same room your father used to stay in when he came to visit me, Celeste."

Celeste smiled and followed Roman. He carried her suitcase and a large duffel bag filled with miscellaneous weapons up the impressive spiral staircase.

As Celeste began unpacking, Roman sat quietly on the bed watching her. She pulled out her sword and laid it carefully under the bed. She could feel his penetrating eyes on her as she moved from her suitcase to the closet, back to the suitcase, to the armoire and so on. She found, to her relief, that the disturbing feeling she once felt when she was around him had pretty much disappeared. Instead, it had been replaced by a sense of longing when he wasn't in her sight. And when they touched, the exciting sparks had returned and become even more powerful. A pleasant side effect of her new Guardian powers, she thought with a grin.

"What are you thinking about?" he asked.

Celeste stopped folding her clothes and stood in front of him. "You." She ran her fingers through his soft wavy hair. A muffled sound of pleasure escaped from Roman's lips as he exhaled.

"What about me?" he asked, trying to keep his composure.

"Just how happy I am that you are here with me."

"About that Celeste," he said pulling away a little, "you know Stellan doesn't want me to stay."

"Well I do. And I'm the trainee. I don't feel safe without you near me, and if I'm supposed to concentrate on training I shouldn't be distracted by concerns over my safety."

"Excellent argument, but I don't know that Stellan will be as easy as I am to convince," he said as he pulled her into his lap.

"But it's true, I never feel as safe as I do when I'm in your arms," she said running her fingers down his bicep.

Roman leaned in slowly, looking into her sparkling eyes as his lips neared hers and kissed her tentatively. His arms enveloped her in a protective embrace as his hands ran through her cascading hair. As the heat of the moment increased, Celeste clung on to him more urgently as his searing kisses intensified. She felt as though time were standing still and all the terrible things that had happened over the past month were magically swept away.

"Roman will you be joining us for dinner or will you be leaving before?" asked Stellan politely. The happy couple had finally descended after a rather intense make-out session, and they were positively glowing.

"Actually, Stellan, I hope you don't mind, but I've asked Roman to stay and help me train," interjected Celeste.

"Celeste, we've already talked about this, and I thought you understood my position on the topic."

"You're right, I have heard your position on this, but you haven't heard mine." Stellan looked at Celeste in surprise then to Roman who responded with a wry smile.

"Firstly, Roman is an excellent fighter, and I could use him as a sparring partner. He is strong, fast and smart. He is a vampire after all, and who better to learn from than the enemy?"

"While that is true--," began Stellan.

"Secondly," interrupted Celeste, "Roman has already saved me from vampires a bunch of times, and I feel safer knowing that he is here. If I'm not worried about my safety, I'll be more concentrated on my training."

"Umhmm…"

"And lastly, I know that my dad didn't want me involved in the supernatural world, but isn't that a bit silly now? I am deeply involved, and keeping Roman or Nico away from me isn't going to change that."

"Is this your doing, Roman?" Stellan shot him an irritated glance.

"Hey don't look at me, I had nothing to do with this."

Celeste watched Stellan, her eyes anxious for a response. "I see you have put a lot of thought into this, Celeste," said Stellan.

"I have."

Stellan sighed. "While it's against my better judgment, I will agree to allow Roman to stay for a few days until you've settled in. Once you become acquainted with your new environment, I assure you that you will have no concerns for your safety and in regards to a sparring partner, you'll find that I am far more nimble than I look."

Celeste looked skeptically at Stellan's wiry frame.

"That seems fair," said Roman.

"But if I find that you are more of a distraction than anything else, I will send you packing immediately, Roman."

"I promise to be on my best behavior."

Celeste and Roman exchanged victorious glances, both smiling happily.

Celeste tossed and turned in her bed that night as a vision overtook her subconscious. She was back in the white circular room, but instead of the tribunal she had seen last time there was a round white table with two people seated. She recognized the portly man and the silver-haired woman from the day she was chosen to be the Guardian. As she looked curiously at them, they stood and waved her toward them.

"Welcome Celeste, my name is Dante, and I am the head of the Council of Guardians. I apologize for not introducing myself when we first met, but the Choosing Ceremony is quite a lot to take in," said the portly man. He had a kind face and salt and pepper hair, but the deep wrinkles on his forehead depicted a life burdened with significant responsibilities. Though he had some extra weight on him, it was plain to see he had been handsome at one time.

"And I am Sierra. It is a pleasure to finally meet you, Celeste." Sierra on the other hand had beautiful smooth skin, her cheeks rosy and her smile sweet. It was only the long silver hair that betrayed her true age.

"Thank you, it's nice to meet you too, both of you," she said extending her hand awkwardly.

"Please sit down."

When she looked down at the white table a third metallic chair had suddenly appeared. She pulled it out hesitantly, afraid it would disappear before her eyes, and sat down.

"You must be wondering why we have summoned you here today," he said.

"Yes, I was. And can I only see you when I'm dreaming?"

"Oh this isn't a dream my dear. We are in another realm – Astor. It is a safe haven where the Council as well as many inactive guardians dwell. It is easier for me to reach into your mind to transport you here when you are asleep. Guardians are rather difficult to influence, so the subconscious state makes for a smooth transition. Eventually you will be able to come in and out of this realm as you please."

"Wow, that's pretty cool. So this is like an alternate universe?"

"Not quite, it is simply a part of the world not visible to others as it is shielded by magic," answered Sierra.

"Okay," Celeste said with doubt.

Dante continued, "In any case, the reason that we brought you here today is to see how your Guardian training has been coming along."

"Yes, we want to make sure that your mentor has been providing you with everything you need," said Sierra.

"Stellan has been wonderful so far. I'm going to be spending the summer with him training," explained Celeste.

"And we couldn't help but notice that you have been spending time with some vampires," said Dante.

Celeste was taken aback, and she shifted nervously in her chair. "Is that against the official guardian rules or something?" she asked.

"No, not exactly, but it has so rarely come up in the history of the Council that we have never had to make a specific rule against it."

"Are you aware that some supernatural creatures are inexplicably drawn to guardians?" asked Sierra. "Has Stellan told you about that?"

She shook her head.

"No one knows why it happens or why it affects some and not others, but it seems that your light attracts their darkness."

Celeste shivered. She wasn't sure if it was from the cold room or Sierra's words.

"I am curious," said Sierra peering through her purple-rimmed glasses, "how can you stand being around them?"

"I've been working on controlling my feelings. Stellan taught me how to."

Sierra shot Dante a look of approval.

"I am impressed that you have been able to master your impulses so quickly," said Dante.

"It's hard, but I have to do it," she admitted.

"Still, we don't see how consorting with vampires could be conducive to your studies and training," he continued.

Celeste felt a twinge of anger bubble up inside of her. "Roman and Nico aren't just any vampires. They are good, and they're on my side. They have been very helpful to me so far, and they've saved my life *a lot*. I may not even be here today if it weren't for them."

"We are familiar with the Constantin brothers. We are also aware of the Patrick and Magnus situations, which is honestly the only reason why we haven't removed these vampires from your life." Celeste was shocked. *Did they really have the power to get rid of them?* "For whatever reason, they seem to want to protect you, which is ultimately our goal as well," finished Dante.

"Then I don't see why we are even having this conversation," said Celeste haughtily.

"It is our duty to check in on you from time to time Celeste," said Sierra. "We only want what is best for you. Becoming the Guardian is a long and arduous journey, and we hope to help you in whatever way possible."

"Your father was an exemplary Guardian, and we have no doubts that you will become one as well," Dante added.

"Thank you," Celeste said, reigning in her temper.

"One last thing before you go, do you have the Wilder family key your father left you?"

"Yes, of course," she said pulling it out from under her shirt.

"Good, if you ever need to reach us, simply hold the key in your hand and focus in on your powers."

As Celeste lay in bed wide-awake staring at the ceiling, she reveled in her discussion with the senior Council Members. She finally felt as though she were a part of something. The idea of being the Guardian didn't seem as scary now that she knew she had a Council she could rely on and a whole secret realm she could visit. But Dante's words about Roman and Nico had her worried. She hoped that her powers would grow quickly so that she could return soon. Maybe she would even be able to see her father there again, she thought. She pulled the covers up over her head and shut her eyes. She couldn't wait until morning came so she could tell Roman and Stellan all about it.

The days flew by for Celeste under the steady schedule of early morning runs, a few hours of sparring with Roman, and evening meditations as her new normal. She could feel herself getting stronger, faster and more confident in handling an assortment of deadly weapons. Her sword was still her favorite, but Celeste now could handle a stake, crossbow or dagger with the greatest of ease. Roman had also taught her how to turn virtually any inanimate object into a deadly weapon. From chairs to tree branches to pens, Roman had borne the brunt of her newfound resourcefulness and ferocity.

"As much as I hate to admit it, having Roman here is proving to be quite useful. The fact that Celeste can stab you with a knife or shoot you with an arrow and you heal within minutes makes for excellent practice scenarios," said Stellan as he watched the two of them go at it in the backyard as the sun began to set.

"You should have seen her try to break my neck a few hours ago. You would have really enjoyed that," said Roman, ducking to avoid a blow.

"I almost got him too. He was just a little too fast for me," Celeste said proudly. She signaled to Roman for a time out, and walked towards Stellan.

"Then we need to work on your speed," he said. "Since most of your opponents will be stronger than you given their supernatural abilities, the Guardian must rely on the element of surprise. You, my dear, are especially lucky as you have been given the gift of premonitions, you must use that knowledge to your advantage."

"How do I do that?"

"You must rely on your instincts. You said that you can feel danger when it is near you so you must listen to your body's natural response. Remember that your enemies do not know that you can sense their true nature. Use that to get the upper hand from the onset."

Celeste nodded listening intently.

249

"I'd like to try something. Roman, go get the blind fold from the weapons trunk in the garage." In a flash, Roman was back firmly tying the black blindfold around Celeste's eyes.

"Celeste, put all your energy in concentrating on 'the feeling' and see if you can detect from which direction Roman is coming at you from."

Celeste stood very still and took a few deep breaths before delving inside herself to find the source of her premonitions. It was difficult since she hardly felt it anymore around Roman. She searched deeper within, and she felt a tiny pang in the pit of her stomach that something wasn't quite right. She lunged to her left just in time, plunging her sword into Roman's chest.

"Bravo!" said Stellan clapping.

"That was dangerously close to my heart, Celeste," said Roman. He pulled the sword out while muttering a few expletives.

She pulled the blindfold up over her head and saw the bloody wound on his chest. "Oops, sorry! I couldn't see with the blindfold on, and Stellan told me to follow my instincts."

"Next time, try to be more careful or you're going to have to find yourself a new training partner."

"That's enough for today. Roman, why don't you go get yourself cleaned up, and I'll finish off with some meditating with Celeste."

"She's all yours."

Roman limped back to the house clutching the open wound in his chest, and Celeste sat down with legs crossed next to Stellan on the lawn.

"Now do you see why the meditating is so important?" Stellan asked.

"Yes, I think I am starting to," Celeste agreed.

"It is very important for your mind to be centered so that you can fully tap into your gifts. I'm sure Dante mentioned that to you as well when you were summoned by the Council. That was another reason why I didn't want Roman to be here during your training. I may be an old man, but I am not blind, and I see the way you look at each other."

Celeste reddened at the thought of having this awkward conversation with Stellan.

"Love is a beautiful thing, my dear, but it can become a weakness. It clouds our judgment, not just yours, but his too. Be careful that it doesn't put you both at risk."

"Is that what you told my father too?"

Stellan chuckled. "You are a quick one Celeste. Yes, of course I did. When your father came to me seeking my counsel about your mother, I had to advise against their relationship. As a member of the Council it was my responsibility to remind your father that his duty as a Guardian came first."

"And what did he say?"

"He didn't listen to me of course. He, and in this you two are very much alike, gave me a list of reasons why he should be with your mother. He was very stubborn, that father of yours, but ultimately he was right. He succeeded in accomplishing his duties as a Guardian as well as a husband and eventually a father."

"Until he was killed."

"Yes, that is true, but had he listened to me he would have undoubtedly died eventually as we all do. But without ever experiencing true love, having a family, and bringing you into this world."

"Then why do you want Roman and me to stay away from each other if you think my father was right in wanting both?"

"Because, my dear Celeste, your mother was not a vampire."

***

"So how is Nico doing with vampire obedience training?" asked Celeste as she and Roman strolled hand in hand through the moonlit woods. The peaceful sounds of the forest drowned out the frenetic day of training. The only sounds that broke the stillness were the crunching of dead leaves underfoot or the occasional mouse scurrying across their path.

"He said he's making some progress. It's slow, but Dani doesn't seem to want to rip every human's head off anymore."

"That's promising. So he's been taking her out in public?"

"Yes, but not in Oak Bluffs. He's been driving her to Falls River or Youngstown at night so that no one will recognize her. As long as she has fed before being near people, she's been able to hold it together."

"I just hope that she can go home one day to her family."

Roman stopped walking and leaned against a towering oak. A hint of sadness flashed through his eyes. "It's hard for vampires to live among humans, even well-adjusted ones. Dani would have to tell her family what she is, and unfortunately that doesn't always go over well. Even if they did come to accept what she is, after a few years the good old citizens of Oaks Bluffs would notice that she hasn't aged a bit and become suspicious. She wouldn't be able to stay there for long."

"Right, I guess I hadn't thought about that," she said. "So does that mean that you and Nico won't be staying in Oak Bluffs for long either?"

"We never really can Celeste. Even if it weren't for Fabian chasing us, after at most five to ten years most people would start to notice that I'm just too devilishly handsome for a thirty-year-old."

"This isn't funny Roman. When were you planning on telling me this?"

"We've only been back in Oak Bluffs for a few months now, Celeste. I figured we still had time. And I thought it would be a little presumptuous of me to start talking about our future since most of our days together involve you kicking, cutting, stabbing or staking me."

Celeste couldn't help but crack a smile.

"Besides, you're the one that is leaving me at the end of the summer when you go off to college," said Roman.

"Leaving you?" she asked. "Are you implying that we are together?" she asked with a mischievous grin.

"I don't know, does it?"

"You are exasperating Roman Constantin!" whined Celeste, playfully punching him in the stomach.

"I love you, Celeste," he said, taking her by surprise. He pulled her close to him and took her face in his strong hands. "I've never loved anyone the way that I love you, and I'm sorry that I waited this long to say it."

Celeste barely waited for the last word to come out of his mouth before jumping into his arms, her lips passionately locking onto his.

The next few weeks continued in much the same way: a never-ending cycle of waking, training, meditating and sleeping. In spite of Stellan's original wishes, Roman stayed with Celeste the entire time. As tough as Stellan tried to be, he couldn't deny Roman's value and he didn't have the heart to kick him out. Celeste was progressing much more rapidly than anyone had anticipated, and Stellan frequently found himself watching her proudly as she pinned Roman to the floor on numerous occasions.

"Nico!" said Celeste as she ran into his arms as he hurried up the walkway.

"Hello little brother," said Roman just behind her. "It's good to see you."

"I think this fresh country air is doing wonders for you. I've never seen you look so relaxed brother," said Nico.

"It's the company," chimed in Celeste with a big smile.

Dani lurked nervously by the car until Stellan finally invited her into the house. Roman stood protectively by Celeste's side watching her every move as she neared.

"Hi Dani Lynn, how are you?" she asked.

"I'm doing a lot better, thanks. I can smell your blood, but I don't have a blinding urge to tear into your neck anymore."

Celeste recalled that subtlety had never been one of Dani Lynn's strong suits, and apparently it hadn't improved when she became a vampire. "That's great to hear Dani. And since we're being up front, I might as well tell you that if you try to bite me, I'll stab you in the heart without blinking."

"Sounds fair," she responded.

"I almost hope she tries," said Nico. "That would be a sight I would love to see!"

"Watch it Nico or else I'll have to show you some of my moves," teased Celeste.

"Now that would be something *I'd* like to see," said Roman.

"I've heard she's been mopping up the floor with you brother."

"I think 'mopping up the floor' is a bit of an exaggeration, but yes, she has come quite a long way – due in large part to my relentless motivational training."

"Oh, I don't doubt that," said Nico.

"Come on now children, enough of that trash talk as they say. Let's sit down for dinner and Celeste can show Nico what she's learned tomorrow morning," said Stellan as he ushered them all into the candle-lit dining room.

The following morning Celeste and Roman were up early for a jog followed by a round of hand-to-hand combat in the backyard. Roman held Celeste with both of her arms immobilized behind her back. She threw herself forward, tucking her chin to her chest and somersaulted to the ground taking Roman down with her. He landed flat on his back with a ground-shaking thud.

"Impressive," said Nico as he came out on the porch to watch.

"Feel free to tag me out," said Roman breathing hard.

Faster than Celeste's eyes could follow, Nico had switched places with Roman and he was coming at her. She ducked and missed his first blow then followed up with a leg sweep that sent him crashing to the ground. She hurdled on top of him and held a stake hovering just inches from his chest, a satisfied grin on her face.

"I was going easy on you," he said.

"Well, don't!" Celeste ordered.

Dani joined Roman on the porch where she was shielded from the morning sun to watch Nico and Celeste now sparring with long swords.

"She's pretty good," she said.

"Yes, she's getting there."

"So guardians are like vampire hunters right?"

"Something like that. They protect the human world from all evil supernatural beings."

"And are they strong like us? She seems to be."

"Not quite as strong, but certainly not your average human either."

"How many guardians are there?"

"It's hard to say exactly, but no more than a dozen around the world at any given time," instructed Roman.

"So if I don't get on Celeste's bad side, I should be pretty safe from getting a stake in the heart, right?"

"Yes, it's pretty unlikely that you will come across another guardian in your lifetime, unless you do something very bad."

"Like what?" Dani Lynn inquired.

"Like go on a murderous killing spree, leaving countless bodies in your wake. Then the Council would send a guardian to find you and end your life."

"You say that like you've seen it happen before."

"I have," Roman said and walked away.

As a reward for Celeste's tireless training and rapid progress, Stellan had agreed to allow her friends to come visit for the day. Natalie had been texting non-stop since Celeste had left town, but she hadn't heard much from Brian at all. So Celeste was surprised when Natalie told her that they would be coming up together.

"Hi!" said Natalie as she ran up the walk. "I missed you so much!"

"I missed you too," said Celeste returning her enthusiastic hug.

Brian came up behind them and nearly toppled them all over as he eagerly joined in the embrace.

"How are you stranger?" Celeste said to Brian, searching his eyes.

"I'm good Cel. It's really great to see you."

"Come on in, I'll introduce you to my Uncle Stellan," said Celeste as Stellan stepped out of the kitchen.

"This is such a lovely home you have," said Natalie as she walked around the large open living room.

"Make yourselves at home children. Celeste has told me much about both of you. I'm sure you have a lot of catching up to do so I will make myself scarce," said Stellan, retreating into his study.

"So how come I never heard about this uncle?" asked Brian once he was out of earshot.

"He's not really my uncle, just an old friend of my dad who recently moved back to the area."

"Can we go outside? It looks so beautiful out back," said Natalie. She had been checking out the backyard through the oversized window.

"Yeah, I was thinking we could go for a hike in the forest. There's a river about a mile away, and we can go for a swim too."

"Sounds cool," said Brian.

Natalie went to one of the guestrooms to change, leaving Brian and Celeste looking at each other uneasily.

"So how's your summer been? Too busy to text your best friend back?" she asked finally.

"Sorry about that. I joined this summer basketball team, and I've been playing every day. Between that and helping out with Maxi the weeks have flown by."

"Okay, I just wanted to make sure you weren't avoiding me or something."

"Maybe just a little bit," he admitted. "I think this is the longest amount of time that we've spent apart, and I figured I should start getting used to being without you. I've spent most of my life in love with you without really knowing it, and now I have to try to move on."

Brian spoke so nonchalantly, and it made Celeste's heart hurt. But she knew he was right. "I understand that, and I'm trying to give you your space. It's just hard because I miss you so much," Celeste admitted.

"I miss you too, Cel."

Trekking through the tranquil forest with two of her oldest friends, Celeste felt oddly normal. The thick foliage overhead provided a respite from the scorching noon sun, but still the drops of sweat trickled down her back relentlessly. She longed to jump into the refreshing waters of the river ahead.

"It is such a perfect day for a hike!" said Natalie.

"Yeah, it really is pretty nice out here," admitted Brian.

"So what have you been doing anyway?" she asked.

"Mostly spending time with Uncle Stellan, like I told you guys. He's getting older and needed some company. Plus he's like a Wikipedia on my dad so it's been really fun hanging out with him and hearing stories about my dad when he was young."

"Well, you look great. Been working out?"

"I've been jogging in the mornings and doing some yoga. It's so peaceful out here, so I started meditating too."

"Not a bad way to spend the summer," she said.

"Enough about me, what's going on in Oak Bluffs? Tell me everything!" said Celeste.

Magnus soared through the air, hovering just below the dense tree line. As powerful as he was, the bright sunlight still bothered him, and he preferred the cover of darkness. Many centuries ago, he had done Fabian a favor and had been awarded an amber amulet that had been spelled to protect him against the sun. No one knew that the necklace hanging around his neck was the source of his day-walking abilities, and he fought to keep it that way. Magnus had been tracking Dani Lynn for the past few hours and had finally been rewarded. Their shared blood had led him right to her. His plan had worked surprisingly well. When he arrived at the house, he immediately sensed that the one he coveted was nearby. He flew in circles around the perimeter of the house until his keen eyesight caught sight of Celeste in the woods.

Celeste wiggled her toes in the cool water as she reclined along the riverbank. Natalie popped up behind her, startling her from her quiet reverie.

"Brian's passed out," she whispered.

Celeste looked back up the path and saw Brian stretched out on a blanket, cheeks rosy from the sun, mouth wide open. She smiled, remembering a similar sight last time they went hiking when they were just in grade school.

"Is everything okay with you two?" Natalie asked, noticing the wistful look that had crossed her face.

"I'm not sure to be honest. I hope so."

"He's tough, he'll get over you."

"Is it bad that I don't want him to? I mean of course I want him to be happy, but things have been so strained lately. I feel like I've lost my best friend."

"I'm sure the weirdness will pass. Once he meets someone it will be much easier. Just like it has been for you – now tell me everything about you and Roman!"

"It's been going really well," she said, unable to hide the huge smile that spread across her face.

"That's great! I knew he liked you!"

"Yeah, but that's what I'm afraid of. Every time we get close, he pulls away. Everything has been going so well for the past few weeks, I'm just waiting for the other shoe to drop."

"Don't be so negative Celeste! You're awesome and he's lucky to have you."

"No, I'm lucky to have you," she said, reaching out to give her friend a hug. "I've really missed you!"

"Me too! Oak Bluffs is no fun with you gone. Brian's been playing basketball non-stop, Nico's been holed up in his house, and poor Jessica is distraught over Dani Lynn's disappearance. Everything's falling apart without you. When are you coming home?"

"Soon, I hope. I want to spend some more time with my uncle. But I promise I'll be home as soon as I can."

Suddenly, a wave of frigid water drenched the girls. Confused, they looked all around searching for the origin of the attack. Wiping the water from their eyes and smoothing their hair out of their faces, they saw Brian emerge from underwater just in front of them.

"How did you get in the river? You were dead asleep a few seconds ago," said Natalie.

"I snuck around behind the trees and swam underwater up the river to scare you," he said, obviously pleased with his clever prank.

"You are so dead Brian!" said Celeste as she leapt into the water with Natalie right behind her.

As the three friends packed up their bags for the hike home, Celeste felt her evil radar (so nicknamed by Nico recently) start twitching. She surveyed the peaceful forest around them, but saw nothing. Wishing that Roman or Nico were with them, she glanced around suspiciously and pulled the knife out from her backpack and tucked it into her jeans pocket.

"Hey why don't we jog back?" asked Celeste.

"Jog? But I'm in flip-flops!" complained Natalie.

"Oh right. Okay, then, let's just walk quickly to get some cardio in."

"Geez, you have become quite the work out nut, haven't you?" she asked.

Celeste picked up a few of Natalie's clothes that had been scattered around the riverbank and hurriedly stuffed them into her bag. Brian shot Celeste a concerned look, but she ignored it and hustled them through the darkening forest and back to the safety of the house.

"Stellan, I felt something when we were out there," she whispered as Brian and Natalie changed out of their wet bathing suits.

Stellan peered over his glasses, dropping the book he had been reading in his study. "What was it?"

"I'm not sure, but there was something evil watching us. I looked around, but I didn't see anyone."

"It can't be Dani, she's been tucked away in the basement all day so that your friends wouldn't see her. And Roman and Nico took the car into town to buy groceries for dinner," he said, puzzled.

"Do you think it could have been Magnus?" she asked.

"Perhaps, but I don't see how he could have found us."

"I'm going to text Roman to hurry back."

"Hey Cel, can I borrow a towel?" bellowed Brian from the bathroom.

"Sure, I'll be right there." Celeste ran over to the linen closet and brought Brian a fresh towel.

"Are you okay?" he asked. "You seemed a little nervous when we were out in the woods."

"I'm fine," she said, changing the subject. "Roman and Nico are on their way over. They're going to have dinner with us."

"Oh," Brian said, suddenly despondent.

"I thought it would be fun if we all got together since I know Nico's been MIA a lot this summer. Natalie hasn't seen him for a while, and I haven't seen them much either."

"But you have seen them?"

"Yes, I have."

"Them or Roman?"

"Both, but look Brian, I want to be honest with you. I don't want to keep things from you, but I don't want to hurt you either."

"Just tell me the truth Cel."

"Yes, I've been spending a lot of time with Roman. He's been coming out to visit me."

"So are you two like together now?"

"Yes," she said, averting her eyes.

Roman and Nico arrived moments later with groceries in tow. Roman's eyes were wild with worry. He immediately looked to Celeste to gauge her emotional state, and she responded with a telling glance confirming she was fine. As she watched him, she thought about how incredible it was to be able to communicate with him without so much as a word. She didn't think it was possible, but she felt more strongly connected to him every day. Brian entered the room and harshly brought her back to the reality that her friends could be in danger now because of her.

"Hello there, Brian," said Nico as he followed Roman in, carrying an armful of groceries.

"Hey Nico, how's it going? Let me help you with that."

"Great, thank you," he said handing him some of the bags, "I'm doing well, doing a bit of traveling over the summer and you?"

"Not too bad, nothing too exciting though."

"Where's Natalie?"

"Here I am!" she said as she came bounding out of the bathroom and into Nico's outstretched arms.

"I've missed you beautiful," he said.

"Me too! Where have you been for the past few weeks?"

"I had to go visit some relatives in Chicago unexpectedly – health issues."

"So are you and Roman going back to Oak Bluffs tonight too?" questioned Brian.

Celeste shot Nico a look, hoping he would get the hint. She didn't want Brian or Natalie knowing the brothers would be staying.

"Not sure yet. We actually have some friends that live a couple hours away from here so we may pop by for a visit."

"Well, you better let me know when you're back home so we can hang out," said Natalie.

"Yes, for sure," he responded.

Roman had snuck away from the conversation to get started on dinner and once everyone was chatting comfortably, Celeste joined him.

"I didn't know you could cook," she said as she watched him skillfully chop up some onions.

"There are many things you don't know about me, Celeste."

"So tell me something I don't know," she said, jumping up to sit on the counter next to him.

"Well, for starters I spent a year traveling through Italy and France learning everything you'd ever want to know about food and wine from master chefs and sommeliers."

"Impressive! And this is the first time you're cooking for me?"

"I have had other things to worry about lately – you know, like your safety, training you, Magnus, Fabian..."

She elbowed him flirtatiously. "Okay, point taken. When all of this craziness is over, I want you to tell me everything about you," she said, leaning into him.

"That could take an entire lifetime," he said, his gaze intent on her.

"I've got time," she said and gave him a gentle kiss.

"Oh, um, sorry," said Brian awkwardly. He had walked into the kitchen catching them mid-kiss.

"No, come in please," said Celeste, hastily pulling away from Roman. "What's up?"

"Your uncle sent me in here to check on the food. He was worried we'd be driving home too late."

"Dinner's almost ready," said Roman. "Why don't you two have everyone move into the dining room, and I'll be out in a minute."

***

"Bye you guys, I'll miss you!" Celeste stood at the door and waved, watching her friends drive off until the Mustang disappeared in the darkness. As happy as Celeste had been to see Brian and Natalie, she felt an immense relief now that they were gone and safe. She glanced around the yard nervously before shutting the door and locking it.

"I think Roman and I should do a sweep of the area tonight," said Nico, getting right down to business.

"I should go too. I'm the one that can feel their presence," said Celeste.

"Yes, your evil radar would certainly come in handy."

"No, Celeste, you should stay here with Stellan. We can fly and cover more ground that way," interjected Roman.

"Ugh, I never get to go anywhere!"

"You can let Dani out of the basement. I'm sure she'll be happy to see you," said Nico.

"Right," she said reluctantly as they flew out the back door. Celeste followed them and stood by the door peering unhappily into the black night.

"He is simply looking out for your well-being," admonished Stellan.

"Yes, I know, but sometimes he treats me like I'm nothing but a fragile human that he needs to keep in a cage to protect."

"That's what happens when you love someone."

Celeste couldn't help but smile.

"Did you hear that?" she asked nervously. "Someone's outside."

Stellan pushed past Celeste and stepped out to the back porch and found Dani in a sort of trance. Her eyes were glazed over, and she wore a vacant expression on her face. Celeste approached her, but Stellan reached out to stop her.

"What happened Dani?" asked Stellan.

Dani turned around, the confused look in her eyes beginning to clear. "I'm not sure," she said. "I heard your friends' car drive away so I started to come up the stairs from the basement and then everything went blank."

"Did you hear anything or see anyone?" asked Celeste.

"I have no idea. I remember thinking that I really wanted to come outside so I opened the back door and that was it."

"Come on ladies, let's get back inside," said Stellan. He ushered them back in, and closing the door he invoked a cloaking spell, uttering, "Vitame nix ingressare." A purple light glowed momentarily around the whole house and then disappeared.

When Roman and Nico returned without finding a trace of a vampire, Stellan called everyone into the living room. "I've been thinking, and I believe it was Magnus that you felt in the woods earlier today. It would also explain Dani's loss of memory."

"How?" asked Roman.

"Magnus is Dani's creator. Having never turned anyone yourselves, perhaps you have forgotten that the creator bond is one of the strongest attachments a vampire can feel."

"What is a creator bond exactly?" asked Celeste.

"When a vampire is made, the creator gives them vast quantities of their own blood. This blood bond allows for the creator and its offspring to be linked forever. Magnus could easily find Dani anywhere in the world because of it. And because Magnus is so old and powerful, he would be able to influence her as well."

"I didn't think vampires could influence other vampires," said Celeste.

"Typically they cannot. But Magnus is extremely old and with age comes power. That coupled with the blood bond makes it possible."

"So Magnus was here tonight, and he wiped out my memories of seeing him?" asked Dani.

"Yes, I believe so."

"What if he brainwashed Dani into trying to kill one of us?" asked Nico, glancing worriedly at Celeste.

"It is not entirely impossible," Stellan responded.

"But I don't feel brainwashed," Dani retorted. "And I swear I wouldn't hurt any of you."

"Unfortunately, it doesn't matter what you want to do. If he is controlling you there wouldn't be a thing you could do about it."

"I'm going back to the basement, aren't I?" asked Dani miserably.

Celeste crawled into bed and let out a huge yawn. She stared up at the ceiling and saw a thin crack in the shape of a V. She wondered if her father had looked at the very same spot when he was here. She closed her eyes and began drifting to sleep when a noise at the door startled her. Instinctively, she grabbed the dagger on her nightstand. The door opened slowly and as every nerve in Celeste's body tensed, she readied herself to lunge at the intruder.

"Whoa, it's me, Roman," he said as his keen night vision caught sight of the blade.

"Oh Roman! You scared me to death!" She dropped the dagger and into his waiting arms. "What are you doing here?"

"I didn't want you to be alone tonight. Not with Magnus lurking somewhere nearby and possibly controlling Dani."

Celeste suddenly became very aware of her thin nighty against Roman's bare chest and arms around her.

Noticing her unease Roman tactfully added, "I can sleep on the floor."

"No, it's fine," she said, getting back under the covers and making room on one side of the bed for him. Uneasily, he lay down next to her on top of the comforter with arms crossed chastely across his chest.

"Thank you," she said and moving his stiff arm put her head on his chest and snuggled up against him.

Chapter 16

Magnus paced back and forth in the damp, abandoned warehouse that he had settled in since his arrival in Oak Bluffs. It had been pure luck that in hunting Dani he had found Celeste, but finding her with the Constantins and the wizard would make things much more difficult for him. After watching her for a few days from afar, he was certain that this was no ordinary girl and was quite sure that she was the new Guardian. If he could kill her before she came into her full powers, he would succeed in ending an entire bloodline of guardians. He knew he had to make his move soon.

***

"I think I had a premonition last night," said Celeste as she walked into the kitchen.

"Tell me exactly what happened," said Roman, rushing over to her.

"It was Fabian - I think and he was here."

"What did you see?" asked Stellan.

"It's hard to explain. All I saw were flashes, really."

"Just tell us what you remember," said Stellan soothingly.

"Well, from how you've described Fabian, it seemed like it was him, but he was with someone else too. It wasn't Magnus, but he kind of looked like him only he was smaller and blonde. He had the same cold, dark eyes though." Celeste shuddered at the recollection.

"What else?"

"They were here in this house and Stellan, you were in the vision too. It was dark outside, and it was raining. I saw a bright flash of light, and my Wilder family key bouncing off the floor. And that's it."

"That's pretty vague. Who do we need to talk to in order to get this premonition power of yours fine-tuned?" asked Nico.

"I'm sorry, I wish I could tell you more, but that was all I saw. So maybe it wasn't Magnus the other day, maybe it was Fabian."

"No, I would have sensed it if it had been him," said Stellan, shaking his head wearily.

"Should we get help from the Council?" she asked.

"No, not yet."

"On the bright side at least her vision didn't include any of us getting killed," said Nico.

"And at least we know he is coming, so we can be prepared," said Stellan. "I will reinforce the spell to cloak the house specifically against Fabian's magic. It won't keep him away forever, but it should buy us some time."

"Roman, are you okay?" asked Celeste noticing he hadn't said a word.

He looked up, eyebrows furrowed in concentration. "Yes, fine. Nico, you should get Celeste out of here."

"No! I'm not going anywhere. I'm going to stay right here and fight with all of you."

"Stellan, please help me talk some sense into her," begged Roman.

"No, I won't let you two send me away. This is exactly what I've been training for. I'm the Guardian, and this is where I need to be. How am I ever going to learn if you protect me from every bad thing that comes my way?"

"Celeste, we know that you are very capable and if this was anyone but Fabian, I would agree with you. But he is much too powerful of an opponent for you to face right now," advised Stellan.

"And how about you, Stellan? If you send me away with Nico that just leaves the two of you to fight him alone. I won't allow it."

"Celeste so help me, if you don't go with Nico of your own accord, I will knock you out and put you into the trunk of his car myself," said Roman bristling.

"Just try it," said Celeste obstinately.

"Obviously we are going nowhere with this," said Nico. "While you three were arguing, I checked the weather forecast on my phone and if Celeste's premonition was correct, we look to be in the clear for the next few days. There's no rain in sight."

"Now there's a smart boy," said Stellan with a grin.

"Fine, then it's agreed. No one is going anywhere right now," finished Celeste.

"Well, I don't know about that," said Roman. "We need to get Dani out of here. I don't trust her being around Celeste since we don't know what Magnus might compel her to do."

"That is true, but I believe we may be able to use Dani to find Magnus. The blood bond should work both ways," said Stellan.

"Let's do it then. The sooner we find Magnus and deal with him the better. One evil immortal is more than enough to handle," concluded Roman.

***

"I hate small-town America," said Alek as he examined the dingy hotel room in disgust.

"No one forced you to come," said Fabian, "and it is essential that we maintain a low profile."

Alek snorted contemptuously. "As if I would miss the final encounter between you and the Constantins."

"Yes, I do imagine it will be a confrontation to remember," Fabian said with a gleam in his eye.

"Should we find that traitor Magnus first?" asked Alek.

"I haven't yet decided if he's more useful to me dead or alive."

Alek peeked outside through the dirt-encrusted blinds. "He may know where they are."

"Yes, that is true. But how difficult could it be to find two wayward vampires in a trifling town like this one?"

"Well, the sooner we finish this, the faster I can get back to my summer vacation in Iceland," said Alek.

"Patience Alek, our little trip will soon be over, and I will have my prize."

"It can't be soon enough."

Fabian crossed the distance between them and towered over Alek scowling. "I have waited a long time for this. Do not provoke me!"

"Yes, of course my liege, I apologize for my insubordinate words."

Momentarily appeased, his tone returned to normal. "The irony of it all Alek, is that they have no idea that their deaths will bring back the object of my desire. The one thing I have longed to possess for over a century – their mother."

***

"Dani you have to concentrate," urged Stellan.

"I'm trying."

Stellan and Celeste crouched beside Dani as she sat pouting on the cold basement floor. Roman and Nico looked on attentively from the top of the stairs. They had been banished when Dani said their hovering was making her nervous.

"Feel the blood running through your veins and focus on it. Then open your mind and follow where it leads you," continued Stellan in his most soothing voice.

"I don't feel anything."

"Please try Dani. This is really important. If we find Magnus and kill him then you don't have to stay in the basement anymore. Don't you want that?" asked Celeste. She had resorted to talking to her like she did to Brian's little sister, Maxi. Strangely, it seemed to work.

"Okay, let me try again," she said, closing her eyes and breathing in and out slowly.

Celeste sat down across from Dani and reached out for her hands, then began to breathe rhythmically with her. Celeste felt a wave of warmth stemming from their joined hands and suddenly, a jolt surged through her body. A clear picture of an old abandoned warehouse flashed through her mind.

"He's in a warehouse!" the girls shouted in unison.

After describing the vision in detail to the others, they narrowed down the possibilities to a few run down warehouses by the pier in Oak Bluffs.

"I can fly back and do a quick recon mission, once I've found him I'll let you know," said Nico eager to finally do something.

"I don't like you going by yourself," said Celeste.

"He won't even know I'm there, trust me," he said with a wink. "Be back soon!"

Celeste trailed after him onto the back porch and watched him take off into the sky. Her concerned eyes followed the white falcon as it soared high above the clouds and finally disappeared.

"Don't worry about him," said Roman coming up behind her, "he can be quite capable when he sets his mind to it."

Celeste dug her heels into the ground, clenched her fists and looked obstinately at Roman and Stellan. "I am going," she announced.

There was no way Celeste was getting left out of this one. After much discussion, it had been decided that she would be allowed to accompany them to join Nico on the hunt for Magnus. Dani Lynn's involvement was another topic of heated debate. To Dani's disappointment, everyone agreed it was too risky to bring her along not knowing the extent of Magnus' control over her.

"How long do you think it will take Nico to find Magnus?" asked Celeste anxiously.

"It shouldn't be long now. He's an excellent tracker, and thanks to Magnus' creator bond with Dani it seems that you two pin-pointed the location rather accurately," said Stellan.

"I should probably call my mom before we go, just in case."

"Just in case what?" asked Roman with an edge to his voice. "Do you think I would ever let you come with us if I thought anything could happen to you?"

"No, of course not. I just meant in case it got late, and I didn't get to talk to her. I didn't want her to worry that's all."

Celeste slipped a reassuring hand in Roman's for a brief moment before walking out of the kitchen and up the winding stairs. He stared after her pensively until she disappeared around the corner.

"Are you really that certain about our chances against Magnus?" asked Stellan.

"Yes I am. We've faced him before and have managed to get away unscathed. This time *we* are going after him so we have the element of surprise on our side. And besides, I would die first before letting any harm come to Celeste."

Stellan put a reassuring hand on Roman's powerful shoulder, and he felt it tense under his grip. "We will need that confidence, but remember Magnus is over a thousand years

276

old. He is strong and smart so we must not underestimate him."

"Can't we have Celeste summon the Council? Isn't it their job to keep her safe?" Roman's hands flew up in frustration.

"Well, yes, to a certain extent anyway. If the Council stepped in every time a guardian's life was in danger, they wouldn't get anything else done. It is the nature of the guardian's job to be constantly at risk."

"Then what are you thinking? How come you agreed to let Celeste come with us?" Roman implored.

"I have a plan, but it's risky and I don't believe you will approve of it," said Stellan.

"Tell me anyway," said Roman, running his hands through his unruly hair in an attempt to calm his nerves.

"In a way, Celeste is our secret weapon. He doesn't know what she is or what powers she has. If we can lure him out, and make him believe that he has a chance at capturing her, we can catch him unaware."

Roman glared at Stellan. "So basically you want to use Celeste as bait?"

"Yes, but we will never lose sight of her. I can open a portal a hundred yards away from the warehouse and watch from there. Nico can be in the air and you and I will be hidden nearby. While Celeste distracts him, you and Nico can catch him off guard, and I will come in behind you if needed."

"I don't like putting her at risk like that."

"I'm in," said Celeste appearing in the doorway.

Roman was not pleased, but with one look at her determined face, he knew there would be no arguing with her.

Stellan filled them both in on the details of his plan while they waited impatiently for word from Nico.

"Nico just called to report that he found Magnus," said Roman. "He's at the warehouse by Pier 11."

"Then it's time," said Stellan.

"Are you ready?" Roman asked Celeste.

"I am," she said reaching out for his hand.

Stellan waved his hand and the portal opened before them in a blue blur. Celeste could feel the whirling vortex pulling her towards it. She gripped Roman's hand tightly and the three of them dove in with weapons in tow.

"Magnus! Magnus come out, I'm here to exchange my life for the lives of Nico and Roman," shouted Celeste. She stood a couple paces from the rundown warehouse and nervously rotated Roman's mother's ring around her finger.

I can do this. I must be strong.

Magnus peeked out of the rusted warehouse door looking perplexed. "What are you doing here, you silly girl?"

Celeste knew her act had to be convincing for them to succeed. She put on her most sincere face and bravely continued. "Roman and Nico are missing, and I know you took them. I'm here to surrender myself, just please let them go."

Magnus knew Fabian had been after the brothers, but was it possible that he was here in Oak Bluffs and had captured them already? A chill went down his spine. Double-crossing Fabian was never a good idea, especially if he was close by, but

Magnus pushed the thought aside. He had to find out for certain if this impetuous human girl was indeed the new Guardian.

"Fine, I admit that I do have them. They are inside. Come with me and I'll show you."

Celeste could feel every nerve in her body on edge, but on the outside she remained calm. Like a duck swimming on a still lake, outwardly she seemed unflustered but just underneath the surface, her feet paddled furiously. This is what it meant to be a Guardian; this is what she had been training for. She felt the heavy weight of her sword in her backpack, and its presence lessened her fear.

"Nice place," she said.

"I was attempting to remain inconspicuous, which I've obviously failed at since you've found me." He paused dramatically. "How did you find me anyway?"

"We all have our secrets," she said. He chuckled, but did not pursue his questioning.

Celeste followed him deeper into the dark, empty warehouse, taking note as she walked hoping she could find her way back out if necessary. Finally they reached a dark room with no windows and only crude furnishings – a couple of folding chairs and a cot on the floor with a drab blanket tossed aside.

Magnus cocked his head arrogantly, and held the door open for her to enter. As she slid by him, her eye caught the glimmer of the amber amulet hanging from his neck. There was something about it that caught her attention. Magnus noticed her interest and swiftly tucked it away under his shirt.

"Please have a seat," he said motioning to the chair.

"No thanks, I'd rather stand," she said, arms crossed obstinately over her chest. "Now where are Roman and Nico?"

"Patience, little girl. I have a few questions for you first."

Magnus eyed her up and down suspiciously and apparently unable to come to a satisfactory conclusion, he continued, "What are you?"

"What do you mean what am I?"

"You associate yourself with vampires and a wizard, so I hardly believe that you are an ordinary mortal girl."

"Think what you want Magnus, but I'm not telling you anything."

Annoyed by her obstinacy, Magnus turned away from her contemplating his options. Celeste looked around anxiously eyeing the blacked-out skylight above her head. Suddenly, Magnus spun around, inches from her face, with a crazed look in his eyes and fangs protruding. She jumped back, startled, but quickly regained her composure. She unsheathed her sword from her backpack, pointing it at him menacingly.

"Oh my, this is just wonderful!" he said with a sinister chuckle. "I was right! You are the new Guardian. I would recognize that symbol anywhere."

Without flinching Celeste asked, "You know my family symbol? Have you met others like me?"

"Of course, little Guardian. I have undoubtedly killed many of your family members along with countless other guardians."

Celeste's head was spinning, but she couldn't stop now. "Were you the one who killed my father?"

"I suppose I might have. It's hard to keep track these days, I've killed so many people in my thousands of years on this earth. What did he look like?" he asked with an evil glimmer in his black eyes.

A blinding anger swelled through Celeste and she lunged at Magnus with her sword. He effortlessly batted her aside, as easily as a horse swats a pesky fly with its tail. But she got back up and charged at him once again. Instinctively, she reached for the amulet around his neck and tore it off the chain. The look of alarm on his face confirmed its importance; although why it was significant Celeste still had no clue. As he was preoccupied with retrieving the jewel, which had clattered onto the floor, Roman and Nico came crashing through the skylight above and landed on top of him.

Magnus was momentarily dazed by the impact, and he struggled beneath the weight of the pair. The bright morning sun filled the dark room, and Magnus shrieked as the scorching rays burned his white flesh.

"The amber amulet is what protects him from the sun! Don't let him get it!" yelled Celeste.

She rushed toward them and plunged her sword into Magnus' chest, but missed his heart. With a howl, he fought off his attackers and broke free to escape into the shadows as the sword clanged to the floor. The burns and wound had slowed him down though, and as he tried to transform, Roman tackled him to the ground. Nico was right behind him about to pounce when Magnus' strength returned and he flung Roman off of him like a rag doll.

"Valiant effort boys," Magnus said mockingly.

His wound was almost healed, and without that advantage it was unlikely they would take him down. Celeste watched wide-eyed as Magnus ran straight toward her. She stood unmoving with sword drawn, the sun bouncing off of her golden curls.

"Ha! You really are the Guardian aren't you?" he said pausing in front of her with a look of admiration. "It will be my pleasure to kill you."

He lunged toward her with fangs bared, pushing her out of the light and knocking her sword to the ground. Out of the corner of her eye, she saw Roman and Nico just a few feet behind him. She hesitated for a moment, and then resolutely shut her eyes and let his fangs clamp down on her neck. Distracted by the frenzy of the bloodlust, he didn't hear the brothers close in on him from behind. Roman hurled himself on top of Magnus who was forced to release his grip on Celeste. She squirmed free and ripped the sleeve from her shirt to staunch the blood flowing from her neck. Roman pinned Magnus' torso to the floor while Nico held his lower half down in the sunlight.

Magnus shrieked in anger.

"Now!" yelled Roman.

With one fierce stab, Celeste ran her glimmering sword straight through Magnus' heart. His black eyes bulged out in shock as he realized imminent death was upon him. He convulsed hideously for a moment and then disintegrated into a pile of ash.

"Wow, that was disgusting," said Nico, covered in dust.

"Are you all right?" Roman asked Celeste.

"I think so. I just need to sit down," Celeste said collapsing to the ground.

Roman sat down on the floor cradling her as a single tear rolled down her cheek. He gently wiped it away.

"Excellent job my dear," said Stellan, appearing out of nowhere with a fiercely proud look in his eye.

"Nice of you to finally show up," said Nico, dusting himself off.

Stellan offered his hand, and Celeste took it, picking herself up off the ground. She looked up at him and couldn't help the smile that spread across her face.

"Well the good part about killing ancient vampires is that there is no body to get rid of," said Nico, stretching out lazily on Stellan's couch.

"Way to look on the bright side," said Celeste.

"We should all be celebrating," said Dani. "Magnus is dead, and I can finally come out of the basement!"

Dani's giddiness was contagious and soon they were all laughing, but in the back of their minds they knew that killing Magnus was only a temporary reprieve. Fabian was still out there.

"Dani is right, let's enjoy our moment of victory," said Stellan. "I believe I have a bottle of champagne I've been saving for a special occasion such as this." Stellan returned quickly with a tray of elaborate champagne flutes, and Celeste helped him pass them out.

"To Celeste," toasted Stellan, "our new Guardian. May she have a long and blessed life and may all of her victories be as successful as this one."

"To Celeste," they all said in unison, clinking their glasses.

"You know, Magnus killed my father," said Celeste, as she and Roman lay in her bed in the quiet darkness.

"He admitted it?" he asked, turning toward her.

"Yeah, pretty much."

"I'm so sorry, Celeste. But now I understand why you attacked him like that. You were incredible!"

"I lost it when he said that. He was so snide about it too, like killing my father was too insignificant for him to even remember. I felt this overwhelming urge to rip his head off. It was much worse than when I was around you or Nico when I first became a Guardian. It was scary," she said.

"It's all part of being a Guardian, I believe. Your powers seem to be fueled by your emotions. But that's a good thing, Celeste. You feel everything so intensely, and if you can focus that energy, you'll be unstoppable."

Celeste rolled over to face him. "Thanks for always making me feel better, Roman. Sometimes I worry that I won't live up to everyone's expectations though."

"You already have," he said kissing her sweetly.

She smiled looking into his deep blue eyes feeling as though she were being swallowed up inside of them – wanting to be.

"You were unbelievable today. It took a lot of courage to do what you did, and you didn't even think twice about doing it. You have the heart of a hero, and I know you are going to be greater than anyone could ever imagine."

"I love you Roman," she whispered.

"I love you more than you will ever know," he responded.

With Fabian's impending arrival looming over them, Stellan had thought it best for everyone to remain at his house for a few more weeks. When Celeste had told her mom that she would be extending her stay, she hadn't taken it well. Celeste tried to spare her most of the details; she didn't want to give her mother more to be concerned about.

"I promise I'll be home soon," she said to her mom on the phone.

"I miss you sweetie, and I know that you're doing very important things, but spending your last summer before college with your friends is important too."

"I know Mom, which is why I was thinking about coming home for the day. Stellan is really happy with my progress, and he said I deserved a break."

"That's wonderful news! I know you'll want to see Brian and Natalie, but do you think you can spare some time for your mother?"

"Of course, Mom. I'll be home around noon, and we can have lunch together."

"Perfect! I'm so happy I'm going to see you!"

"Me too, Mom. See you in a few hours," she said. After she hung up the phone, she realized she was nervous about returning home. She had changed so much in the last few weeks, and she wasn't sure she would fit back into her old life anymore.

"It's not fair that I can't go with you guys," said Dani pouting. She had strategically positioned herself in front of the door with her jaw clenched and arms crossed.

285

"I'm sorry you can't come Dani, but you know that if you go out in the sunlight you'll burst into flames," said Celeste, trying to sound sincere.

"This sucks! Being a vampire is no fun at all. I can't go out in the daylight, I can't see my friends or family, and you won't even let me bite people!"

Nico attempted to suppress the smile that was forming at the edge of his lips. "Well maybe if you're a good vampire, Stellan will work on a spell to let you walk in the daylight," he said.

"You can do that?" she asked.

"There are many things that I can do, but sometimes there are things that I shouldn't," responded Stellan with a reproachful glance at Nico.

Dani crossed the room in an instant, imploring Stellan with hands pressed together tightly in supplication. "Oh please Stellan, if you can make it possible for me to go outside in the day, I promise I will never drink blood from a human again. I'll even try to survive off of squirrels, birds, or even rats – I'll do anything!"

"I don't doubt your intentions Dani," he said, pausing to pry his hands away from her iron grip, "but your instincts concern me. Bloodlust is a very powerful thing that most vampires are not strong enough to overcome."

"But look, I've been around Celeste for days and I haven't tried to bite her, not once!" claimed Dani.

"Yes, but Celeste can cut your head off with a single move," said Nico. Dani looked over at Celeste in desperation, but she only shook her head discouragingly.

"I'm sorry Dani, it is simply too soon. You are still a very young vampire, and you need to get a handle on your emotions before I give you the ability to daywalk," concluded Stellan.

"And besides Dani, even if you could come back with us, what would we do if someone in Oak Bluffs recognized you?" asked Celeste.

"I'm never going to get out of this stupid house!" Dani said in frustration as she stormed down the stairs.

Pulling into her driveway, Celeste was overcome with nostalgia at the sight of her home. She had only been gone for two months, and yet so much had happened that it felt more like years. She sat unmoving for a moment taking in all the emotions. Roman leaned across her and unbuckled her seat belt bringing her back to the present. Celeste turned to him, giving him a quick kiss and hopped out of the car.

"Mom! I'm home!" Celeste stepped inside and was greeted by the familiar scents of her childhood home. The smell of chocolate chip cookies came wafting out of the kitchen followed by her mother. She smiled at her wistfully and raced into her open arms.

"It's really great to be back home," said Celeste. She and her mom sat in the sunny backyard and nibbled on warm chocolate chip cookies after lunch.

"Then why don't you just come back already?" asked her mom.

"There are some things going on that I need to take care of, Mom. I can't come back here until I do. It's not safe for you or anyone."

Her mom gave her a worried look. "And how about you, who is going to keep you safe?"

"You don't have to worry about me, Mom. I have my Guardian powers now and everyday I'm getting stronger. Plus I have Stellan, Roman and Nico to protect me."

"I don't know Celeste. You are still my little girl, and I'll always want to protect you."

"I killed a vampire," she blurted out.

"You did what?" she asked leaping out of her seat.

"I killed him, Mom, the vampire that killed Dad."

Saying the words out loud opened a floodgate of emotions that she hadn't realized she had been suppressing. Quite unexpectedly, she found herself sobbing like a baby in her mother's comforting arms. Feeling embarrassed, she said, "I'm okay, I just feel everything so strongly now. It's part of being a Guardian I guess."

"Who was this vampire that killed your dad? And how in the world did you kill him?"

"It's a long story Mom, and I promise I'll tell you about it later. I'd rather not think about it right now," she said pausing. "I had lots of help though; I couldn't have done it without Roman, Nico and Stellan."

"You are a very brave young woman. Your father would be so proud of you."

"Remember how I told you I was having dreams about him? I see him all the time now. He's been helping to train me. It all seems so real, it's like he's really there with me."

"I'm so glad that he is helping you through this."

"Me too. I guess it's one of the positive side effects of being the Guardian."

Her mom smiled ruefully. "I wish I could see him. I miss him terribly, you know?"

"You never really talk about him. You're always so busy with your patients and the hospital. I used to think you had forgotten about him."

"Of course not, Celeste! I'm sorry if how I acted made you think that. It's easier for me not to think about him or talk about him. It hurts too much," she said with tears in her eyes.

"I thought maybe you didn't talk about him because he was a Guardian, and you were mad at him for that. And that you'd be mad at me too."

"I could never be mad at either of you for that. I may not like the idea of it, but I know it's a very important duty that you were chosen for."

Celeste smiled at her mother gratefully.

"I don't know if Stellan shared this with you, but he's been keeping me updated on your progress."

"No, he didn't tell me that," said Celeste. She wondered why he hadn't.

"You think I'm just going to send you off to live with a man I hardly know without keeping an eye on you?"

Celeste laughed.

"It's been very enlightening. He's been very helpful actually in making me understand all of this."

"I'm glad, Mom."

"Tell me the truth though, how do you really feel about all of this?"

"It's hard. Sometimes I just want to run away from it all, the responsibility, the training, the fear, all of it. But then other times when I have my sword in my hand and I'm swinging it through the air, everything just feels so right, like this is what I was born to do."

Celeste's mom looked at her proudly as she continued.

"Stellan has been great. He's taught me so many things. He always seems to know the right thing to say. I could see why he and dad were close, and why he chose him to train me. And Roman, I don't think I'd still be here today if it weren't for him. He makes me stronger, like I can do anything when I'm with him. And he's the one who gets me through all of this craziness."

"Yes, Stellan has told me that he has been quite instrumental in your training."

"He has been." Celeste couldn't help but smile when she thought of him.

"You're in love with Roman aren't you?"

"Yes," Celeste admitted, her face reddening.

"First loves are very important, Celeste. I know I haven't been as supportive as I should have been, but I trust your judgment. If you love Roman, I know he must deserve it, even if he is a vampire."

"Thanks Mom, that means a lot to me."

"Maybe when you come back home in a few weeks, we can have him over for dinner so I can get to know him a little better. He does eat, doesn't he?"

"Yeah, he does. That would be really great," she said.

"You know, you've grown up a lot these past few weeks. I can see it in your eyes. Something has changed."

"I'm not a little girl anymore, Mom."

***

"How is it possible that that traitor has gone missing?" asked Fabian, clenching his fist angrily.

"The word underground is that he's dead – killed by the Constantins," said Alek.

"That's impossible! Magnus was over a thousand years old. Those two boys were no match for him."

"Perhaps they had help."

"Stellan?"

"That would be my guess," said Alek.

"But it is not Stellan's style to involve himself in this sort of thing. I know he cares for those boys, but he's practically retired."

"One thing is for certain: there is no way that the Constantins took Magnus out on their own. There must be a new player in town."

"Whoever it is, we will have to make sure they do not interfere with my plan. There is too much at stake, and I will not risk losing my chance at finally being reunited with Lilliana," finished Fabian.

***

Roman and Nico had been driving in silence each lost in thought. Nico turned to look at his brother and noticed a smile on his face.

"You seem different, you know?" said Nico, breaking the stillness.

"How so?"

"Happier I suppose, and more determined."

"Umhmm..."

"I don't know exactly, but it's good to see you like this. It's like you have a renewed purpose in life. I take it things are going well with Celeste?"

"Don't be nosey, little brother," Roman said with a grin.

"Oh come on Roman, it's the least you can do considering you pretty much stole her out from under my nose."

"I did no such thing," he said defensively. "Don't forget who spent nearly every night in a tree for weeks watching over her."

"Aha!" Nico announced victoriously. "I knew you felt something for her even back then!"

"Fine Nico. Yes everything is going well with Celeste, and I am happy. I feel like I finally have a purpose in this eternal life we are forced to lead, but all of that terrifies me. I have so much more to lose now."

"You're not going to lose her."

"You don't know that Nico. Fabian is coming—he could be here already for all we know. And who knows what he will do once he finds out what she is. Assuming he doesn't kill us all, what kind of life could we even have together?"

Putting a hand on his brother's shoulder, Nico said, "Roman, you need to stop and take a breath. Let's focus on one thing at a time, okay? First we'll find Fabian and kill him, just like we did with Magnus. And then you can worry about living happily ever after with Celeste."

"If only it were that easy," said Roman.

Chapter 17

As Celeste drove to the quaint town square for the annual end-of-summer barbecue to meet Brian and Natalie, she thought about the orientation package she had just received from NYU. For as long as she could remember all she had ever wanted was to go to college there, and now it couldn't be further from her mind. It wasn't that she didn't want to go; she simply couldn't imagine juggling college with her duties as a Guardian. Celeste wished that her father were here to talk to, since he was the only one that would truly understand.

How did he do both?

And then there was Roman: how could she leave him? Celeste was relieved to see the park up ahead so she could put off her worrying to another time. All she wanted was to enjoy this beautiful summer day with her friends like a normal teenager.

"Celeste, over here!" said Natalie as she waved her over eagerly.

Celeste crossed the grassy lawn to join her and Brian and a group of their former classmates. They all hovered around a long picnic table clad with a red and white checkered tablecloth and covered with half empty plastic cups and barbecue favorites.

"I'm so glad you made it home for the barbecue—it is an Oak Bluffs summer tradition after all," said Natalie, "and this could be our last one together."

Celeste looked at her friend sadly and stuck out her lower lip in a pout. "I know."

"Celeste! You made it!" said Brian as he stumbled over.

"Whoa there, are you okay?" She grabbed him by the shoulders to keep him from toppling her over. His bright green eyes were shinier than normal and there was a noticeable slurring of his words.

"Yeah, great, never been better!"

As the words came out of his mouth, Celeste was overcome by the intoxicating smell of beer. "Are you drunk in the middle of the day?"

"No, of course not," he said with a big goofy grin.

"He's been drinking for hours," said Natalie with a scowl.

"Nothing wrong with that," he said. "We are celebrating right? Summer's almost over, and everyone's going away to college, and I'm going to be stuck here in Oak Bluffs for the rest of my life while you all move on without me." There was an awkward silence as everyone seated turned to stare at Brian.

"Hey, why don't you come with me, and we'll get you some water," said Celeste, grabbing his hand like a disobedient child.

"I don't want any water. I'm going to sit right here with my new friend, Lacey and drink my beer," he said, as he plopped down on the bench and put his arm around the girl.

Celeste recognized Lacey from one of her classes. She was a junior – semi-popular with a cute blonde pixie cut hairstyle.

"Come on Celeste, let's get you a drink, then maybe Brian won't seem so obnoxious," said Natalie, glaring at him.

Celeste poured the frothy beer into her cup and as it slowly filled she thought about Brian. She couldn't remember the last time she had seen him like that. Sure, he would get drunk sometimes, but never like this and never so full of hostility.

"What is going on with him?" Celeste wondered out loud.

"He's been having a rough time lately, I think," said Natalie. "With you being gone and the summer ending and everyone getting ready to go away for college, he's been acting weird." She shrugged and dropped the spout hastily back on the keg.

"Did he say something to you?"

"No, of course not. He's too proud to admit it when he's sober anyway."

"I had no idea he was feeling that way."

"Have you talked to him much at all lately?" Natalie asked her.

"No," Celeste said. "And thanks for making me feel like a bad friend!"

"You're not a bad friend, and he knows that. You just don't love him the way that he loves you and that's bound to make things weird."

"Has he said anything about me?"

"He told me that you told him that you and Roman were together. He said he was okay with it, but I know he's not," said Natalie, pausing to take a sip of the beer.

"I don't know what to do Natalie. I can't help how I feel, but I don't want to hurt Brian. Everything I do or say is wrong. How can I fix this?"

"I don't think there is anything you can do, Celeste. He has to move on, and it's just going to take some time."

"I should go talk to him," Celeste said as she turned back toward the picnic table.

"I don't think now is the best time. He probably won't remember most of the conversation anyway."

"That's kind of what I was hoping for," said Celeste.

Sitting at the edge of the table, Celeste took a gulp of her lukewarm beer and picked at the coleslaw on her plate. She tried to enjoy herself, but she had so many things running through her mind it was almost impossible. She glanced over at Brian who had his head buried in his supersized cup. Seeing him so upset was killing her inside, and not knowing how to fix it was even worse. She watched her classmates from afar, so happy and carefree, and she felt a twinge of envy. Part of Celeste wanted to be like them – their biggest concern was deciding their fall class schedules. Then she thought about Roman and Nico and even Stellan, if she hadn't been chosen, she would never have met any of them. Roman made her feel whole again, and if she had never met him, she was certain that she would have spent the rest of her life feeling incomplete. She took another sip and as if he had sensed that she was thinking of him, she felt a vibration in her pocket and saw a text message from Roman.

How's the picnic?

She quickly typed out a response and forced herself to snap out of her funk and went to join her friends.

"Look at that junior, Lacey, all over Brian like a cheap suit!" said Natalie.

She and Celeste were sitting across from Brian and his new friend and had a front seat view of the drunken flirtations. "At least it looks like he's having fun," said Celeste.

"He has no idea what he's doing. Brian would flirt with an inanimate object at this point."

The girls sat watching the incoherent encounter between Brian and Lacey for a while longer until Celeste couldn't take it anymore and decided to intervene.

"Hey Brian, I'm going to have to leave soon, and I was hoping we could hang out a bit before I did," said Celeste.

"Why don't you come sit with my new girlfriend and me," he said, patting the empty spot next to him. Lacey, also highly inebriated, flashed a huge grin and looked adoringly at him.

Oh barf... "I'm fine right here, thanks."

"So you wanted to talk about something?" asked Brian slurring his words.

"Not in front of her," she said.

"Why not? Anything you have to say to me you can say in front of my girlfriend, Lacey," he said and proceeded to sloppily make out with her.

Celeste felt an overwhelming feeling of jealousy take root in her stomach and spread throughout her body. She inhaled a deep breath and fought to suppress the urge to strangle Lacey on the spot.

"Okay Brian, that's enough. I'm taking you home." She crossed over to the other side of the table and yanked him off of her.

He looked up at her in surprise, trying to get his eyes to focus. "I'm not ready to go, and you can't tell me what to do. You're not my girlfriend or my mother!" he said, pulling his arm out of her grasp.

"No, but I know your mother, and if she saw you like this she'd drag you out of here kicking and screaming if she had to." Celeste's voice had risen abruptly, and looking around she noticed everyone was staring. She lowered her voice, and tried to sound sweet and convincing, "Brian please, let me take you home."

He turned back to Lacey and enjoyed a last sloppy make-out session before letting Celeste lead him away.

Celeste buckled her seat belt and reached over in front of Brian to make sure his was securely fastened as well. He could barely hold his head up.

"What am I thinking? I can't take you home like this. Your dad is going to kill you and as much as I'd like to see that right now, I want to spare them," she said thinking out loud.

"Whatever," he responded.

As Celeste backed the car out, she took one last rueful glance at her happy classmates and turned towards home.

Moving Brian out of the car quickly and quietly was harder than Celeste had expected. She threw his arm over her shoulder and hauled his dead weight around the back of the house so his parents wouldn't see him. She was thankful for her Guardian strength for the ability to move his 170-plus pound frame. As soon as Brian hit the couch in her living room, he passed out cold. Shaking out her sore shoulders, she was relieved she wouldn't have to deal with drunk Brian for a while. She ran up the stairs to her room to gather some things she needed for her return to Stellan's.

***

"How is it possible that we haven't been able to locate the Constantins?" asked Fabian furiously. He was pacing the length of the grimy hotel room.

"Perhaps your magic is waning," said Alek.

"Your life will be waning if you dare to be insolent with me! I am the most powerful wizard alive. No one is greater than me!"

"Stellan must obviously be hiding them. He must be the *second* most powerful wizard," he said with a smirk.

"Instead of aggravating me, perhaps you could make yourself useful for once."

"Of course, my liege, what would you have me do?"

"Get out there and search for them. Something is blocking my magic from finding them perhaps you can locate them the old fashioned way," ordered Fabian.

"Of course," said Alek instantly transforming into an enormous vulture and flying out the door.

"Roman," said Stellan's holographic form, as it appeared in the middle of their apartment, "I've found out some information about Fabian." Nico overheard Stellan and came hurdling down the stairs. "Fabian is here in Oak Bluffs, and he's with Alek."

Roman's naturally olive complexion turned a pale white. "Who's Alek?" asked Nico.

"He's Fabian's apprentice, for lack of a better term. He's young but also quite powerful and utterly devoted. He was spotted by one of my informants not far from Celeste's house. It's imperative that we get her out of there and back here where it is safe."

Roman had already dashed to the door with his keys in hand. "Celeste isn't home—she's at that picnic in the town square with Brian and Natalie."

"Wherever she is, find her and bring her back here as soon as possible," warned Stellan.

Brian started to stir at the sound of Celeste's footsteps coming down the stairs. She looked tenderly at him and ran her hand through his unruly hair. She thought about the sight of Brian kissing Lacey and felt the jealous twinge again. She had to stop that, though, Brian wasn't her boyfriend and he could kiss whomever he wanted. *But then why do I feel this way?*

Brian cracked open one eye and, realizing where he was, attempted to sit up. "Oh man that was a bad idea," he said slumping back down dizzily.

"How are you feeling, drunko?" she asked, sitting down next to him on the sofa.

"Like I've been hit by a Mack truck," he said, rubbing his head.

"Good," she said whacking him in the stomach.

"Ugh! Are you trying to make me puke? What was that for anyway?"

"You were a world-class jerk today," she said. "All I wanted was to spend a nice afternoon with my best friends, and you ruined it!"

"I'm sorry okay? I wasn't really feeling like myself."

"Yeah no kidding, and you were making out with that Lacey girl all over the place. It was disgusting!"

"Oh right, so it's okay for you and your boyfriend to make out, but it's not okay for me?" he said.

"That's totally different--"

"It's not," said Brian interrupting. "You're the one that told me to move on, so that's what I'm doing and now you're upset at me for it?"

"That's not why I'm upset. I'm just mad that we didn't get to spend any time together because you were wasted and making out with some random girl."

"Cel, you can't have it both ways. I can't be in love with you forever and wait on the sidelines while you make up your mind."

"It's not like that. There's just so much going on right now that you don't know," she said with tears in her eyes.

"So tell me then!"

"I can't!" she said angrily wiping the tears away.

"Why not?"

Celeste considered all the practical reasons of why she shouldn't tell Brian, but in the end her heart won out. She was tired of lying to her best friend. "You know what, fine, I will tell you. I hated not telling you the truth. And it's probably a good thing that you are still drunk for this."

"Why aren't you picking up, Celeste?" said Roman desperately to her voicemail. He was speeding out of the town square back toward Celeste's house.

"She must be at home or at Brian's house. Natalie said they left the barbecue a while ago," said Nico.

"What if Fabian or Alek found her?" asked Roman with a look of panic in his eyes.

"Just drive faster Roman; we'll be at her house in five minutes."

"So Roman and Nico are vampires, your Uncle Stellan is a wizard and you're a vampire hunter of some sort?" Brian asked incredulously. "I just want to make sure I've got this all straight."

Celeste had already repeated the story a few times, and Brian was beginning to get past his skepticism. "I'm a Guardian, a protector of the human race against all things evil," she said matter of factly.

"So why didn't you take out our Vice Principal when you had the chance?"

"I'm glad you think this is a laughing matter, Brian."

"Look Cel, I don't know *how* to take all of this, but at least it explains why you've been acting so weird the past few months."

"I really wanted to tell you, but I just didn't know how to, and I didn't want to put you in danger. Stellan is not going to be happy with me for sharing."

"I promise I won't say anything, not that anyone would believe me anyway. I hardly believe it myself."

"I know what you mean. It all came as a pretty big shock to me too, especially finding out about my dad."

"I just can't believe those guys are blood-sucking vampires like in *Dracula.* I always knew there was something weird about them."

Celeste rolled her eyes at him.

"And you – I can't believe my best friend can kick demon ass. That's kind of hot actually."

Celeste shoved him playfully. "I'm super strong too."

"I was wondering how I got to the couch..."

"So now do you see why it could never work out between us?" she asked, looking at him seriously.

"No, not really. I mean, what are the chances that things are going to work out between you and a hundred-year-old vampire?"

"Brian, I'm not talking about that with you. And anyway my duties as a Guardian have to come first now. I don't even know if I'm going to go away to college anymore," she said.

"But you have to! It's what you've always wanted. You said your dad was a guardian and he still had a life. You can too. You don't have to be the Guardian and choose to be with a vampire, you can have a normal life with me."

There was such a hopeful look in Brian's eyes, and it broke her heart. She didn't know what else to say. Looking down at the table, she noticed that her phone had died. She hoped Roman hadn't been trying to reach her.

Roman and Nico burst through the front door of Celeste's house, the door barely remaining on its hinges. Celeste and Brian, who had been chatting obliviously on the couch, jumped up in surprise at their sudden entrance.

"Why didn't you answer your phone?" asked Roman, running to her and wrapping his arms tightly around her. "I thought something happened to you."

"Roman, you're crushing me," she said trying to wriggle free. "I'm okay, what's going on?"

Brian stared uncomfortably at Roman. Hearing about vampires was one thing, but being in a room with two of them had him slightly disconcerted.

Roman seemed to have noticed Brian's presence for the first time, and said, "We need to talk in private."

"It's okay, you can tell me in front of Brian. I told him everything."

"You did what?" asked Roman, letting go of her abruptly.

"I told him everything, Roman. I was tired of lying to my best friend. He deserved to know."

"What were you thinking? Are you going to tell Natalie too? How about your mailman?" He began to pace the living room waving his arms in the air agitatedly.

"Calm down Roman," said Nico.

"No, this was a mistake. Humans aren't supposed to know about the supernatural. It's against the rules," said Roman.

"You of all people should probably not be too concerned about breaking supernatural rules considering your current situation. What's that saying about throwing rocks at glass houses?" said Nico. Roman glared at his brother, and he immediately stopped talking.

"Anyway it's my secret, and it's too late because I already told him," interjected Celeste defiantly.

Roman stalked up to Celeste and stood inches from her face. "It's not too late. I can easily compel him to forget everything you said."

Celeste was not so easily intimidated. "Don't you dare," she said, finger pointed at his chest. "He's not just some human you can manipulate, he is my best friend and I need him to know. I need someone to talk to about all of this."

"So I'm not enough?" asked Roman, doubt creeping into his eyes.

"This isn't about you Roman! Keeping all of these secrets has really been weighing on me. I've always told Brian everything, and it's important to me that he knows."

Brian stood speechless, watching the heated exchange. Nico had also been holding his tongue.

"We can discuss this further on our way back to Stellan's," Nico interrupted. "Fabian is here in Oak Bluffs, Celeste. That's why we stormed into your house like the SWAT team. We've gotten a bit off track, but we have to leave *now*."

Celeste's face paled at the mention of Fabian being so close by. "I want to come with you," said Brian.

"No!" said Celeste, Roman and Nico in unison.

"I'm sorry Brian, but it's too dangerous, and I don't want you involved. It was my fault for telling you about all of this in the first place, but I won't let you get hurt because of me," she said.

"What if that wizard guy hurts you?" asked Brian, taking a step towards her.

"I won't let that happen," said Roman, stepping in front of him.

"Well that's comforting," he said.

"I'll be fine, Brian. I've become a pretty awesome fighter. I promise I'll show you my moves when I get back," she said, attempting a smile.

"We have to go," Nico implored.

Brian pulled Celeste into his arms and squeezed her tightly as Roman glared at him from the door.

"Be careful," he said, ignoring Roman's scowl.

"I will. I'll see you soon, I promise."

Brian watched worriedly as the three of them rushed into the car and sped out of the driveway. As he watched the car disappear down the road, he looked up and saw a massive vulture flying overhead.

Roman drove all the way to Stellan's house in silence. Celeste hadn't said a word either. Only Nico made an occasional quip from the back seat. It wasn't the first time that she and Roman had fought, but for some reason it felt different this time. She could tell that Roman was hurt, but she didn't understand why. Being a Guardian was her secret, and she didn't know why he had gotten so upset that she had told Brian.

307

Was Brian right? Is my relationship with Roman destined to fail? Can I really be the Guardian and have a normal life?

"Thank goodness you made it back safely," said Stellan as they rushed up the drive just as twilight set in.

"I'm so glad you guys are finally here. I've been so bored," said Dani Lynn, popping up from the basement.

"I'll grab the bags from the car," said Nico. "It looks like it's starting to rain."

Without a word, Celeste went to her room to unpack her things, and Roman took a bottle of vodka out to the back porch.

"Well, they're in a mood," said Dani walking away dejectedly.

"What's the matter with them?" asked Stellan.

"Lover's spat," said Nico.

"This isn't exactly an appropriate time for that."

"Tell that to them."

"Can we do anything to remedy the situation?" asked Stellan.

Nico replied, "Doubtful. I'm pretty sure they don't even know why they are fighting. If you want to know my opinion – Roman thinks that Brian is better for Celeste than he is. Seeing them together just makes it worse so fighting with her is easier. Celeste loves them both in different ways and is having a hard time choosing the right path given her new supernatural reality."

"You are wise beyond your years my boy," said Stellan with an affectionate pinch to Nico's cheek.

"I   try,"   said   Nico   with   a   grin.

As Celeste hung up the last of her clothes, she heard a light tap on her door. Her stomach clenched uneasily.

"Come in," she said, trying to keep her voice from shaking.

Roman walked in and she could smell the faint scent of vodka emanating from his lips as he exhaled. "Do you love him?" he asked abruptly.

"What?" asked Celeste, turning to face him.

"You know exactly what I mean. Do you love Brian?"

"Roman, I am not having this conversation with you, especially not when you've been drinking."

"Please, just answer me. I need to know."

She looked into his tormented blue eyes and felt like she had been punched in the stomach. She knew she had to be honest with him.

"Of course I love him. He's my best friend. I've known him since we were three years old! He's like a brother to me."

"And you're sure that's it? You only love him like a friend, a brother?" he asked desperately. "Because if it's more than that, it's okay Celeste. I want you to be honest with me, and be honest with yourself."

Celeste stood there speechless.

"You could have a normal life with him. You can be the Guardian and still go to college, get married, have a family. I can't give you those things. I wish I could, I would want nothing more in this world than to be able to."

"Roman..." she said with tears running down her face.

"You need to think about it Celeste," he said taking a step toward her and wiping a tear from her cheek affectionately. "I love you, but your future and your happiness is more important to me than mine is."

"Roman, no--" she said.

He put a finger to her lips quieting her sobs and kissed her sweetly on the forehead. "Just promise me that you'll think about it." And he walked out the door.

"What do you think Fabian is really doing here?" asked Nico.

"I wish I knew," answered Stellan.

"It's odd right? He could have come after us ages ago. It's been decades since he killed our parents, and why come after us now?"

Stellan shook his head, gazing into the crackling fireplace, deep in thought. He was trying to decide whether or not to share what he had learned. Decision made, he took a deep breath and said, "I've heard some rumblings from the underground. I can't confirm their accuracy, but they say he is attempting a spell of some sort."

"A spell that he needs us for?" Nico asked, leaning forward intently.

"Yes apparently. It's very dark magic from the sounds of it."

"Why didn't you tell us?"

"As I said, nothing has been confirmed, and I didn't want to worry you for nothing. I was hoping I'd be able to discover his purpose, but I haven't as of yet."

Suddenly there was a loud burst of thunder and a brilliant flash of lightning darted across the dark sky. They heard the rush of feet on the stairs and Celeste appeared in front of them, eyes wide with panic.

"Something very bad is here," she said as Roman came running behind her.

The front door flung open and landed in the living room with a crash as its hinges went flying through the air. Roman ran to Celeste and placed himself as a barrier between her and the open doorway, while Nico appeared at her flank seconds later. Outside two dark figures slowly approached.

"Get back," said Stellan as he muttered a few words and a glimmering force field appeared where the door used to be.

"Oh Stellan, don't make me laugh," boomed Fabian's voice from outside. He held up his hand and swiped it to the side and with a flash the force field was gone.

"What do you want?" asked Roman stepping forward.

"Roman Constantin, my, my how confident you've become – or is that just stupidity?" asked Fabian. "You've come a long way from that sniveling little brat I met over a century ago."

Roman's fangs dropped and a terrifying growl emanated from the depths of his core. Celeste had never seen that vicious look in his eyes before; an icy chill swept through her.

"You are not welcome here Fabian. Leave now or there will be consequences," warned Stellan.

"I believe he has threatened you, my liege," said Alek, his small frame overshadowed by Fabian's impressive one.

Fabian let out a wicked chuckle and continued, "I don't want to hurt you Stellan or that human girl. Get out of the way.

This is not your fight. This is between me and the Constantins." Fabian and Alek moved inexorably closer, two dark ominous shadows, as the wind and rain whipped around them, bending to their will.

"We are right here," said Roman. "Again I ask, what do you want from us?"

"That is something you will find out in due time. But for now, I need you both to come with me without a fight."

Roman looked at Nico, who gave him a faint nod. "Fine. As long as you don't hurt them."

"No!" said Celeste. She hurled herself in front of the brothers and unsheathed her sword, thrusting it into the air.

Roman lunged after her trying to hold her back, but as she pointed her sword at Fabian a blinding white light shot out of it that sent both Fabian and Alek flying back onto the wet lawn. Stunned, Fabian and Alek remained on the ground for a few seconds scrambling to get back to their feet.

"Stellan, get her out of here!" roared Roman.

"No, I'm not leaving you," she said, reaching for his hand.

"Celeste go now, please!" he begged.

Fabian and Alek were back on their feet and they were racing towards the open door. Nico stood in front of it, fangs bared, poised to attack. The wind was picking up and Celeste had to dig her heels into the ground to keep from getting swept away by it. She clung desperately to Roman's hand, as he pulled her towards Stellan.

"Stellan, now!" Roman yelled.

Stellan waved his hand and a swirling blue portal opened before them. Celeste squeezed Roman's hand and released it with one last look at his frantic face. Alek had reached Nico, and the two were grappling on the ground. Celeste prepared to jump into the blue abyss, Stellan right behind her. Out of the corner of her eye, she saw Fabian lunging toward her, but Roman threw himself on top of him. Fabian dodged the assault and sent Roman sprawling through the air with a flick of his finger.

"No!" cried Celeste, pausing to look back as Stellan attempted to force her through the portal.

Fabian sprung up, faster than human or supernatural eyes could follow. He shoved Stellan out of the way and grabbing Celeste, they jumped through the portal, leaving everyone else behind.

Chapter 18

"No!" growled Roman as the portal disappeared before his eyes, and he crashed onto the cold tile floor. As he pushed himself up, he felt something familiar on the ground. Picking it up, he saw it was Celeste's key which must have come off in the struggle. "Stellan, quick—open the portal. We have to go after them!"

"I can't Roman. Fabian hijacked control of it. I have no idea where they went," said Stellan.

"Where's Alek?" asked Nico.

They looked around but it was no use, Alek had disappeared into thin air.

"This can't be happening," said Roman throwing a chair across the room and smashing it to bits. "How could we lose Celeste?"

"Roman, you must calm down. Destroying my house isn't going to help her," he said, placing a wrinkled hand on his shoulder.

"Then what can we do?"

"Give me a moment. We must think rationally. Up until a few moments ago, Fabian had no idea who Celeste was. Assuming he will soon figure it out, he will then realize how valuable she is. He dare not kill her and incur the wrath of the Council."

"We need to tell the Council what happened," said Nico.

"Yes, that is exactly what we have to do. And remember, Fabian doesn't really want her; it's the two of you that he needs. He has to know that without her he would lose his leverage."

"So you think she is safe for now?" asked Roman, a glimmer of hope in his weary eyes.

"Yes, I truly do."

"Well, since no one else brought it up, what in the world was that burst of light that came out of Celeste's sword?"

"I am not sure to be honest," said Stellan. "I have never seen a guardian do anything like that."

"So it wasn't the Wilder sword?" asked Roman.

"No, Celeste's father Kristof never wielded that power."

"So you're saying it came from Celeste?"

"Yes, it would appear so. We will have to take a look back in the guardian journals to see if anything like it was ever recorded in the past."

"Whoa, what in the world happened in here?" asked Dani coming up from the basement.

"Fabian happened," said Nico. "Where have you been?"

"I was hiding in the basement. I heard all the commotion up here and I got scared." She looked down feeling embarrassed.

"They took Celeste," said Roman.

"Oh no! What are we going to do?"

"We are working on it."

"Actually Dani, if you'd like to help, you could do a little research for me," said Stellan.

"Sure, I'll do anything."

"Very good, and I am going to contact the Council right now, and then work on a tracking spell to find where Celeste has been taken. Roman, find me an article of her clothing to use for the spell."

"I have something better than that – I have the Wilder key."

***

Celeste opened her eyes and looked around groggily. She was surrounded by impenetrable rocks and towering mineral formations. Due to the damp, chilly air, she reasoned she was in a subterranean cave. But exactly where, she had no clue.

Are those stalactites or stalagmites? I should have paid more attention in geology class.

Celeste stood up and searched frantically for a way out, but the only exit was blocked by an enormous boulder. She pushed against the cold, rough surface with all her strength, summoning her newfound powers, but it was no use; it wouldn't budge. She suddenly remembered the flash that had emanated from her sword before Fabian had forced her through the portal, and began searching wildly for it. It was gone. Celeste had no idea what caused the flash of light, but whatever it was, it was powerful enough to have stunned both Fabian and Alek.

Too bad it ended up backfiring on me and getting me captured. But it was worth it if Roman and Nico are safe.

As she searched around the cave she found nothing but a few rocks and a torch to provide some light. Not finding anything she could use as a weapon, like Roman had taught her, she slumped down on the ground hopelessness setting in.

"Oh wonderful, Fabian will be so happy to see that you are awake," said Alek, appearing where the boulder had been just seconds ago. Looking at him closely for the first time, Celeste noticed how young he appeared. And had he not been the apprentice of an insane wizard, he might have even been attractive. His platinum hair contrasted his dark sparkling eyes and his mischievous grin was quite appealing – in a frightening way.

"What does he want with me?" asked Celeste, quickly getting back on her feet. She stared at the young man contemptuously; his platinum hair slicked back perfectly not a single hair out of place.

"Originally, you were simply a means to an end. But after that light show that your sword produced, he has some questions for you."

"I have no idea what that was," she said truthfully.

"Right. Come this way, then, we don't want to keep Fabian waiting."

Celeste could hear the echo of her footsteps as she followed Alek through a dark passageway, which opened up, into another cavernous chamber similar to the one where she had woken up. Seated before her on an impressive throne carved out of the rock was Fabian. A smug smile crossed his face at her approach.

"Please excuse our humble abode. I would have taken you to our motel but I couldn't risk you being tracked there, not that it was any better than this honestly."

"They'll find me wherever I am," said Celeste defiantly. She surveyed the cave, determined to find a way out or at least a weapon of some sort.

"She's got spunk," said Alek amused.

"I am counting on them to do just that. I only needed to buy some time to figure out what it is that you are."

"She is something special, it's clear," said Alek. He caressed her cheek, making Celeste's skin crawl. She whipped her head out of his grasp before he could continue.

Looking at Fabian in disgust, she asked, "What do you want with me?"

"My initial purpose for you was simply to lure out the Constantins, as our mutual friend Patrick discovered their fondness for you from the beginning. I always found it quite curious, and it wasn't until seeing you in action today that I am beginning to understand it," said Fabian.

"Yes, no wonder they were protecting her," said Alek, his dark eyes filled with excitement.

"You must be the one, the new Guardian," said Fabian almost reverently.

Celeste considered denying it, but figured it would be pointless; so instead she stood resolutely glaring at Fabian.

"Why are you with the Constantins?" asked Alek. "Aren't you supposed to kill their kind?"

"Yes and why are they protecting you? It seems that there must be more to this story, don't you think Alek?" echoed Fabian.

He nodded and looked questioningly at Celeste.

"I'm not telling you anything," she said stubbornly.

***

"What did the Council say?" asked Roman as he stopped his anxious pacing when Stellan finally appeared at the top of the steps. Celeste had only been gone for an hour, but it felt like a lifetime to Roman.

"They are using their considerable resources to track Fabian down. Making an act of aggression like this against the newly chosen Guardian will surely unleash a furious retribution on them," said Stellan.

"Fabian had to know that this would happen. What could he be up to that he would be willing to risk all of that for?" asked Nico.

"That question is precisely what worries me."

"So what are we supposed to do in the meantime, just sit around and wait?" asked Roman, who had resumed pacing.

"Technically yes, that is exactly what we are *supposed* to do. Now that the Council is involved, they will want us to stay out of it – especially the two of you."

"Well, I certainly can't sit around here doing nothing."

"I agree. That is why I started a tracking spell, and we should have some results shortly," said Stellan. "Fabian has been blocking my magic, but I think I've found a way around it."

319

"Please hurry Stellan. If anything happens to Celeste--"

"Nothing is going to happen to her Roman," he interrupted.

"We need a plan," said Nico. "When Stellan finds her, we can't just go in there blind."

"I want to help," said Dani coming down the stairs. "I read through some of those journals, but they're so long and there are so many of them. I couldn't find anything about a sword that shoots light out of it. Isn't there anything else I can do?"

"We could take her with us," said Nico. "At the very least, she could be a distraction."

"Sure, why not," said Roman. "But Nico I want you to understand something – I won't hesitate to give up my life for Celeste's. It is *us* that Fabian wants after all, but I don't expect you to do the same."

"I would do it for her anyway," said Nico, his dark eyes unwavering.

"You know there are ways we can make you talk," said Alek as he stroked the dagger on his hip.

"Don't threaten her. I will handle this," said Fabian, shoving Alek aside.

"You are no fun at all," he whined like a spoiled child.

"Celeste, I apologize for how we've been treating you," he whispered soothingly as he took a few steps toward her. "Perhaps I have gone about this the wrong way. You know, I too was once part of the Council."

"You were?" she asked.

"Yes, I was head of the Council for many years in fact. I oversaw the wellbeing of all the guardians in the world at one time."

"And what happened?"

"My colleagues and I had a difference in philosophy. I believed that guardians were no longer needed in this world, and that supernatural beings should no longer have to hide in the shadows. I wanted humans, guardians and all supernaturals to co-exist and share the world."

"But wouldn't they just kill each other?"

"Maybe at first, but I believed that over the long term we could have reached a balance of power."

"Meaning all the humans would have been dead and the supernaturals would have taken over?"

"Obviously you are just as closed minded as my colleagues at the time were. As a result of this disagreement, they banned me from the Council and sought to strip me of my powers. But I was too strong for them, and I escaped with my powers intact, as I'm sure you've noticed."

"I'm pretty sure the Council won't be happy when they find out you've kidnapped me."

"Of that I'm certain you are correct. But the Council rarely intervenes and even if they would, they have become old and weak; while I have only grown in strength, they will be no match for me."

"We'll see about that," she said.

"I see that trying to rationalize with you is getting me nowhere so I will have to try a more invasive approach," said Fabian. He stretched out his long gangly arms and grabbed hold of her head.

Celeste struggled to break free of his grasp, but he was surprisingly strong. Out of the corner of her eye, she could see red light surging from his hands as he squeezed her head with an iron grip. It felt like thousands of volts of electricity were shooting through her skull. She bit her lower lip to suppress a scream, not wanting to give him the satisfaction. When he finally let go, the cave spun before her and she collapsed to the hard rocky ground.

"What did you see?" asked Alek.

"Nothing. It cannot be. No one can close their mind off to my influence," said Fabian stunned.

"She is a Guardian: doesn't that make her immune?"

"Maybe to you or some vampire, but not to me."

"And yet, here we are..." he said with a sarcastic smirk.

Celeste's head had stopped throbbing and she had managed to pick herself off the ground along with a jagged rock that she clenched tightly in her fist.

"No matter. Whatever the reason is that the Constantins are protecting you, they should be here soon, and it will mean their imminent demise."

"I've discovered her location!" said Stellan, racing frantically down the stairs.

"Finally, let's go!" said Roman. "Are you ready little brother?"

"Of course," he said with a smile.

Roman took the Wilder family key out of his pocket and hung it around his neck for safekeeping.

"Don't forget about me!" said Dani as she came running.

Stellan waved his arms and an enormous portal opened in front of them.

"Whoa, that's pretty cool," said Dani.

"Is everyone ready?" asked Stellan.

"Yes," they said in unison, and they disappeared through the portal.

Chapter 19

"Ouch!" cried Dani as she skidded to a stop on the rocky ground. She had landed unceremoniously on her backside and was grimacing in discomfort. Stellan had managed to land on his feet, as he always did when portal jumping. Roman and Nico were already inspecting their new surroundings trying to get their bearings.

"Where are we?" asked Nico.

"It appears to be an underground cavern. The tracking spell had us hovering somewhere over the Ural Mountains right before we left," said Stellan.

"We are in Russia?" asked Roman.

"Cool, I've never even left the United States!" said Dani.

"Well, there's no time for sightseeing now. Which way do we go?"

"Follow me," said Stellan as he led the way through the dark and dank passage.

They trudged along in silence as the blackness enveloped them. The only sound was the echo of their footsteps and occasional pitter-patter of water droplets from melted ice seeping in through the cracks.

"So what's the plan?" asked Dani breaking the eerie stillness.

"There is no plan. We are going to surrender ourselves in exchange for Celeste," said Roman.

"And let him kill you?" she asked, stopping abruptly to face him.

"If that's what he wants. It doesn't matter as long as she is safe."

"Geez, maybe I shouldn't have come. How do you know he won't double cross us and kill us all? That's always what happens in the movies with these evil villains."

Nico cracked a smile. "We don't really know what's going to happen."

"So don't you think we should have a back-up plan at least?"

"Dani, that's enough! No one said you had to come. You can still turn back," rebuked Roman. With an exasperated sigh, Dani shrugged her shoulders and followed Stellan further into the darkness.

"They're here," announced Alek. "A portal was opened at the mouth of the cave. They should arrive momentarily."

Fabian grunted. "That was quicker than I thought. Stellan's magic must not be as weak as I had imagined."

Celeste thought she saw a flash of concern in Fabian's hard eyes, but it was gone now. He reached for her and grabbing her by the arm shoved her toward Alek.

"Do something with her so that she doesn't interfere."

"My pleasure," said Alek with a wicked grin.

With a flip of his wrist, Celeste found herself in some sort of invisible cage. She banged against the clear walls and felt a lapse of hysteria set in as she pictured a pantomime she had once seen as a child. She paced around the cage determined to find a way out, no matter how ridiculous she looked. She was still holding the rock she had picked up earlier and tightly held it concealed in her fist. She knew Roman and the others would be here soon and the thought of what Fabian might do to them terrified her. Suddenly, she heard a loud explosion and saw rocks crumbling down at the edge of the chamber. Through the rubble came Stellan followed by Roman, Nico and Dani trailing behind. Celeste's heart plummeted.

"Finally! I thought you would never get here," said Fabian. He had a malicious grin on his face and his eyes were twinkling in the torchlight as he slowly walked towards them.

"Have you come to join the party?" asked Alek with his usual glibness.

"We are here for Celeste," said Stellan, his stern eyes unblinking.

Celeste caught Stellan's eye and tried to send him a wordless warning from her invisible prison. They were stepping right into a trap, and she was helpless to stop them.

"Ah yes, your precious little Guardian. Well as you can see, she is perfectly fine," he said with a nod towards Celeste.

"Fabian, don't be a fool. Now that you know who she is, you would be wise to let her go immediately," said Stellan.

"Now what would be the point of that? I've come so far; I don't think I can turn back now. Besides, having the Guardian under my power could prove to be quite useful."

"This was never about her," said Roman stepping forward. "You came for us, and here we are. Let her go with Stellan, and my brother and I promise not to put up a fight."

"As if you could," added Alek. What he lacked in height, he more than made up for in bravado.

Celeste looked desperately to Roman and she could see the torment in his steely eyes as he returned her gaze. She couldn't let him do this. She wished she had her sword more than anything.

"Fine, it's a deal," Fabian said extending his hand. "Alek, put the Constantins in the cell with Celeste."

"Let her out first," said Stellan, ignoring his overture.

"But why? I thought they would want to have a moment to say goodbye. And besides she is my insurance policy that the boys behave. You, Stellan, I have no further use for."

And with a wave of his hand, he flung Stellan like a ragdoll against the side of the cave where he landed on the floor with a crash. Roman's fangs extended and he let out a vicious snarl.

"Uh, uh, uh," said Fabian wagging his finger at Roman. "You promised you would not fight me. Stellan will be fine, he just needed a little time out."

Celeste looked on in horror as Alek escorted Roman and Nico toward her and opening an invisible door shoved them in. Celeste ran to Roman wrapping her arms around him. As she did, she felt the leather string around his neck and saw the Wilder key tucked under his shirt. Pretending they were engaging in a romantic embrace, Celeste slipped the cord over her head. She quickly clasped the key in her hand, and focused all her power into summoning the Council as Dante had taught her. All she could do now was hope that it worked.

"Roman, I won't let you do this. I won't let you both die for me," she said, holding his face between her shaking hands.

"It's not up to you Celeste. It is our choice, and this is what we have decided. We've both lived very long lives. Your life has just begun, and I want you to live it to the fullest," he said, his voice thick with emotion.

Celeste looked over at Nico who nodded in agreement.

"But I can't imagine a life without you in it," she said as a tear rolled down her cheek. "I don't want to live without you. I can't."

Their private moment was shattered by a burst of laughter from Fabian. He had moved across the room and his loathsome face hovered just inches from them.

"Oh Alek, aren't we dense? All this time we were searching for a hidden reason as to why the Constantins protected her, and we missed out on the most obvious one of all. Roman is in love with her!"

"Love? Well that is preposterous, who ever heard of a vampire being in love with the Guardian?" asked Alek chuckling.

"And she loves him too!" said Fabian. "This is just too much!"

Celeste's blood was boiling; she wanted nothing more than to rip that smug smile off of Fabian's face. In a fit of anger, she hurled the rock she had been gripping and it tore through the invisible barrier. The rock flew through the air so quickly it caught Fabian entirely off guard hitting him squarely on the forehead.

"You insolent thing!" yelled Fabian, holding his head where the blood had started to flow.

At the sight of fresh blood, Dani who had been huddled in a corner frozen in fear, momentarily lost control. With a savage growl, she lunged at Fabian, knocking him to the ground. Everything had happened so quickly that she was able to get a bite into his neck before he zapped her sending her crumbling to the floor.

"Alek!" roared Fabian furiously as he held onto his neck to try and stop the bleeding. "Enough of this, we must start the spell immediately."

"How did you do that?" asked Nico.

"I'm not sure," said Celeste. "I was just so angry, so I threw the rock as hard as I could. I have no idea how it broke through the barrier."

"Can you get yourself through it?" asked Roman.

"I've been trying, but I haven't been able to."

"You have to keep trying," said Roman with an encouraging touch to her shoulder.

"Did you see Dani take out a chunk of Fabian's neck?" asked Nico. "That was awesome!"

"Let's keep the celebrating down for now, since we are still stuck in this cage. A little vampire bite isn't going to keep Fabian down for long," said Roman.

Fabian remained on the ground scowling, fastidiously wiping away the blood from his black robe.

"I've been trying to summon the Council, but I don't know if it's working. I've never done it before; shouldn't they have answered me by now?" Celeste clutched the key and focused intently. Again, she fervently wished for her sword.

329

Alek had appeared with an ancient leather-bound book, and was flipping through it expertly. The worn cover was filled with dark symbols that Celeste immediately recognized as black magic. Once he found the page he was looking for, he helped Fabian off the ground and placed it in his arms.

"Get me the first one," he said to Alek.

Alek appeared inside the cage and taking hold of Nico popped back out taking him with him.

"No!" said Roman, trying to reach out for Nico, but he slipped right through his fingers. Roman hurled himself at the invisible wall with a growl, but it remained unmoving.

"Don't worry, you'll be next," said Alek with an evil grin.

With a flick of his hand, Fabian snapped Nico's neck and fastened him standing upright to the cave wall with iron restraints around his limp neck, wrists and ankles. He took out an ornate dagger and sliced open each of Nico's wrists, inserting a pin in the wound so that the skin couldn't heal itself. As the blood came gushing out, Alek positioned an ancient looking vessel on each side to contain the dark red liquid. Roman began pacing desperately inside the cage. He bit his lower lip to keep from screaming.

Celeste could feel the pain radiating from him at the sight of his brother's suffering. She grasped her key tightly and summoned the Council again, repeatedly imploring that they come to her aid. Celeste placed her arm around Roman's broad shoulders, holding him as he watched in helplessness as Fabian tortured his brother.

"I'm so sorry," she whispered.

Fabian began to read from his book in a strange language, and as he did Nico began to come to. "Demonium resurectus omniam filibus..."

"What are you doing?" he asked weakly.

Fabian ignored him and continued the chant as Nico's blood continued to pour into the vessels.

"Alek, I'm ready for the next one."

Celeste looked at Roman terrified. She couldn't lose him, not now and not like this.

"Everything's going to be okay," he said. "He'll let you go once he has what he wants. I'll make sure of it." He caressed her cheek lovingly, looking deep into her eyes.

"No, Roman, please don't leave me. You have to fight him!"

"I'll always be with you Celeste, I love you," he said as Alek yanked him out of the cage while Celeste scrambled to hold on.

"No!" screamed Celeste. "No!"

As Roman was dragged away, Celeste looked down at the beautiful ring he had given her and couldn't believe how useless she felt. There was nothing she could do but watch in disbelief as Fabian took the lives of those she loved most.

No! I won't let this happen!

Celeste plopped down on the hard floor and shut her eyes. She envisioned being back in Stellan's sun-filled yard meditating like he had taught her. She focused all of her power and for what felt like the millionth time, Celeste clung onto the Wilder key desperately reaching out to the Council and wishing for her sword.

"My brother and I have done everything you wanted Fabian. Now let Celeste, Stellan and Dani go," said Roman. His voice was calm but forceful.

"Alek, chain him to the wall."

"Wait!" said Roman planting his feet firmly in the ground. "Give me your word that you will let them go."

"Fine, fine, you have my word that I will let them go as soon as I get what I want from the two of you," conceded Fabian.

"Okay, then let's get on with this," he said with one final rueful glance at Celeste.

Fabian repeated the exercise with the dagger on Roman as he was restrained against the wall. The blood flowed rapidly and filled the vessels as Fabian continued his chanting. Nico had become very pale, and could hardly hold himself up any longer. Celeste noticed a slight movement from where Stellan lay, and to her relief she saw that he was waking up.

"That's enough!" cried Celeste. "You're killing them!" She jumped to her feet and threw herself against the invisible barrier. She hit it with a smack. Dazed, she knelt down on the floor, willing herself to stand back up. She put her hand down to push herself up, and felt something icy and metallic under her hand.

It can't be...

It was her sword! It had appeared from thin air as if by magic. She glanced around cautiously and saw that no one had seen it. She left it where it was, partially submerged in the dirt. She had about five seconds to come up with a plan.

"Alek, it's time. Bring her," said Fabian.

Roman looked worriedly at Celeste, but noticed that Alek didn't make a move toward her. Instead, he suddenly disappeared from the chamber and returned moments later wheeling in a shrouded body prone on a table. Fabian carefully removed the sheet, gazing intensely at who or what lay underneath. Roman, nearly unconscious from blood loss, looked up in shock when the cover was removed.

"Mom?" he asked and then everything went black.

Celeste picked up the sword and holding it high over her head focused all of her power into it. She felt a surge of energy flow through her and a blazing white light shattered the invisible barrier. Fabian, momentarily distracted from whatever was under the shroud, spun toward her.

Simultaneously, Stellan sprung up and unleashed a fiery flash of lightning blinding everyone around him. Celeste put her arm up to shield her eyes from the bright lights and out of the corner of her eye saw Dante, Sierra and the other three members of the Council (whom she didn't know by name) crash through the outer wall of the cavern.

In the midst of the chaos, Celeste ran to Roman and Nico. She removed the pins from their wrists to stop the blood loss and began working on freeing them from the restraints.

"Are you okay?" she asked. Nico looked deathly pale, and though she had removed the manacles, he hadn't moved.

"Of course. See, we're starting to heal already," said Nico with a forced smile and then collapsed to the floor.

"Nico!" she cried.

"I'm okay, I just need to rest," he said and curled up into a ball against the rock.

Roman looked as white as a ghost, and didn't say a word. She helped him down and was rewarded with a reassuring smile. She propped him up against the wall next to Nico.

"Stay here, I'm going to need some help getting you out of here." Celeste ran over to Dani shaking her vigorously until she woke up. "Get up! We have to get out of here."

Dani opened her eyes and looked around dazed.

"Come on Dani, you have to help me get Roman and Nico out while Fabian is distracted. I can't do it by myself. They've lost too much blood."

"Okay, okay, I'm up. I'm coming."

As the Council members came crashing through the wall, Fabian attempted to pick them off one by one. There was a frightening glint in his eye as he prepared for battle.

"It's been much too long, Seraphina," he said to a fearsome raven-haired woman, and with a wave of his hand sent her flying across the room. Dante leapt up in time to catch her before she hit the stone pavement and lowered her gently to the ground.

While Dante tended to his companion, Fabian moved on to the next one. "Balthazar, I didn't think you were still alive," he said derisively to an elderly graying Council member. Before he could repeat the move on Seraphina, Balthazar lunged at him with his spear.

"My, you are pretty spry for such an old fellow," taunted Fabian, dodging the assault.

Suddenly, Alek appeared in between Fabian and his attacker. Balthazar paused, spear in hand ready to strike at either foe.

"Alek, get Dante! He's been meddling in my affairs for far too long. I'll handle this old man," instructed Fabian.

"It would be my pleasure," said Alek. He crossed the room in a blur and flung himself on Dante. Dante struggled to regain his balance and unsheathed his sword just in time to strike at Alek. With a mighty swing of his arm, he slashed Alek across the chest. Reeling from the blow, Alek took a few steps back then raised his hand to hurl a large boulder at his attacker. Dante sprang away just in time to avoid the blow as the rock hit the cave wall and smashed into a thousand pieces sending shrapnel across the room. Seraphina, who had been unconscious, now rose to her feet to help Dante. Faced with two angry guardians wielding hefty swords, Alek stopped.

"Wait!" he said, holding both hands up.

"Finish them!" shouted Fabian from across the cavern. Balthazar was slumped in a corner and Fabian had another Council member on his knees. With a terrifying gleam in his eye, he looked at Dante and then back at the man kneeled before him and with a wave of his hand snapped his neck.

"Bastard!" screamed Dante.

"No! Markus!" cried Seraphina, running toward her fallen companion.

Alek considered the situation at hand, and with a sly twitch of his mouth disappeared into the wall in a puff of smoke, leaving Dante frustrated and Fabian outnumbered.

Stellan, Dante and the three remaining Council members had Fabian cornered and successfully pinned up against the wall. He fought back with black magic of his own, dark flashes of light emanating from his hands. Celeste looked on in amazement at what would have been a spectacular light show had the circumstances not been so dire.

"You fools!" said Fabian. "You think you can defeat me?"

He summoned a whirling tornado that ripped through the group of Council members, tossing them unceremoniously about the cave. In the midst of the fighting, Celeste and Dani each took a Constantin brother and tucked them safely away in an alcove away from the chaos. They were still too weak to move.

"Stay here, I have to go back and help," said Celeste.

"Celeste, please be careful," said Roman, but he didn't try to stop her.

Celeste sprinted back towards the fighting, firmly gripping her sword. She could feel the adrenaline coursing through her veins, and it felt good. Something had clicked inside of her, and she was in full on Guardian mode.

When she reached the others, she found Stellan barely holding himself up by a wall. His clothes were tattered, and there were cuts all over his worn face. The rest of the Council members were in no better shape; some had been badly injured by the tornado. The winds, having been swallowed up by a portal opened by Sierra, had started to die down, but Fabian was nowhere in sight.

"Quick, Celeste, you must find him before he gets away," said Dante, struggling to get to his feet. "We'll be right behind you." He had a large, bloody gash across his forehead.

Celeste nodded and took off in the direction he had pointed. She sped through the dim, winding passageways guided only by the light of her sword and her instinct. She could feel Fabian's evil presence nearby. She slowed and crept silently through the shadows. Turning a corner, she saw him bending over the body on the cart. He stared at it reverently, gently caressing the arm which hung limp at its side. It was a look she had never seen in Fabian's eyes, and for a moment she pitied him.

Behind her, Celeste heard a rush of footsteps approaching; Fabian reacted to them as well and turned around, finally seeing Celeste. Dante and the others rounded the corner, swords in hand ready to resume the fight.

"Give up now, and we will spare your life in return for your years serving on the Council," said Dante. He stood poised for battle, back straight and shoulders high. Stellan, Sierra and the others flanked him on both sides, faces unflinching.

Fabian let out an ominous chuckle. He made a move towards the body, but Dante stopped him, crossing the distance between them in the blink of an eye. He clutched Fabian by the neck and held him high in the air.

"Surrender," hissed Dante.

"And what live powerless for the end of my days in a prison? I'd rather die."

"If that is what you wish," he said coolly. All of the Council members pooled their energy and a powerful force swept over Fabian.

"No! You can't take away my powers!"

As he struggled futilely against Dante's iron grip, Sierra approached him, wielding a sword similar to the one Celeste

337

had but with its own unique hunter symbol. With a sharp thrust, she drove it into his heart. His body contorted unnaturally then began to shrivel leaving only a charred black corpse in its place.

Standing behind Stellan, Celeste let out the breath she'd been holding as she saw Fabian's lifeless body crumple to the ground. Dante hovered over it, mumbling a few words Celeste couldn't make out. The other Council members had gathered around it as well. They formed a circle and with hands held tightly they stood together in silence.

Celeste needed to get back to Roman and Nico. She turned away, leaving the strange and unfamiliar scene in front of her to hurry back to the center of the cave. As she ran, she looked around for Alek of whom she had lost track of since the appearance of the Council, but he was gone.

"It's finally over," she said letting relief sink in.

"I knew you could do it," whispered Roman.

Looking down she saw Roman's haggard expression, and crouched down to sit next to him. She picked up his head and cradled it in her lap. He still looked so pale, she thought worriedly.

"Roman, please take some of my blood," she said, offering her wrist.

"No, I can't," he said shaking his head.

"You are going to need your strength to get through the portal – both of you are."

"I'm feeling better Celeste. Dani and I shared a blood bag that she had brought for a snack," said Nico.

"And you didn't save any for Roman?" she asked indignantly.

"Sorry, that was my fault. I didn't realize how hungry I was," said Dani, flushed with embarrassment. "After I gave the Council my blood to heal them, I needed to replenish."

Celeste could see that Roman was having a hard time sitting up, and he was doing a poor job trying to hide it. "Oh this is ridiculous," said Celeste picking up the dagger from the floor and slicing her wrist.

"Celeste, don't!" said Roman.

But it was too late. She put her bleeding wrist up against his mouth, and he was unable to control his reaction. His fangs fastened onto her soft skin and the blood he desperately needed trickled into his mouth.

"Don't worry, I'm fine. I'll tell you when to stop, and you will. I trust you," she said looking into his worried eyes.

"What do you think you are doing?" cried Dante as he walked over to see Roman feeding from Celeste.

Roman quickly let go of her arm and retracted his fangs, a mortified look crossing his beautiful face.

"I'm saving his life!" Celeste insisted.

"Do you know how precious Guardian blood is? And you are wasting it on a vampire!"

"A vampire saved *your* lives today, too. If Dani hadn't given all of you her blood, you wouldn't have been strong enough to defeat Fabian." Dante had the decency to look down, slightly abashed.

"And I don't care what you think. It is my blood and I will do with it whatever I feel like," she continued defiantly.

"Roman was willing to give up his life for me today – they both were. There aren't many humans I know that would do the same."

Backing down, he said, "Still, you must know that this sort of thing is unconventional and of course frowned upon." Dante looked at Stellan with a smirk. "It looks like you will have your hands full with this one."

"Yes, I am quite aware of that. Thank you for intervening Dante. I know it is not something the Council does frequently," said Stellan looking at Celeste with a frown.

She suddenly felt guilty for being so rude; they had just saved all of their lives. "Yes, Dante, Sierra and everyone, thank you," she said with all the sincerity she could muster.

"Well I am happy we were able to avert a disaster. The end of the Wilder family bloodline would have been an immeasurable loss to the world," Dante said. With a parting bow, all four of them, carrying their fallen companion, vanished in a burst of light just as quickly as they had appeared.

"I don't know about you guys, but I am so ready to go home even if that means spending the rest of my days in the basement!" said Dani.

"Go ahead; we'll be right behind you. You can see some of Russia while you're out there waiting," said Roman.

"Are you okay?" asked Celeste.

"Yes, I'm fine. Dante was right, your blood really is...special. I feel different somehow," he said with a smile. "There's just something I need to check before we leave."

Roman stood up slowly at first but in seconds his color and his strength had returned. He walked over to the table that

Alek had wheeled in moments before the Council's arrival, but the body was gone.

"Stellan, did you see what I did? I know I was at the point of losing consciousness, but I know what I saw," said Roman.

"What?" asked Nico.

"It all happened so fast, I can't be sure," said Stellan, shaking his head.

"But it can't be. I buried her behind our house in Oak Bluffs decades ago. But you thought it was her too?"

"It certainly did look like her."

"What are you two talking about?" asked Nico perplexed.

"Fabian had her—he had our mom's body."

"Well at least what looked like your mother," added Stellan.

"What?" asked Nico. "How is that possible?"

Stellan walked over to Fabian's book of spells and skimmed over the page to which it had been opened. "It's a resurrection spell," he said amazed, "which is very dark magic. It looks like he needed your blood to complete it."

"Why would Fabian want to resurrect your mother?" asked Celeste.

"Yeah, that makes no sense," said Nico.

Roman's puzzled look slowly turned to a knowing smile. "I think I know why. He loved her. Even after all that time and everything she did to him. He still loved her and wanted her back," said Roman with a furtive glance toward Celeste. She caught his eye and warmth flooded over her.

"So where is her body now?" asked Nico.

341

"I don't know. I lost track of it in the struggle," said Roman.

"Do you think Alek took her?" asked Celeste. "He was out of here in a flash once the Council showed up."

"Perhaps, but it wouldn't make much sense," said Stellan. "I can try to track him down when we get back home." Roman scanned the area around the cavern one more time, then Celeste took his hand and led him out.

Chapter 20

Waking up in her own bed still felt strangely unfamiliar to Celeste even though she'd been back for days now. After weeks at Stellan's she had become used to the lumpy mattress and timeworn smell of the guest room, which she had begun to relate to her new life as a Guardian. Her bed seemed much too luxurious and her room too bright and colorful. As she rolled over and saw the picture with her parents on the nightstand, she stared longingly at it. That was her old life, a life she hardly remembered anymore; it seemed more like a beautiful dream she once had. Her new life as a Guardian was filled with adventure, danger, fear and excitement, nothing what she had imagined her life to be.

"Good morning sweetie!" said her mom peeking in through the door.

"Hi Mom."

"Do you know what day it is today?" she said, sitting down on the edge of the bed.

"Monday?"

"Yes of course silly, but what I meant was that it's exactly one week from today that you start at NYU!"

"Wow, is it really? The past few days have been such a blur, I can't believe how quickly it went by."

"Well, you did practically sleep through them all. I'm not surprised that you lost track of time. Stellan must have really run you ragged with all that training."

"He sure did," she said with a half-hearted smile.

Celeste hadn't told her mother about Fabian and Alek and her near-death experience. Knowing that her daughter was the Guardian was one thing, but telling her all the dangerous details was quite another.

"Don't you think you should at least go see Brian or Natalie?" she asked. "You haven't seen any of your friends since you've been back."

Celeste had been lying low since her return to Oak Bluffs. An extreme sense of guilt washed over her as she realized she didn't have much time left to spend with her friends before leaving for college. She hoped that things wouldn't be so strained with Brian now that she had told him the truth. And then there was Roman... He hadn't been the same ever since their talk about Brian back at Stellan's house. She had spoken to him a few times, but he seemed distant, and there was no doubt in her mind that he was avoiding her.

Real boys really are nothing like what they are in the movies.

Celeste knew she had to face reality soon, and as her father used to say, "There's no time like the present." Her mind was made up. She was going to get up, get dressed and stop hiding out in her room. Brian's house was the first stop on her list.

"Hey Cel!" said Brian with a big smile as he opened the door. "I heard you were back. I was wondering when you'd come by."

"I'm sorry it took me so long. I've just been exhausted and catching up on some much needed sleep. Being a 'you-know what' is quite draining," she said lowering her voice.

"I bet. Don't worry, you don't have to whisper. No one's home but me. Come on in."

Celeste followed Brian into the familiar living room. Countless picture frames covered the coffee table and the walls, many with pictures of her and Brian as children. They sat down on the worn out couch. When they were kids they used to pretend the couch was a fort and had spent hours battling imaginary villains. Being here brought back many sweet memories.

"So how have you been?" he asked.

"Okay, I've just been getting settled back in at home, and now I can't believe I have to leave again."

"Yeah, that's right," he said, pretending he had forgotten. "You're heading off to the big apple in a few days."

"That's the plan."

"You know Natalie is leaving this weekend too. We should all hang out before you abandon me here."

"Absolutely! And enough with the guilt trip, you're the one who decided to stay in Oak Bluffs," she said.

"I know, and I'm actually okay with it now. I made the Oak Bluffs Community College basketball team so that should be cool."

"That's great Brian, congrats! I'm sure you will be their star player."

"Right…So are you going to tell me about what happened with that wizard guy or are we just going to skirt around the subject for the rest of the day?"

"I don't even know where to begin…" and Celeste recounted the entire harrowing tale.

***

"How is Celeste doing – happy to be home?" asked Nico. He had just come back from a jog and little beads of sweat dripped from his forehead.

"Yes, I'm sure she is," said Roman as he sat looking pensive.

"That sounds like you don't know. Are you avoiding her again?"

"I'm not avoiding her exactly," he said standing abruptly. "I'm simply giving her some space so that she can make a decision."

"What kind of a decision?"

"Why must you be so nosey, Nico?" Roman chided.

"Because I care about your happiness Roman, and if I didn't interfere in your love life, it would be non-existent like it has been for the past hundred years."

"Maybe there is a reason for that," he said sullenly, staring out the window.

"Just tell me what sort of ultimatum you gave her now."

"It wasn't an ultimatum; I simply gave her an out. She's leaving for college in a week for goodness sake. What kind of a life can she have with me? I know she has some sort of feelings for Brian, and we all know he loves her. They could be happy together and lead a normal life."

"Is that what Celeste wants?"

"She says it's not, but she's not being rational. She's not thinking about the long term. She has no idea what it's like for us, Nico. She doesn't belong in our world."

"Whether she belongs in it or not is not your decision to make. And let's be honest, being the Guardian is not going to lend itself to a normal life either."

"No, but without me in her life, she'd have more of a chance," Roman conceded.

"I don't understand why you insist on punishing yourself. You've convinced yourself that you don't deserve her, and it's just not true. There is no doubt that she makes you a better person, but you make her better too. Don't you see that?"

Roman just shook his head. "Shouldn't you be getting in the shower?"

"Don't you let her go, Roman. It will be the biggest mistake you've ever made."

"That sounds like a story right out of *Buffy The Vampire Slayer* – the TV show not the movie," said Brian when Celeste finished.

"Yeah, only there were way fewer hot guys!" said Celeste laughing. It felt good talking to Brian like this, not having to keep anything from him.

"I'm really glad you're alive, Cel. I know I joke around about it, but that is some pretty crazy stuff."

347

"I know, but it's my life now." She paused and took a sip of her iced tea.

"What are you going to do when you're in college? I bet there's a ton of demonic activity in New York City."

"Great, thanks Brian. I hadn't even started thinking about that yet."

"So how does Roman feel about you leaving?" he asked, trying to be nonchalant.

"I don't know. We haven't really been talking much lately," she said, looking away.

"Why not?"

"It's complicated…"

"Come on Cel, you can tell me."

"It's kind of about you," she said awkwardly.

"Me?"

"He thinks that I would be better off with you than him…"

"Well, I can't argue with him there," he said with a smirk.

"He knows how you feel about me, and he wants me to be happy, have a family and all that. He can't give me that so he thinks he should let me go."

"This guy is already planning a family for us?"

"Brian! Stop joking around, this is serious," Celeste demanded.

"Okay, okay, don't hit me! You know I love you Cel, and I probably always will. But I've been thinking about you a lot over the past few days, and I don't want you to choose me because I'm the safer choice or the more comfortable option. I want you to choose who you love and who you can't see yourself living without."

"But I love you both, and I can't imagine my life without either one of you in it," she said, taking his hand in hers and squeezing it tightly.

"But in different ways, right? I see the way you look at him, and I've never gotten a look like that from you."

"Brian…"

"It's okay, though, because I want someone who *will* look at me like that."

"You will Brian, I know it. You're going to make some lucky girl very happy one day. I just hope it's not Lacey Green."

He chuckled. "And don't worry Cel. I'll always be there for you, especially now that you're going to be living in New York City. I'll be coming up to visit every weekend!"

Celeste took a couple deep breaths and gathered her courage as she stood in front of Roman's apartment. As she lifted her hand to knock on the door, it swung open and Roman stood in front of her wearing the same fitted black t-shirt and dark blue jeans he had worn on the first day they officially met. His stunning looks still had the same effect on her, even after everything they had been through.

"Hi," she said slightly breathless. "Are you going somewhere?"

"Yes, actually I was heading over to your house," Roman admitted.

"Really?" she asked.

"Yes, I wanted to talk to you. Come in, please." He took a step back and opened the door so that she had to brush against him as she entered. A wave of electricity surged between them as their skin touched and their eyes met fleetingly.

"I've missed this place," she said, looking away.

"It is nice to be back," he said, gathering his composure. It had only been a few days since he'd seen her, but he'd already forgotten the intense effect she had on him.

"Is Nico home?" she asked.

"No, he went over to Natalie's. He's been over there a lot since we got back. Now that I think about it, I think he may have a thing for her."

"You're just realizing that now?" she said with a giggle.

"I suppose so," he said grinning.

"So, you wanted to talk to me about something?" she asked. They had stopped in front of the floor-to-ceiling window, and they both stared out onto the tranquil lake ahead.

"Yes, I do, but if you came all the way over here, I imagine you have something to say as well?"

"Fine, I guess I'll go first," she said, steeling her nerves. "I've been doing a lot of thinking lately, about college, about my life as a Guardian, about Brian and about you."

"And?"

"At first I didn't want to listen to what you were saying, but after these past few days of reflecting on the realities of my new life, I realized you were right."

"I was?" he asked, a look of disappointment crossing his face.

"Yes, I should be able to have a normal life, go to college and be the Guardian. If my father did it, then I know it's

350

possible for me. I still want to have the whole human experience."

"You should. It's what you deserve," he said, turning away from her.

"But I want to have it with you," she said, reaching for his face and turning it back towards her.

"With me?"

"Yes Roman. A normal life wouldn't mean anything to me if you weren't in it."

"But--" Roman interrupted.

"Let me finish," she said placing a finger on his lips to silence him. "I know that you are trying to protect me from a dangerous life filled with supernaturals, but don't you see that that is the life I was destined for? And I need you to protect me from it, to stand by me and make me stronger. I can't do this without you."

"Celeste, you have no idea how happy I am to hear you say that, but how about five or ten years from now? What sort of future could I possibly give you?"

"While I'm flattered that you are already thinking about us in the long term, technically we haven't even been on our first date yet!"

He couldn't help but smile. "You are *all* that I see in my future, Celeste. You have been since the first day I met you, but--"

"No, no 'buts' Roman," she said taking hold of his face and looking into his troubled eyes. "I'm a Guardian, and as much as I hate to admit it, I don't think we have the longest life span. Let's just think about now. You asked me to make a decision and I did so now you have to respect it. I choose *you*, I want to be with *you*, and I love *you*."

"I love you too Celeste, so much," he said. His body longing for hers, he wrapped his arms around her and kissed her desperately.

Celeste looked into his smoldering blue eyes and could feel all the love that he felt for her and the pain that haunted him. She never felt so close to anyone in all her life. As they kissed heatedly the rush of emotions that took over her were more powerful than anything she had ever experienced. Celeste finally understood what real love was. It truly was nothing like in the movies; it was a thousand times better. So when he looked up at her questioningly, she nodded smiling and he picked her up in his arms and carried her into his bedroom.

When Celeste opened her eyes, she found herself in front of Dante and the rest of the Council.

"What am I doing here?" she asked nervously.

"Congratulations Celeste Wilder, you have passed Guardian training successfully. In fact, you have done better than most of our candidates ever have. You have a bright future ahead of you," said Dante smiling proudly.

"Yes, congratulations," echoed Sierra, Seraphina, and Balthazar, whose names Celeste had recently learned after the battle with Fabian.

"Thank you," she said. "I didn't know I was being tested."

"Well it's more of a trial period really," said Sierra.

"There is just one more thing before you officially become the new Guardian," said Dante.

"What's that?"

"You have to make a choice." Celeste looked at him with a confused expression on her face. "We chose you to become the next Guardian, and I believe we made an excellent decision. But now it is your turn to choose whether you want to accept this duty."

"You mean I don't have to be the Guardian?"

"No, Celeste you don't," said Sierra.

"It has always been our custom to select a Guardian, but it is ultimately their choice to commit to the responsibilities," explained Dante.

"What would happen if I didn't accept it?"

"Your powers would disappear, and your memories of everything that has taken place over the past few months would be erased. You would no longer have any knowledge of the supernatural world, and you would simply go back to being an ordinary human."

"You can do all that for me?"

"Yes, and we have. It hasn't happened very often, but once in a while a nominee is not suited for this life, and they are set free."

"Can I have a moment to think about it?"

"Yes certainly, take all the time you need Celeste," said Sierra with a warm smile.

Celeste's mind was racing as she thought about the possibility of a life without the responsibilities of being a Guardian. She could go to NYU and have a normal college experience, she could live a long life, get married, even have a family. She wouldn't get terrifying premonitions anymore or have to spend hours training or living in constant fear. All of it would be over.

But all of my memories would be gone too…

Celeste wouldn't remember anything about the supernatural world including the existence of vampires like her love Roman and her dear friend Nico. And if she wasn't the Guardian, Stellan, her mentor, would never have existed for her either. And she would lose all of her gifts and the incredibly empowering feeling she felt when she held her sword. She would also undoubtedly lose her ability to visit with her father in her dreams. Celeste didn't know if she could give all of that up to go back to being just a normal human. Suddenly, the thought of being normal didn't look so attractive to her when she realized all that she would lose. It ended up being a much easier choice than she had expected.

"I accept. I want to be the Guardian," she blurted out loudly.

All of the Council stopped their idle chatter and stared at her in surprise.

"We are very pleased to hear that," said Dante. "You were born to be the Guardian, and of that I am sure."

"So what happens now?" she asked.

"You go on living your life, and on occasion we will summon you if you are needed. And of course you will continue to have premonitions, which will help guide you to those that are in danger. It is your duty to help them wherever they may be. And if you ever need our counsel, you know how to contact us."

Celeste unconsciously reached for the Wilder key hanging from her neck. "Okay, thank you Dante. Thanks to all of you. I will do my best to make you proud."

***

"Listen up everyone, I have an announcement!" said Celeste. She looked gratefully around the table at her dearest friends. They were all together at Ralph's for a farewell dinner for Natalie, but all eyes were on Celeste.

"Natalie, I want to wish you all the best at Richmond College. They are so lucky to have you, and I'm really going to miss you!"

Natalie smiled with tears in her eyes.

"And about college," continued Celeste, "I've given it a lot of thought, and I've decided to postpone going to NYU."

"What?" everyone said in unison.

"Why aren't you going?" asked Brian.

Out of everyone there – Roman, Nico, Natalie, Brian, and Dani Lynn (Stellan had cloaked her with a glamour spell so she could go out in public without being recognized), Natalie was the only one who didn't know the truth about who Celeste was. Celeste knew she had to be careful about what she said in front of her.

Roman glanced at her and gave her a reassuring smile, and she continued.

"Before everyone freaks out, I'd like to point out that I said 'postpone'. I already spoke to the university, and they have agreed to defer my enrollment for a year. As all of you know, I've been having some family issues to deal with, and I thought

355

it would be a better idea for me to stick close to home for a year until I figure a few things out."

"So does that mean you will be going to community college with us?" asked Nico.

"Exactly. I enrolled this morning, and starting next week I will be an Oak Bluffs Gator!"

"Wow Cel, that's awesome news for us anyway. It looks like you're stuck with me for at least another year," said Brian.

"So now I'm the only one that's leaving?" asked Natalie. "I'm going to miss out on all the fun!"

"Don't worry, I'll come visit you," said Nico with a wink.

"We'll all come visit you," echoed Celeste.

"And you have to come to my games now that I'm going to be leading the Gators to victory," said Brian. "I'm thinking a regional championship at least!"

As everyone chattered happily about the future, Roman turned to Celeste and whispered to her, "Are you sure about this?"

"I've never been more sure about anything," she said and leaned in for a sweet kiss.

"Aww!" said Natalie. "I think it's more than just family reasons making you stay in Oak Bluffs."

Celeste smiled happily.

"Excuse me," said a pretty girl with fire red hair as she approached the table. "I couldn't help but overhear you all talking about college. I just moved into town, and I'm starting at Oak Bluffs Community College next week too. My name is Marie."

As Marie introduced herself to everyone, Celeste's evil radar gave a slight pulse. She looked around in alarm, and not seeing any immediate danger she focused back in on Marie. She had a sweet smile and a few cute freckles on her nose, so she seemed harmless enough. Still, Celeste was definitely getting a vibe from her: it was clear Marie wasn't a vampire or a wizard, but also that she definitely wasn't human. Celeste looked over at Roman for assurance, and he smiled casually.

"What is she?" she whispered under her breath.

"A fairy."

"A what?"

"Shhh... they have excellent hearing," said Roman. "We can talk about it later."

When Celeste looked up, Marie was looking at her quizzically with big emerald green eyes.

"Sit down with us," said Natalie. "We'll tell you all you need to know about surviving in Oak Bluffs."

As everyone sat around the table, Marie explained what had brought her to the small town. Celeste eyed her skeptically, but Roman seemed to be at ease so she took that as a good sign. She glanced over at Brian to see that he was gawking at the cute girl hanging on her every word. For some reason Celeste realized, his smitten gaze made her happy. She leaned over to give Roman a quick kiss on the cheek, and he reciprocated with a squeeze of her hand, which he was holding under the table. All of a sudden, a searing pain tore through Celeste's head. She bit down hard on her lower lip to suppress a scream as a terrible vision flashed through her mind.

***

Outside a dark figure loomed in the shadows. Watching the happy group of friends and seething with anger, he vowed to get revenge on them all.

Want to find out what happens to Celeste next? The next book in my series will be released later this year. Sign up to my mailing list to be the first to know when it is out! www.wilderbook.com

Acknowledgements

A special thank you to my loving and supportive husband who always understood my need for escaping into a good book (or TV show!) And of course my mother who is the guiding force behind everything I do. And to my father who will always live on in my dreams.

A huge thank you to everyone that had a hand in the creation of this book. I could not have done it without you! To Robin Wiley, the first person to read *Wilder* and Celeste's biggest supporter from day one. I don't think I would have gone forward if it wasn't for your constant encouragement. It means the world to me. To my dearest and oldest friend Dorothee Leiser who spent hours reviewing my manuscript and providing invaluable input as well as grammar and punctuation edits!

Thank you to all my friends, family, co-workers who let me bounce ideas off of them and listened to my struggles as a first time author and self-publisher. I appreciate it more than you all will ever know.

Author Biography

G.K. De Rosa has been an avid reader from a very young age. At the precocious age of two, while living in Italy, she had memorized an entire children's book in Italian and expertly turned the pages at the exact right moments of the story. As she grew up, she always enjoyed literature, no doubt having been instilled with a love of story telling from her early years in Catholic school where she was greatly influenced by exemplary teachers who taught her the value of English and Literature. Though she did not pursue writing in college and instead went for the more traditional route of International Business inspired by her love for travel and all things foreign, after a move to New York City, she found her creative writing side calling once again. She began writing a restaurant review blog, City Lights and Tasty Bites, detailing her other passion – food! The hectic hustle and bustle of the city, combined with long commuting times gave her the opportunity to spend more time reading and rekindled a lost love. After reading countless books in many diverse genres over the two years in New York City, and returning to her home state of Florida, she felt compelled to write something for herself. She had always felt particularly drawn to Young Adult novels and having been an eternal romantic at heart, a fantasy romance was a natural choice. She currently lives in South Florida with her real life Prince Charming and their fur baby, Nico the German Shepherd.

Contact me:
Website: www.wilderbook.com
Email: gkderosa@wilderbook.com
Facebook: www.facebook.com/wilderbookseries
Twitter: vampgirl923
Goodreads: G.K. DeRosa

51179814R00217

Made in the USA
Lexington, KY
14 April 2016